Gestation Seven

Gestation Seven

One Was Black and
One Was White

J. Stewart Willis

DEDICATION

TO EVE, FOR ALL THE GOOD YEARS

plastic. She wondered if her parents, without plastic, had ever gone anywhere.

She returned to Brenda. "I'll stay with the kids. As soon as I get Little Dave in the high chair and Billy settled on my lap, will you get some nuggets for Billy and a salad for me? Italian dressing. Milk for Billy and an orange soda for me." She set her pocketbook on the table, fumbled in it with one hand, pulled out a twenty, handed it to Brenda, and hoped she would see some change.

She then pulled some wipes from the plastic bag, wiped down the high chair and half the table, settled Little Dave in the high chair, pulled it to the table, took Billy from Brenda, and settled him on her lap. While Brenda went to get the food, Linda kept her eye on the other two high chairs, mentally willing the people to go. She would have loved to have two hands with which to eat.

Brenda returned with the food after Linda had dug out a baby bottle for Little Dave. She had warmed it before she left home and stored it in the plastic bag. She knew it would bounce on the floor a few times and had brought a washrag, partly soaked in dish detergent, and another that was just wet.

Brenda set the food tray on the table and went off with the paper cups to get their drinks. Linda spread some napkins on the table in front of Billy and opened the nuggets so he could get to them, play with them, and maybe eat some. She picked up her box of salad, fumbled with the box with one hand, and popped it open. Next came the package of dressing. She reached around Billy so that she could work on the dressing with two hands, managed to tear the serrated edge, shook it on the salad and then tried to work on the fork in the plastic package, gave up, and decided to wait for Brenda.

She put the baby food and fork on the tray for Brenda to open. She would also have to get Brenda to open a straw and put it in her drink.

When Brenda came back, she automatically did all the opening, set the jars in front of Linda, stuck the plastic fork in the salad, stuck the straw in the orange drink, pushed it over to Linda, pulled the tray to herself, and began eating her Big Mac and fries.

"Jesus! What would we do if I also had two kids? You should have spread them out a little. You waited all through graduate school. You obviously know how not to have kids. I think you lost your sanity when David went to work."

"I know. It's hell at times. The first was planned, but Little Dave was a surprise." *Never again,* Linda thought. *Drank too much at a party. Fourth of July. Lost the control I had in college.*

Brenda looked at her hard, eyebrows raised above her made-up eyes. "So what's the sudden need for a break from the house? You've been home moping for weeks."

"Just bored to death. David's been working late so much the last year, sometimes weekends. This past weekend just seemed worse than usual. Thought this was all over when he finished his research for the PhD. Now he's away so damn much it makes graduate school seem like paradise."

"Uh-huh. Wasn't what you were expecting?"

"No. It was supposed to be just a standard job, eight-hour days. I knew that if he did well and got into management, there might be long days. But not in the beginning. Thought we were going to have kids and a routine for a while. The first year was like that, but things have changed." She had reviewed it in her mind. *The first year had been good after all that crap of graduate school.*

"So what's changed? Has he got a new boss? His lab mates dumping on him?"

"Don't think so. At least, not that I'm aware. He's not complaining about anything. When I complain, he just says it's work that he has to do, that it will be over soon. Shit, I don't understand what he does anyway."

"At least that might be better than trying to discuss work with a guy who punches an adding machine all day like Eddie does. You ever call David at work?"

"Sometimes, but he doesn't answer his cell phone, and when I call the office, the secretary answers and has to call him. I don't like that, and I'm not sure he does either."

"Yeah, how about when he's working late?"

"I tried, but no one answered. He said he can't stop his work to answer."

Linda continued feeding Little Dave throughout the conversation. She had learned to do that, with little thought, so she could think about what she was saying.

Suddenly, Little Dave dropped his bottle on the floor, and she got up, holding Billy on her hip, and scooped up the bottle. As she did so, out of the corner of her eye, she saw a high chair becoming free.

She plopped Billy in Brenda's lap. "Brenda, hold the kids!" she shouted as she dashed across the restaurant and grabbed the high chair as soon as the other baby was lifted free.

"Thank you," she blurted at the startled couple and slid the chair away.

Brenda had dumped her hamburger in the middle of the tray, knocking over her little container of catsup. She was holding on to Billy for dear life and steadying Little Dave's high chair with the other hand.

"Jesus, give me some warning. You dashed off like a mad woman."

"Yeah. Well, that's what kids do to you. It's called survival," Linda summarized as she settled Billy in the high chair.

Brenda was silent for a moment, looking thoughtfully at Linda.

"So you think he's running around?"

"Maybe."

"Is he still screwing you?"

Linda had been uncertain about answering. This is not what she had planned to discuss during lunch.

"We make love."

"I'm not talking about you. Is he interested? Is he screwing you?"

"Uh yes." Linda looked around to see if anyone was listening. They weren't. "Brenda, I don't think we should be talking about this."

"Sweetheart, you brought it up. How long have you been married—seven years? Even Marilyn Monroe had to worry about that. Don't you get fidgety now and then? Hell, I do. Bet David does too. But the screwing's a good sign." With that, Brenda went back to chewing on her fries.

Linda decided not to talk about it anymore.

Not Brenda. "Tell you what. Here's a plan. Do you know who he works with?"

Linda nodded.

"Okay. The next time he works late, give them a call at their homes. If they don't answer, it's a good sign but doesn't really prove anything. If they do answer, tell them that David is working late, and you need to get hold of him. Say he doesn't answer the phone, and you don't know what to do. See what they say. You can probably tell if they lie."

Linda nodded and sighed. "Yeah, it might be worth trying. Now let's get out of here. I need a new pair of shoes. These are cramping my toes."

So they had packed up, reversing the whole procedure, and headed for Fair Oaks Mall. They needed an indoor air-conditioned mall to fight the heat and a parking space on a level where they wouldn't have to take the baby stroller up or down an escalator or look for an elevator. They rolled the stroller across the parking lot, a small armada in a vast sea of cars. At least everyone gave them a wide berth. Fortunately, a guy held the door for them. She had Brenda, but if not, getting through the door would have been hell.

Inside the mall was fairly quiet. The teenagers weren't out of school yet. There were just some slow-moving women milling around, some geriatrics and recovering surgery patients getting their exercise, and a few people who looked homeless.

In the shoe store, Linda tried to keep the children in the stroller, but Billy threw a fit, and she set him free. He headed for the shoe display and began knocking the shoes off, with Linda following behind picking them up. She grabbed him and sat down with him on her lap.

"Here, I need you to help Mommy try on some shoes." She kicked off her right shoe. She hadn't worn socks or panty hose and now regretted it. She looked around. The one salesman was involved with another woman who had a pile of shoes on the floor in front of her. Linda decided the salesman would be a while.

"Brenda, those shoes over there. See if any of them are eights?"

Brenda went over and started looking. "Just these green ones. They all right?"

"Yeah, I'll give them a try."

She tried them on, holding Billy with one arm and reaching down with the other. The shoes weren't great, but they felt all right. She stood, wearing one new shoe and one old shoe, and walked four steps one way and four back.

The shoes still weren't great, but they didn't pinch.

"Yeah, I guess I'll get them."

She sat down and started putting the shoes back in the box.

Meanwhile, Brenda started inspecting shoes. She picked up some low heels. The salesman had finished with the woman and was checking her out. Brenda walked over. "Hey, can you get these in an eight-and-a-half?"

The salesman glanced at the shoe in her hand. "Yeah, as soon as I pack this lady up."

Brenda came back and sat down. "Cheap place. Won't pay for two salesmen."

The salesman finished with the sale and vanished into the back of the store, brought out the shoes, and fitted one on Brenda's foot. She looked at it, walked a few steps, and sat back down.

"Thanks, but they don't look the way I thought they would. Guess you better let my friend pay for her shoes."

Linda paid for the shoes, holding Billy on her hip, while Brenda watched Little Dave.

As they left the mall, Linda asked, "Did you need shoes? Do we need to try another place?"

"No. I just wanted to make that guy work a little. Give him a hard time. Can't imagine him staying in that job long. Who would?"

They drove home, and as they parted in Linda's driveway, Linda thanked Brenda for going with her and helping with the kids.

"No problem. Just fuck the hell out of David, and I expect that everything will be okay."

Linda wished that she had kept her mouth shut.

CHAPTER TWO

MONDAY - MARY MURPHY

Mary Murphy didn't like her name. It meant being cute, which she was. It meant having freckles, which she did. It meant having light brown hair bordering on red. It meant being five feet three. What she wanted was to be tall and sophisticated with dark hair, someone to be respected and admired when she walked into the room. But she was Mary Murphy, and that meant she had to work to get anything important.

She was twenty-three, one year out of college with a journalism degree and still trying to figure out how to translate that into some modern job with an online journal. She had landed a job with an Alexandria, Virginia, newspaper, staff of twelve. Even the secretary outranked her. She went for the bagels, wrote about garden tours, interviewed the high school graduates, etc., and occasionally reported on the opening of a new business—if it wasn't too big a business. All the while, the old reporters gave her a hard time, even though their industry and jobs were on the verge of oblivion. Most didn't have the skills to adapt to a new world.

Still, she was like all ambitious young reporters, always looking for an opportunity to write articles for the front page.

As long as she was with the paper, it seemed the only way to get ahead. That wasn't going to happen with the assignments Editor Dan Jenkins was giving her. She needed to make her own break or change jobs. She was always looking.

As she was driving home down US 1 after work Monday afternoon, thinking about going out to a bar alone, she was passed by a police car, its siren screaming, lights flashing. Then another police car roared past. Maybe it was something interesting.

A moment later, she could see three, maybe four, police cars ahead, off the road to the right, lights flashing and people scurrying about. The cars ahead of her were being stopped. She pulled off the road into a drugstore parking lot, jumped out, and started walking toward the commotion. The police cars all seemed to be parked next to a barbecue joint, two cars and an ambulance parked in the rear of the parking lot, and two others parked in front. The police were in the middle of the road stopping the traffic. Another cop was on the sidewalk blocking her path and that of a couple of other gawkers.

"What's going on?" she asked the policeman.

"Just, everyone, stay back," he replied. "If you have another way to go, you had better do it. You're not going through here for a while."

"Okay, but what's going on?"

"Police investigation."

"Yeah, I can see that. Must be serious, though, if you're stopping all of us."

More people started gathering, probably coming out of the local stores. A guy asked her what was going on.

"I have no idea, but there's a lot of commotion."

She pulled out her press badge and held it up the cop. "I'm a reporter. Can I get through?"

"No, lady. No one gets through. When we know something, I'm sure the word will be passed out."

Mary pulled out her cell phone and started taking pictures— pictures of the police cars, pictures of the barbecue joint, pictures of the cops, pictures of the crowd, pictures of the stopped cars, pictures of cars trying to turn around, pictures of everything moving and everything standing still. The cops seemed to be crowded around a dumpster in the back of the parking lot. She wished she had a camera with a long-range lens or binoculars or something.

A police SUV pulled into the back of the lot. Yellow tape was being stretched out around the dumpsters. People in white plastic suits and gloves got out of the SUV and headed to the dumpsters.

"Hey. This is a real crime scene," someone commented.

"Just like TV," someone else said.

People were all stretching their necks to look.

A young guy joined the crowd. "Have you seen the body?" he asked.

Mary moved toward him. "What body?"

"My scanner said a body had been found. Police are coming from all over. Most excitement I've had on the scanner in a long time."

"Hey, officer, know anything about the body?" someone shouted.

"No, nothing about nothing. I'm sure someone will say something when the time's right."

A television van arrived—ABC. A man got out and came over.

Same questions. Same answers. He moved back toward his van. A cameraman had gotten out. He handed the first man a microphone. The man holding the mic positioned himself with his back to the crowd and the police. The cameraman held up the camera. They were doing their preliminary thing, just like the radio reporter had.

After a few minutes, the man came back, and he and the cameraman pushed through the crowd. The cameraman focused on him while he raised his credentials and shouted at the cop. "Officer, I'm here from ABC news. You're live on television now. Can you tell us what's going on?"

Mary doubted it was live and thought it was just intimidation to get things moving. How she wished she had a microphone and a camera. She eased over and showed her credentials. She wanted to be part of the action and wanted to take advantage of the camera's presence.

The cop gave the same answer. He turned his back to the crowd and began to talk into a handheld radio. He nodded a couple of times and put the radio down to his side. People near the police cars huddled. Most were dressed in civilian clothes. A woman—thirties, Oriental—left them and started walking over.

She talked briefly to the cop and then walked over toward the television people. The radio reporter pushed in, waving her credentials. Mary did too. The whole crowd pushed.

The cameraman went to work. The microphone was poised, ready to be held up to the new woman. The woman stood back to address everyone. The TV reporter adjusted the microphone. He needed every bit of power he could get.

"Good evening. My name is Charlotte Wong. I'm acting today as spokesperson for the police department. As you can see, we have an active crime scene investigation going on."

Just then, she hesitated for a moment and watched as the SUV drove off, lights flashing as it entered the highway.

She then continued. "911 was called a little over an hour ago by an employee of the barbecue restaurant you see over there." She pointed but didn't need to. "He said he had found the body of a baby in the dumpster when he went to take the garbage out. It turns out he found a bundle wrapped in white cloth in the dumpster. It didn't look like any garbage the restaurant would have thrown in there. Out of curiosity, he pulled out the bundle and began unwrapping it. When he realized what it was, he set it down and ran to the restaurant, pulling out his cell phone as he ran, and called 911. When the police arrived, we sealed off the area and waited for our forensic people and detectives to arrive.

"Once the scene was investigated and photographed, we removed the baby and began investigating the contents of the dumpster. When we did so, we found another bundle in similar white wrapping, photographed it in place, and then removed it. When we unwrapped it, we found a second baby that was also deceased. Neither baby seemed to be physically harmed. The cause of death will have to be determined. Of interest is the fact that the first baby was Caucasian. The second was Afro-American. We ask anyone who might have any information regarding this crime or who might have seen any activity around the dumpster or the barbecue's parking lot in the last twenty-four hours to contact the police department. That's all the information we have now. We will provide further information as it develops."

Mary shouted, "How do you think they died?"

The radio reporter shouted, "How long have they been dead?"

The television reporter shouted, "When's the next briefing?"

The cameraman recorded Charlotte Wong walking back to the remaining police cars.

Mary Murphy thought to herself, *Bundles wrapped in white! Shit. I bet I have the only photographs!*

CHAPTER THREE

MONDAY - DAVID NEALE

Summer had come. It was late June in Washington. As David left work, he saw his car in the distance shimmering liquidly, the light refracting to his eyes. He was crossing the huge patched, warped asphalt parking lot of the Northern Virginia Annex to the National Institutes of Health, a yellow brick box of a building on Route 7 out beyond Tysons. It had been built before the notion developed that buildings should have architecture, glass, manicured grounds, and white-lined, curbed parking lots.

He had left work as soon as he thought it was reasonable. Something was wrong. Seth and Doc Gill weren't at work. They had all worked together the day before, had worked all weekend, and David knew it had not gone well. In truth, it had gone very badly. He had been awake all night, the details going through and through his head. Every word that was said repeated over and over—all the images becoming more and more engrained in his mind. How had he gotten himself into this mess?

He punched the button to unlock his car, got in, started the engine, rolled down the windows, peeled away the sun shield, and got the air-conditioning going. As he drove out of the lot, he could feel the wheels sticking to the molten tar.

He drove down Route 7 past the car dealerships and into the ever-growing new metropolis that was Tysons Corners. The Volkswagen ahead of him stopped quickly at a yellow light. He braked hard and was almost rear-ended by the man in the Lincoln behind him who thought he could beat the light. In his rearview mirror, David saw the guy throw up his hands and mouth a few choice words. All David needed was to be hit by that guy.

As he drove, he wondered, *Where were Seth and Doc Gill?* Last night, Seth had said he would take care of everything. *Not to worry. Go home. I'll see you in the morning.* David had been more than happy to oblige, to get out of there, but it wouldn't leave his mind. He wanted to talk more about it this morning. He was at work early and waited for the other two, trying to get the research under way but missing details and having to repeat steps. Periodically, he stopped and sat. He tapped his fingers, shifted his feet, and then paced. No one came. He asked Lourie, the office administrator, if she had heard from them. She had not. She said it seemed strange. David agreed.

Next, he came to the ramp on to the Beltway, carefully working himself into a small break in the traffic, glad that a big truck was a lane over. He worked his way one more lane to the left to avoid the vehicles exiting and entering, maintaining the speed of the traffic to survive. He exited onto Interstate 66 and repeated the process. No speed now. The traffic started and stopped, started and stopped, everyone inching their way home.

He had tried to phone Seth and Doc Gill—home phones, cell phones. He had texted them. He had e-mailed them. No

reply. Where were they? Had they run away? Had they left him?
Was he alone? Where did he stand? Should he look for them?
Should he leave it alone hoping all was solved—hoping it was
all a bad memory?

He exited Interstate 66 on to US 50 and stopped at the
cleaners in a shopping center. There were few cars and fewer
people. It was just too hot. The heat jolted him as he left the
air-conditioned car. The air-conditioning in the cleaners was
fighting against the heat of the machines in the rear of the
building. The girls behind the counter were sweating, their
light blouses sticking to their skin. He felt sorry for them. He
dropped his laundry on the counter, gave his name, waited for
the moving racks to grind away, paid, hung his clean suits and
shirts in the back of the car, got in the driver's seat, and started
the car's air conditioning as quickly as possible. He was glad he
didn't have to get groceries tonight, but he wasn't in much hurry
to get home either.

Linda was already mad that he had worked all weekend.
Fortunately, she hadn't tried to call him at work. He knew she
really didn't care that much about what he did. She just wanted
him home to share the children. She didn't think she should
have to handle them alone, even though it was all she had to do.
She just got tired of the same thing, day after day after day. He
understood that. But he worked and got tired too.

He parked in the driveway of his townhouse, put the
sunscreen back over the car window, got out and picked up
some toys from beside the front door steps, opened the garage,
and shoved them in. Storage was what the garage was for. After
all, it was all the storage they had. Architects and builders don't

seem to worry about storage. *What do you do with your stuff? Everyone has stuff.*

Linda was sitting in a kitchen chair, leaning back, looking beat, her legs spread under her dress to cool her legs. It appeared the air-conditioning wasn't doing its job.

"Hi. What's with the air-conditioning?" He didn't kiss her. He hadn't done that in a year. It was no longer part of the routine.

"Damn thing hasn't worked right all day. You're lucky you work in a big government building. I called the repairman this morning. Got the answering machine. He called back about an hour ago. Says everyone is broken down. Always happens the first hot day. He'll come as soon as he can—whatever that means."

"Is he going to phone first?"

"Didn't say. I'll be here anyway."

"What's wrong with Little Dave?" He was sitting in the playpen looking at David, his face red and his eyes watery.

"Been crying. Doesn't like the heat. Hasn't slept. Got tired and grouchy. Best thing about your coming home is that he's stopped."

Billy was sitting on the floor wheeling around his toy trucks with appropriate sound effects. That would get you after a while, but Linda seemed to be accustomed to it. David picked up Little Dave out of the playpen. "Had a rough day, Tiger? I'll throw you in a cool bath in a minute, and you'll feel better."

With Little Dave on his hip, David went to the refrigerator, took out a can of beer, set it on the table so he could open it with one hand, and sat down to drink it.

"How come you're wearing a dress?" Linda usually wore shorts. She liked to show her legs. She had good legs. Dave remembered the first time he met her. She had crossed her legs sitting at a cafeteria table. She didn't look good in a dress. She slouched a little. If she stood straight, she'd look good in anything.

"Oh, Brenda and I took the kids shopping. Ate at McDonald's and later got a pair of shoes at the mall. Big day, huh?"

Brenda DeHaven was the woman next door. Eddie, her husband, worked for a department store at Fair Oaks Mall doing accounting or something to do with the money.

Brenda thought she was pretty. Maybe she was a little—just borderline. But it was enough to make her self-confident—a little pushy. She stood straight. Nothing shy about Brenda. At least she got Linda out.

"No. That's good. I like to see you get out. Maybe Friday we can take those new shoes and go to dinner and a movie. How about calling the sitter?"

"Okay. But if the air-conditioning isn't fixed, we may never get her back again. Cheryl likes her comforts."

"Hell, it's bound to be fixed by then." *For our sakes too,* thought David. "So what's for dinner?"

"The rest of that meatloaf we had Friday night. You weren't here to eat it, so I saved it. Over the weekend, I just had some crackers and cheese. I'll defrost some beans to go with it."

"Okay. You do that while I bathe the kids." David usually bathed the kids when he got home to give Linda a break. It wouldn't last long because after the baths, they would feed the kids in their high chairs while they ate their own dinners between the children's bites. It didn't really matter much what they had for dinner.

David and Little Dave headed upstairs and started the water running in the bathtub. When the temperature and water depth were right, David dumped in all the plastic toys from the edge of the bathtub and went back down to get Billy in his other arm. Thank goodness, Billy could sit by himself now, but he still held Little Dave up while he washed him. With the other hand, he washed Billy. Billy's bottom didn't get washed very well. With only one hand available, David could only do so much.

David carried both children, naked, into their bedroom, found their pajamas, got them dressed, and hoped their bibs would keep them clean. Downstairs, as he settled the children into their high chairs, Linda set their microwaved food on the trays in front of them. The meatloaf would go into microwave next. David attached the children's bibs, found the small plastic spoons, and went to work. Some food went in, some dribbled, and some were spit out. Most landed on the trays where it was wiped around by little hands. David's parents, when they visited, left the room during the children's dinners. They preferred to forget that David had done the same thing.

Linda had turned the television on while preparing the dinner. David vaguely heard a discussion of the Metro's problems.

As Linda put his dinner on the table, she started talking about all the people who had been in the mall today trying to beat the heat. "Some of them were real scruffy. Looks like that's where the homeless go. Then the high school kids began showing up. The place became so jammed you could . . ."

While listening, David had heard "Breaking News!" on the television, along with a blast of dramatic music; and while Linda talked, he half listened to the news. "There's been a terrible discovery down along Route 1 south of Alexandria. Meghan Harding is on the scene—Meghan, are you there?"

"Yes, Jim. I'm just up the block from where you can see the police cars with their lights flashing. US 1 is temporarily closed, and the police are holding everyone back to where I'm located. A police spokeswoman came over briefly and spoke to us a few minutes ago. An employee of the restaurant, Danny's Barbecue, was taking out garbage this afternoon and found a white bundle wrapped in cloth in the dumpster. Since the restaurant didn't use table cloths or anything like that, he thought it was strange. He pulled the bundle out, discovering there was some weight to it. He partially unwrapped it and found a baby who appeared to be dead. He ran back to the restaurant and called 911. When the medics arrived, they confirmed that the baby was dead. Later, a second bundle was found. It turned out that it too contained a dead baby. The spokeswoman said that was currently all she had to report, except for the strange fact that one baby was black and one was white . . ."

David shouted at a startled Linda, "My god, Linda, you're drowning out the news, and I'd like to listen!"

"Why the hell are you shouting at me like that? It's just another crime."

David drew a deep breath. "Just hush, Linda! I want to hear this!"

CHAPTER FOUR

MONDAY - DAVID NEALE

Linda was startled. "Don't talk to me that way! Who do you think you are? What's so damn important? They're just talking about more murders."

"I just want to hear. You can't even think around here, much less listen to the news."

"Damn it. You've got children. Take care of them and quit the bitching. I do this all day, and I don't gripe when you come home."

"Yes, you do. Most of the time, when I come home, you complain about your day. I have to tune it out."

"Well, my days aren't wonderful. You should try it day after day. You feed the kids!" And with that, Linda stormed out of the room and went upstairs.

The television was now on the commercials, but he had heard the words *one black and one white,* and it stayed with him, storming into his mind, sinking to his stomach. He was going to be sick.

He tried to concentrate on dinner. Both his children were crying, confused. They wouldn't eat.

He threw down the spoons on the table and walked to the bottom of the stairs. He shouted, "You take care of them! I'm going out! Can't stand it here anymore!"

With that, he went out, slamming the door behind him. He got in the car and backed out of the driveway. He shifted gears and realized the sunscreen was still in place. He pulled it off and parked at the curb. He didn't know where he was going. He couldn't go back to the house. That would be hell, a long night of fighting.

He had to think. He couldn't stay here. He began to drive back toward the highway and then over to the mall. He parked and went in, barely seeing the people who passed. He sat on a stone bench. People swirled around him, mere blurs in his mind.

One black and one white.

They had to be the babies that were born this weekend. Two of the three. Where was the third? A white boy and a white girl were born. He wondered which was missing, which was dead. Two dead babies. One black, one white.

It had all gone wrong. Now it was murder. He was involved in a murder. The thought raced through his mind, ricocheting back and forth. He wanted to scream. He wanted to cry. He slouched and breathed hard.

"You all right, mister?" A woman holding two bags was leaning over, looking at him, concerned.

He focused on her face and took a deep breath. "Yes." He nodded. "Yes. Just had some bad news. Have to think."

"Okay. You're sure?"

"Yes. Just have to sit a while."

She nodded. "Okay." She turned and shuffled off.

David saw other people looking. Then he lost his focus again.

He remembered sitting in the lab's café with Seth and Doc Gill almost a year ago. He had been out of college for about fifteen months and had been assigned to Seth's lab from the beginning.

Dr. Sidney Gill was the medical doctor, an OB-GYN who had bailed out of private practice because of pressure, high insurance rates, government paperwork requirements, etc. He was bald with a little fringe of white hair around the sides of his head. He wore rimless glasses. His skin was pale, and he looked every bit of his sixty odd years. Doc was the team member responsible for the medical aspects of their research. Seth was a chemist and Dave a microbiologist. They worked with rats and mice, giving them diseases, studying the effects, applying proposed medicines, and looking at responses.

Seth O'Halloran had curly red hair, a red mustache, and a forehead that was permanently wrinkled. He was the lab team chief. He had high energy and was constantly in motion, often swearing under his breath as if things weren't moving fast enough or were all wrong.

David remembered that Seth had been thinking hard. He had taken a bite from his sandwich, licked mayonnaise from his fingers, and turned to Doc Gill.

"Doc, do you remember that idea I talked to you about a while back about replacing the cytoplasm in a woman's egg?"

"Yeah."

"Guess what? David helped me. My damn Guinea pigs had their babies in forty-five to forty-nine days. Done it four times. Should have been sixty-five days or so. We inserted cytoplasm from a rat. They have babies in twenty-two days. Looks like by using the cytoplasm of an animal that has one gestation period and putting it in an animal with a longer gestation period, the latter's gestation period gets shorter. You know what that could mean to women? Not having to carry a baby for nine months would be a godsend."

David had felt nervous, and Doc Gill had asked, "What do you mean you inserted cytoplasm? Did you just stick it in?"

"No. It's a little bit more complicated. We had to remove some from the target egg first. Didn't want to remove it all. I was afraid of doing damage, so we took just a little and replaced about the same amount." Seth had looked pleased with himself.

Doc Gill had looked thoughtful. "That's interesting. You going to publish it?"

Seth had looked concerned. "No way. That would let someone else get the jump on me. I want to make it work on humans first."

David had leaned forward. "How the hell are you going to do that?"

Seth had looked around to see if anyone else could hear him. "I'm going to get some volunteers."

"Seth, there are rules about using humans for research. Lots of rules."

Seth had shaken his head. "No. This is not like developing new medicines. I'm not proposing dumping new chemicals into people. This is just a human egg taken from the woman's own body. If her body doesn't like it, she'll just abort it. No damage done."

Seth had then looked around the table, looking for responses. Doc had looked concerned. "Why are you telling us this, Seth?"

"Because I need your help."

David had bitten his lip. "I don't know, Seth. Sounds a little dangerous to me. Where would we do the work?"

"The work on the eggs we'll do right here in the lab."

"I don't know that government property should be used."

"Hell. It's not as if we're going to destroy anything or even use government materials. Anything we need to buy, I'll pay for. And we'll do it off hours, so there's no misuse of government time. It'll be fine."

Doc had been thoughtful. "This is going to cost money. I can't put anything into this. Doubt if David has any money either. He's got a pregnant wife, and I'm sure he needs everything he's got."

"Look, guys," Seth had reasoned. "I've been a bachelor for more than forty years. Lived a dull life, but I've saved money. Long ago, I gave up the idea of being married. Always had a dream of doing something big. When this works, none of us are going to have a problem with money. We'll have the patent."

*   *   *

Someone broke into Dave's thoughts. "Hey, mister." David focused. It was some security guy in a uniform. "The mall's closing in a few minutes."

David looked around. He was almost alone. "Sure, officer. I'll move on."

David hurried to the mall door. An officer waited for him there, ready to lock the door behind them. The parking lot was nearly empty. Very quiet. David sat in his car and thought. He wasn't ready to go home. Facing Linda was all he needed. Couldn't handle it. He started driving and found a restaurant open late. He went in and ordered coffee and asked what time they closed.

"Twelve."

"Okay. Thanks."

That would be a lot of coffee, or he'd have to find somewhere else to go.

He added sugar to his coffee. He swished it around with his spoon, and his thoughts returned to the lunch at the NIH café.

*   *   *

Seth had been so enthusiastic. David hadn't been sure and asked, "What would you want me to do?"

"I want you to handle the eggs, like you've been doing. I could do it, but I'm a little awkward. I'm getting gibbon cells from a primate institute. They think it's for NIH research, and I think it's a one-time opportunity. I can't afford to waste them."

"Why gibbon cells?"

"First, because I can get them. Second, gibbons have a seven-month gestation period. Chimps, unfortunately, have an eight-month cycle, and I don't know if we'd see enough effect."

Doc had been listening intently. "And what's my job?" It had sounded to David like Doc had already bought in.

"You're the doctor. I'm hoping you know about babies."

"Been some time, but go on."

"We'll have to get you to take the eggs from the women, reinsert them, manage the pregnancies, handle the deliveries, and work with the mothers and babies afterward. We'll also need you to handle getting the medical equipment, beds, stirrups, etc. The whole works."

"What if something goes wrong during the births?"

"If that happens, we'll take the women to the hospital. By then, we will have proven ourselves."

Doc nodded. "Yeah, I can probably handle that. I'm sixty-two. Seems like I ought to have a little excitement before I retire."

"You in then?" Seth had looked thrilled and relieved, as if he was amazed that he had gotten this far.

"Yeah. Why not?"

"David, what about you? You've got the easy part."

"This is all too fast. Let me think about it."

Seth had looked disappointed but not discouraged. "Don't think long. This is a Nobel Prize opportunity. They don't come along every day. I'll check with you in the morning."

*　　*　　*

After two cups of coffee, David left the restaurant. The management had kept watching him. They probably thought he was loitering. It shouldn't have bothered him, but it did. Guess he was feeling guilty. He was, but not for loitering.

He drove home and parked in the driveway.

He remembered the night after the NIH café lunch. He had fretted over the whole idea. Such a wild idea. Yet didn't it take wild ideas, gambles, to become successful? He knew if left alone, he would never do anything great. That took nerve that he didn't have. Unless something shook him, he'd be in the same job in twenty years. Even moving to another job took courage. A management job might come up. That would be the only change he could foresee.

The front light to his house flashed on and off. Linda appeared in the door. He opened the car door while she held the storm door open by the handle. "Are you going to come in so I can go to sleep?"

She closed the storm door and went in, leaving the main door open. He opened the storm door and went in. She was standing at the foot of the stairs, looking annoyed and angry.

"I'll throw down some pillows and sheets. I don't want you waking the kids. You can sleep on the sofa."

With that, she turned and climbed the stairs.

So what? he thought. *I've got bigger problems than you.*

Chapter Five

MONDAY - LINDA NEALE

After David left, Linda sat down and took a deep breath. *What the hell was that all about?* she thought.

Her body sagged, and she stared blankly. The children were quietly looking at her. Then they began to whimper. She went to work, feeding Billy before everything fell apart. Another night like last night. She had to do it alone. But this time, the waiting for David would be different. Not something to look forward to. Who the hell did he think he was? Did she ever storm out of the house and leave him alone to take care of everything, an evening with children involved? Hell no. Someone had to be responsible. But why her? Maybe she'd try walking out the next time. See how he'd like that.

She went through the routine with the kids. At least they had had their baths. She finished feeding them. She carried Little Dave upstairs. Billy crawled up. She thanked God for that. Carrying two by herself had been a challenge. She put Little Dave in the crib and read Billy a book. She thought, *When will I start saying a prayer with him?* She settled him in, covered him, and told him she loved him. Then she turned out the light, making sure the night-light was on. She left the door open so she could hear them and turned out the hall lights.

All the time, she kept thinking of what she was going to say to David. She was mad. He was so unfair, so self-centered. She had put up with so much over the years. Five years of graduate school.

She thought of five years of being jammed in small, one-bedroom student housing, her only friends being other student wives jammed into other one-bedroom student housing. As undergraduates, she and David had gone to university activities, fraternity parties, sporting events, and dances; and she had her own classes. During those five years of graduate school, they didn't go anywhere.

Dave spent long hours in the lab, often late at night, while she watched television—alone—because her friends' husbands either didn't work in labs or were on a different schedule. She dealt with David when he was a nervous wreck and short-tempered before his exams, for days before his qualifying exam and for a month before the defense of his thesis. She thought it would never end.

She had gotten a job in a clothing shop, on her feet all day, dealing with customers—some nice, some abrupt, some downright rude and mean. She didn't need them taking out their problems on her. But it got her out of the house and into the world, however limited that might be.

She had looked forward to the end of graduate school. David would get a job. With a PhD, it should be a good job. They could start living a normal life, maybe get a larger apartment and then a house. Somehow, it hadn't gone exactly like she planned.

She remembered when she started dating David. His major had seemed like a good one, one that should lead to a solid future. He had been quietly attractive and seemed fairly ambitious. The PhD he wanted had seemed like a great idea. He had looked like the answer to a lot of her hopes.

In those days, she didn't have many dates. She had worried she wasn't pretty enough. She didn't have much money. Her parents were doing all they could to pay her tuition. She worked summer jobs and saved enough for books and food. She wasn't a sorority girl. Her mother hadn't gone to college, so there was no sorority in her background. She really hadn't understood the pledging process. At least, not until it was too late. She wasn't into sports. She was just one of the other girls on campus.

As such, she had developed her own process for getting dates. She ate in the cafeteria and looked for males who were sitting alone at tables. She would sit down, asking if it was all right. She didn't say anything right away but eventually found an excuse to open a conversation. Some were nerds, sitting alone because they had few or no friends. Some had girlfriends who were doing something else. A few were nice. She managed to get some to ask her out, sometimes being blatant about it. She dated some nerds, some nice guys, some bastards. A few dates were good, but most were not.

Finally, she met David, a fraternity man in a good academic program. He was by far the best who had come along. She had still thought so all during graduate school, but it wasn't easy. She had often wondered if there was really light at the end of the tunnel.

Where was he now? Where was her golden future? Was he sitting at a bar, drinking and worrying about something she didn't know about? Was there a dark secret he couldn't share? Was he with another woman, David crying on her shoulder? Was her marriage coming apart in ways she didn't understand at all?

As these thoughts raced through her mind, she remembered Brenda's advice to phone David's work partners. She almost never saw or talked to them; she hardly knew them. What she did know was what David told her about what they did at work, what personal problems they were having, what their backgrounds were. It was about the only part of David's work she could talk to him about. The rats and mice she understood but had no desire to discuss. *Yuck*, she thought. *That's not my thing.*

She got out the phone book and looked up O'Halloran and Gill's phone numbers. What was she going to say to them? "Is David there?" "David's missing. Have you seen him?" Or what? "Is David out with another woman?"

It all seemed absurd.

She decided on a question that was based on fact. She'd say, "I've been trying to phone David at the lab, and he doesn't answer. Do you know any other way to get hold of him?" It wasn't direct, but she hoped in answering her question, they'd give out some helpful information.

She dialed Gill first. He seemed like the nicer of the two. The phone rang until the answering machine came on. Not a personal message. Just what the phone company provides. She didn't leave a message. She thought it would sound dumb.

She sat for a minute and tried to get her thoughts back together. Then she dialed O'Halloran's number. Again, the phone rang until the answering machine came on. "Hi, friend. This is Seth. Leave me your wise words, and I'll give you a shout back." She thought as she hung up, *I sure don't have any wise words. Not even dumb ones.*

They were all out. She didn't have their cell phone numbers. Maybe that just saved her from sounding foolish. Oh well. What did it mean? Were they out with David? No way to tell. She hadn't learned a thing.

What's next? Linda was at a loss.

What had set this off? The news about murders. It was five minutes until ten. She flicked on the television in the bedroom. She'd get the ten o'clock news.

She got out her nightgown so she could put it on while watching the news. She checked the blinds and stripped down. She looked at herself in the mirror. There were certainly more beautiful women, but she thought, *I'm not bad.* She felt she was a loving, caring wife, one David could certainly be proud of. Someone he could show off when they went out. She played that part.

The news came on, and she slipped her nightgown over her head while she watched. The dead babies were the lead story. No news yet as to how they were killed. The police weren't saying. There were pictures of the police cars with lights flashing in the barbecue parking lot, obviously repeats of the afternoon's scene. Lots of talk but few details.

She kept thinking. *Yes, this was upsetting, but why would it have set David off? He couldn't have anything to do with it. He dealt in mice and rats. Maybe the incident just set off something in his mind, just a catalyst. But a catalyst for what?*

No answer came.

Well, she thought, *I'll be darned if he is going to keep me up all night. I don't care whether he comes home or not.*

She cleaned her face, brushed her teeth, and climbed into bed. She rolled on her side and thought some more about what she was going to say to him. After a while, she rolled on the other side. She thought, *Yeah. I'm going to give him hell. But I'm going to get answers too. I'll stay on it until he can't stand it anymore.*

And so it went for what seemed like forever.

Then the room lit up. The ceiling was momentarily brilliant. He obviously was pulling in the driveway.

The lights quickly went out. She thought, *Why isn't he turning off the engine?*

She lay there listening to the car idle. *What time is it?* She reached over and punched the clock, so it lit up. One ten. *Christ, why doesn't he come in?* She just wanted to get some sleep.

She got up, grabbed her robe from the back of the bathroom door, and went down the stairs. She didn't turn on the lights. She didn't want the neighbors to see her in the doorway.

She sighed. *Let's get this night over with. I'll give him hell in the morning.*

She opened the door and stood inside the storm door. *Wish we had a screen door,* she thought. She flicked the front door light on an off, opened the storm door, and shouted. He finally got out of the car. She turned her back and walked to the stairway.

Chapter Six

MONDAY - MARY MURPHY

Mary hurried back to her car, cell phone in hand. She reviewed her pictures, getting more and more excited.

She scrolled down to Dan Jenkins's phone number at work. She knew he'd still be there trying to get the morning edition ready.

"Yes, Mary. Whatcha got?"

"You heard about the babies' bodies they found on Route 1?"

"What babies' bodies? Just heard they'd found a body. Figured it was too late for this edition."

"Well, you better turn on the TV. Two babies. One black and one white. Bet it's the biggest news on television."

Dan replied with mild interest, "Okay. But what have you got to do with it?"

"Boss, I was there. Got pictures on my cell phone. They'll need to be blown up, but I bet they're the only pictures there are."

"Damn it, Mary. If you do, that might be big. If they're any good, we may be distributing to other media. You say you got them, and the TV cameras didn't?"

"The bodies were gone before TV got there. I've got the only ones."

"Get in here quick. Sounds like you lucked out."

Mary was miffed. "'Lucked out,' nothing! Give me credit. I found a story and jumped on it."

"Okay, but move."

"Hey. You just get Pete, the photo guy, ready and warm up my computer. This has got to be in tomorrow. Front page. With my byline!"

Mary pulled her car to the entrance of the drugstore parking lot. Traffic was still locked up, blocking her from crossing into the next lane. She motioned to the guy ahead of her to pull ahead. He nodded. As he moved forward, the next guy in line also started moving forward. She cussed out loud and leaned hard on her horn, over and over. He stopped, and she charged forward, barely squeezing by in front of him.

When she got to the office, she slammed on the brakes, turned off the ignition, jumped out, slammed the car door, took two steps and went back, opened the door, and got the cell phone. She cradled it like gold as she headed for the office.

Dan and Pete were waiting for her.

Dan was excited. "We've been watching the TV news. If you have pictures of more than just police cars with flashing lights, then it could be big."

He took the camera and handed it to Pete. "See what she got."

Mary headed for her computer. "I'll start writing the story."

Dan shook his head. "No. Go work on it with Charlie. He's been watching the news and can blend your story with what's already being said. You need his experience so that it all doesn't sound the same as what's on TV."

Mary was mad. Charlie was the one in the office who gave her a hard time. He was the one who was always telling her to get her sweet young ass out and report on the parades, the local theater productions, or whatever. This was her story. She didn't want to share it with Charlie, of all people. Damn it; she could write it. She had seen the white bundles, the police climbing into the dumpster, the SUV being loaded, the SUV leaving. Most of that had happened before the TV crew arrived. Mary didn't know how much the radio reporter had seen. She needed to listen to the radio report. Still, the pictures were hers. She could beat them all.

Sadly, she understood Dan's logic. Charlie had experience writing this sort of thing, and it needed to be written quickly to be in the morning paper.

Charlie was waiting for her.

Mary challenged him. "How's my young ass doing today?"

"*Sweet* young ass," Charlie corrected her, leaning back.

Mary shook her head but couldn't help smirking. "Now maybe you'll see another side of me."

"Yeah, it sounds like you're revving." He leaned forward toward his keyboard. "I've started the lede. You need to tell me what happened. From the beginning. All the details."

"I'll do that, but we need to find a radio. Listen to the news station. WMZI. Their reporter arrived after me but before the TV crew. We need to know what they're saying."

Charlie tuned the computer into the news station and turned up the speakers.

Mary started describing what happened, trying to figure in her mind when the news reporter arrived, when she fit into the chronology.

Mary's story came out fast. What was she missing? What was she skipping? Her mind was spinning.

Charlie told her to slow down and began typing.

The radio finished the traffic report and went into the "breaking news."

The reporter transferred to what she had recorded earlier and talked about what the police spokeswoman had said, described the police cars with their flashing lights and the yellow tape, commented that some of the cars and an SUV had not left, and went back over what had been learned about the bodies. When she came back on live, she noted that there had been a crowd, but most were now gone. She also said that US 1 had been closed but was now reopened, although the traffic was moving slowly past the police commotion. That was the only new thing they could report.

In the modern age of fast communications, the murdered babies were already becoming old news. The radio reporter said nothing about the white bundles or the plastic packages being loaded into the SUV. Mary sighed. She was safe. The details were all hers. For once, the paper was ahead of the instant news.

Charlie typed and asked questions. She answered, repeating things over and over. Fortunately, she didn't make many additions and only a few corrections in chronology. She had done well the first time through.

Dan came over. "How much copy?"

Charlie bit his lip and stared at the computer screen. "I'd say ten grafs' worth. Suggest a headline, 'Black and White Murders on Highway One.' Sound all right to you, Mary?"

She was startled. It was an acknowledgment she hadn't expected. "Sounds great!"

"So add a headline to the grafs."

Mary's stomach tightened. "How's Pete doing with the pictures?" Her success depended on the answer. She and Charlie could describe things, but the pictures gave the jolt. They represented the big story.

"He says they're good. He needs to crop them and blow them up. We may use two or maybe three. I'll put them out to other media after we've hit the street in the morning. You did good, Mary." And he charged off to rearrange the paper. *Thank goodness for the abilities of the computer.*

Charlie got up. "Here, sit at my computer and read it over."

She did so, made a couple of corrections, and reviewed them with Charlie.

"You satisfied?" he asked. She nodded, and he sent it off to Dan. "Okay," he sighed. "Our job's done."

Mary and Charlie waited for Dan to give a thumbs-up. Charlie then turned to Mary and asked, "You had dinner?"

She shook her head and mouthed, "No." She hadn't even thought about it.

"Then let's go get a burger."

He got up, grabbed his suit coat, and started walking. He then looked back to see if she was coming. Her mind clicked in, and she got up to follow. She realized she had never taken off her dress jacket.

They headed for the fast-food restaurant a block over.

"You did good tonight, Mary."

"Sweet young ass and all?"

Charlie grinned. "Well, if I were twenty years younger?"

Chapter Seven

TUESDAY - DAVID NEALE

David hadn't slept well. Not surprising. With everything else, he now had an angry wife to face.

He heard her in the kitchen. He heard the children. She had gotten them up by herself.

He had slept in his underwear. He slipped on his pants. He needed to put on some clean ones.

He entered the kitchen, remorsefully. "What can I do to help?"

She looked at him, almost with pity. "You can feed the kids."

He guessed he looked pathetic, guilty. He guessed he was guilty. He just wasn't sure of all he was guilty of. He was afraid time would tell. "I'm sorry about last night."

She glared. "You don't have any business talking to me that way. I'm not going to put up with it."

"I know."

"What the hell was so important on television? All I heard was the murder of two babies. There are always murders on evening television. If they didn't have murders, I don't think they'd know what to talk about. The way you reacted, you'd think you were involved."

"It just sounded so bad. Awful. It got to me. I'm sorry."

Linda made a disgusted face with her mouth and turned back to the stove. David heated the children's food in the microwave, checked the temperature, and began the feeding. The children seemed very quiet, as if they knew something was wrong. They ate without enthusiasm, leaving food on their faces and high chair in excessive amounts. David kept trying to spoon it back in and finally gave up. He cleaned them up, put Billy in the playpen and Little Dave in a little swing on the metal frame sitting on the floor.

"I need to get ready for work."

"You do that." She kept her back to him.

In the car, he thought about Linda. Dating her, his senior year in college had finally broken his need for blind dates. He really didn't care for blind dates a whole lot. During his freshman year, the fraternity vice president fixed him up for a house party with a friend of his girlfriend, Dottie. The blind date hadn't been pretty, a little on the heavy side. They hadn't had much to say. He tried to be polite. She had drunk beer, but he hadn't. Back then, it hadn't tasted good to him, and he had hated being out of control. Later, he would learn to drink, to adapt, but he hadn't as a freshman.

They danced some, talked about where they were from, where she was going to school, where she had known the VP's girlfriend, what they hoped to do in the future. They talked until they had exhausted the standards.

After the party, he walked her back to the dorm where she was staying with the VP's girlfriend. She was a little wobbly, and he was glad when he got there and told her goodnight. He had crossed it off as another failed, even lonely, evening.

The next day, he was eating lunch at the frat house when the fraternity president said he would like to talk to him in his room. When David had gotten to the room, he had found the vice president waiting for him. David had thought, *This is not good.*

"I'll put this straight to you," the VP had said. "The girl you dated last night had a lot to say to Dottie. Told her how you led her into the woods and tried to make out with her. Says you pushed hard. Put your hands where you shouldn't have. Said she had to run out of the woods with you shouting for her to stop."

The president had spoken up. "We want to make it clear that is not the way we act toward our dates, especially those who are friends of the other girls who come to our house. It's bad for the fraternity, embarrassing to all of us."

"It's downright humiliating when you get chewed out by your girlfriend because of what a brother has done," the VP had scolded. "We don't need this. Now get out of here before I punch you. I'm so mad."

David had been embarrassed. Flabbergasted. Then he was angry. "I didn't do a damned thing to that girl. Don't know why she would say that. You're making a big deal over her imagination." He turned and left the room. Then, he left the house.

He had wished he said more. He had known they considered him guilty. Why had the girl said those things? Why had she said things that weren't true? It had to be she was trying to make herself look important. Maybe to be able to talk like the other girls. She wasn't pretty. Maybe nobody had ever made a move on her. Or maybe she just didn't like him and wanted to hurt him. He suspected it was more about her than about him. It didn't matter. In the eyes of some members of the fraternity, after that, he was always looked upon as guilty.

Thus, he had been careful. He had depended on blind dates because he had not been good at approaching girls. Funny because he had nice conversations with the brother's girlfriends.

So when he had met Linda Davis, in his senior year, he was surprised at the ease of their attraction and the life that ensued. He had been eating in the cafeteria, alone. There had been almost an hour until his next class. While taking a bite of his sandwich, he had felt a presence across the table. She had been standing there, tray in hand, looking at him.

"Do you mind if I sit here? There don't seem to be any empty tables."

"Oh sure. Have a seat." It had come out weak. He moved his tray out of the way, taking off his coffee and setting it in front of him. He could have left and given her the table, but he hadn't anywhere to go.

He had looked down at his coffee.

Then she had said, "I haven't seen you around before. I'm studying English. It's such a big campus. I guess I shouldn't be surprised."

He looked up, and her eyes were directly on him. "No, it's not surprising. I'm in biology and usually eat at my fraternity, but my classes have me off cycle on Thursdays, so I eat here."

"Biology sounds like a tough program. Not my thing." She then had looked down and picked up her sandwich. "What year are you in?"

"I'm a senior."

"Me too. It's kind of scary. I mean, what do you do with an English degree? Teach, maybe, but that doesn't sound very exciting."

David had thought a moment. "Maybe not, but it's important. We need good teachers. Don't put yourself down."

"Oh, I'm not. I'm sure there are lots of jobs I can do. Most probably don't have anything to do with English. It's really not that defining." She had taken a couple of bites of her sandwich, looking like she was thinking of what to say next. "Biology sounds pretty defining. You must have to be specific about what you do with that. What are your plans?"

David had felt she was getting a little personal. "Someday, lab work. Could teach too, but I don't think so. Right now, I'm planning on a PhD. I think you need one in science to get anywhere."

"Oh. Where are you going to go to school?"

"Here. I'm already working in one of my professor's labs, working on a paper. Want to graduate with honors and probably continue with him."

She had nodded and stuck out her lower lip a little as if she had been impressed. "That sounds great. What's your name? I'm Linda, Linda Davis."

With that, she had put out her hand. David had been slow reacting to the formality and then had reached across the table to shake the extended hand. "David Neale."

"Okay, David Neale. I've always heard that fraternity boys are pretty wild and sloppy. Are you one or both?" She had looked as if she was trying to tease but appeared a little uncertain at the same time.

David had smiled. "I guess not much of the former and a little bit of the latter."

She had looked down, slid her chair back from the table, and crossed her legs. Dave had considered her and admired her legs. "You don't sound like you've been to fraternity parties?"

She looked back up at him, maybe a little defiantly. "No. But I've had lots of dates. Been to all the big dances. Believe it or not, there's a life here that doesn't involve fraternities."

Dave had thought, *Well, why not?* "I'm sure there is, but I just can't figure out how the fraternity guys have missed a pretty girl like you."

He watched her to see her reaction. A slight smile curled the corner of her lips, a little shy, but her eyes sparkled. "I guess they just don't know a good thing when they see it."

He smiled. "I guess they don't. Looks like you and they need to be educated. May I ask what you're doing Saturday night?"

From then on, senior year had gone well. He had a pretty girl to take to all the fraternity activities and no longer felt out of place. She wasn't perfect. She slouched a little, but a lot of girls did. Otherwise, she was pretty damn good. And she didn't report him when they necked. Life had been good.

David's mind snapped back to the present as he pulled into the lab parking lot, fit his sunscreen, and got out into a day that was starting to turn to steam.

In the lab, he checked on his animals and started to take some blood samples for testing, but then sat down. What was he supposed to do next? Could he just continue to work and pretend nothing had happened? Maybe he should go to the police. What would that mean? Would he lose his job? He thought hard. Had he broken any laws? Was he a criminal? Could he go to jail?

The door opened, and Lourie stuck her head in. "Morning, David. By yourself again, I see. It's worrying Solomon. She wants to see you."

She didn't have to say "now." He understood it. Bev Solomon was the lab director. David was surprised she took only one day to realize something was amiss. Maybe Lourie had pointed it out. She was pretty good. Her parents had thought she was going to be a boy named Lou, and she had spent her life proving a girl was just as good. She had changed the pronunciation from *lou-ree* to *law-ree*.

The door to Solomon's office was closed. BEVERLY SOLOMON, PhD., LABORATORY DIRECTOR was emblazoned in two lines of black across the glass.

David knocked on the wooden part of the door. He wondered to himself if the glass would break under a knock.

"Come in."

David opened the door and went in.

Solomon was looking thoughtfully at the wall. "Have a seat."

David thought it couldn't be too bad if he didn't have to stand.

Solomon looked at David. "Lourie tells me that Seth and Doc Gill haven't been in this week. Says they didn't tell her they weren't going to be here. Have you heard anything?"

David was glad Solomon didn't know anything and hoped it would stay that way forever. "No, they didn't say anything to me either. Caught me by surprise. I've tried to phone them both. No answer. They're both bachelors, so if they don't answer, there's no one to answer for them."

Solomon looked like she wondered what to say next. "It's not like someone at work is supposed to report missing persons. I think that would be unusual. But it seems someone should be worrying about this."

David wanted to close the conversation. He didn't want people looking into this too closely. Certainly not the police. "Maybe I should swing by their apartments tonight and see what's going on."

Solomon nodded. "Good idea. Let me know what you learn."

With that, David was dismissed. No small talk. There never was with Solomon. Not much discussion of the lab work. David and his lab partners received written instructions each week and submitted weekly reports in return, which David guessed Solomon expanded into larger written reports. They also made written recommendations about things they might do or how they might modify or improve what they were doing. It all got discussed in meetings Solomon went to. David didn't know what went on in the meetings, but they seemed to result in written directions. Seldom was he verbally asked for input, although his group was periodically asked to make verbal presentations on what they were doing; the number of which seemed to increase as the annual funding of the lab approached each year.

Occasionally, Solomon stuck her head in the lab door as if she was fulfilling something on a checklist. She wasn't a bad boss. Just not directly involved. David preferred it that way. He didn't object to having a woman as his boss. It just occasionally felt uncomfortable. He had been raised to hold doors for women, to help them when they were being seated at a table, and to address older women as ma'am. He knew he would always be uncomfortable objecting to a woman's directives. He inevitably said, "Yes, ma'am." With a woman, he didn't know another way.

David went back and tinkered around the lab. He realized he had a job, and the lab needed to stay viable. He had no idea when, or if, Seth and Doc Gill would be back. Meanwhile, the whole thing was up to him.

He ate lunch by himself in the café. One of the lab techs stopped at his table. "You look lonely. Where are your partners?"

"They're off today. Should be back in a couple of days."

"Must be depressing, rattling around your lab by yourself."

"Yeah, it is."

"Well, I'll see you."

Meaningless words. Maybe a kind of polite routine. Or maybe just being nosy. Whatever. David wished everyone would leave him alone, not expect for him to give explanations for the partners who weren't here, partners who may have committed murder, and partners who may be implicating him. The less people asked, the less they investigated; the less they wanted to know, the better.

David finished a long afternoon. He thought it would never end. The only break came when Felipe Hernandez, the lab tech, came in to clean up and prepare petri dishes for future use.

Finally, the day ended, and he left, going through his usual routine of getting his car under way and the air-conditioning blowing hard.

Seth lived in a high-rise on Seminary Road. David tried the parking lot. All the visitor's spots were full. He went back to the road and parked about a block down. There were two buildings. He took the walk between the two parking lots and noticed there were a fair number of people at the pool, some toasting in lounge chairs, some shining with suntan lotion and sweat, and some in the pool, not swimming, just staying cool.

He entered the lobby of Seth's building, noting the polished concrete floor—light gray in the middle, dark border around the outside. There was a meeting room to the left and a little gymnasium to the right. Slender people who, it seemed to David didn't need to, were working out. The air-conditioning felt good. David took the elevator to the tenth floor. Seth's apartment faced the other building. Seth said it was prime telescope territory. Old bachelors had to do something.

David knocked on the door. No answer. He hadn't expected any, but he knocked again. Still no answer. Made sense. Why would a murderer be at home? David had brought paper and a pen. He put the paper against the door and wrote a note. "Please call me. Need to know what's going on."

He wondered if he really wanted to know.

He added his name and his cell phone number, not the home phone number.

No need to involve Linda.

Next, he headed for Doc's. It was a two-story older apartment building near Seven Corners. He hated Seven Corners. It felt like cars were headed at you from every direction.

Doc's apartment had an outside entrance. No lights were on. Not a good sign. He knocked. No answer.

Without lights, he had to go back to his car to write a note. He stuck it in the mailbox next to the door.

He checked his cell phone. All he could do was wait.

He found a Chili's, went in, sat at the bar, and ordered a beer. He sipped it slowly and sat there as if he were waiting for something. *Stupid. What are you waiting for? They're not coming home. They're not going to call you. They've left you. You're holding the bag.*

He didn't know what the future entailed, but he knew it was not going to be good. In fact, it was probably going to be pretty bad.

He looked around. Five others at the bar. Three guys in a group. One woman with a guy. Both looked in their forties. They weren't talking, just stirring the cherries in their drinks by the toothpicks. Didn't look like a big night out. Looked like they didn't have anything else to do.

He ordered a hamburger and fries. When they came, he took a bite out of the burger, sucked on a fry, and asked for catsup. He picked up a fry and pushed the others around with it. *At least,* he observed, *it isn't soggy.*

He ate a couple of fries and pushed his plate away. He drained the beer and left.

He sat in his car. Morosely, he thought, with trepidation, *No place to go but home.*

CHAPTER EIGHT

TUESDAY - MARY MURPHY

Mary was flying high.

Her name was on the front page of the paper. Her paper's pictures had been picked up by all kinds of news outlets. No longer her pictures, but her name went with them.

There was going to be a news conference regarding the two dead babies. Maybe the mayor would be there. The conference was at Alexandria City Hall, and she was going. Dan gave her the assignment, said it was her story and that she had earned it.

King Street was within walking distance. She grabbed her notebook, camera, phone, and pocketbook and set off. The heat was still bad, and she hoped she wouldn't be too frazzled by the time she got to the City Hall. She turned left as she departed her building and noted someone across the street start off in the same direction. Young black kid, fifteen or sixteen—the age when kids needed to prove something. Two blocks up, she turned left. She stopped to look through her pocketbook and pulled out sunglasses as she glanced back. The kid had crossed the street and was now behind her on her side. When she finally got to the City Hall entrance, she glanced back across the plaza and noticed he had stopped by the fountain and was looking casual.

She lay her pocketbook on a tray while she went through the metal detector. She removed her press pass, keys, camera, and phone from her pocketbook so they could be seen. She let the security person look inside the pocketbook at the mace. After going through, she clipped on her press pass and asked the guard where to go. She hadn't been there before. Other reporters at her paper handled the government activities.

She entered the conference room and was surprised at the size of the crowd. She was fifteen minutes early and still too late. She realized there was national interest in the two dead babies. She just hadn't realized how much. The discovery of the babies had occurred too late for last night's national evening news, but it was on all the major networks today. Her newspaper staff had all watched the news briefly at the office. Mary's still pictures had made it. Mostly, the newscasts just ran film taken of all the police cars, with lights flashing, sitting next to the barbecue restaurant. They preferred pictures with action. Maybe she should have taken pictures that way, but she had been thinking about the newspaper. Still, her pictures were used so that the white bundles could be shown.

Mary noted that all kinds of reporters were jammed up front, cameramen standing around the sides of the room or sitting on the floor. She squeezed down the back row of seats and found a place in the corner. It looked like a row of seats that had just been added to handle the crowd.

Some guy in a shirt and tie but no coat came out and approached the podium. It was a brown shirt and yellow tie.

This was not the mayor. He tapped the microphone. "Hello. Hello. Can you hear me in the back?"

There was some murmuring, and someone shouted, "It needs to be a little louder with this crowd!"

The fellow in the shirt and tie went to a panel at the side of the room and made some kind of adjustments. Back at the microphone, he asked, "Can you hear me now?"

The man who had shouted before gave him a thumbs-up, and the man in the shirt and tie left the room.

Several minutes passed, and the level of noise in the room grew louder as the reporters and others became more and more impatient.

A door opened with a crack.

The room grew quiet.

Alexandria Mayor Dana Robbins, in a neat two-piece gray suit, panty hose, short-heeled shoes, and a black ribbon at her lapel entered the room followed by two men in suits and two uniformed police officers. The Mayor approached the podium, again tapped on the microphone and opened a leather folder. The four men lined up shoulder to shoulder behind her.

Mary stretched up and took a picture.

The Mayor looked around the room and wet her lips. "Ladies and gentlemen, as you all know, a very upsetting and tragic finding took place late yesterday behind a restaurant on US 1 south of the City. The bodies of two newborn babies, discarded in the restaurant's trash dumpster, were discovered by a worker who called 911. Originally, he reported only one body, but when our police officers arrived, they found a second baby in the dumpster."

Mary was standing. It was the only way she could see over the crowd. She hated being short.

The Mayor continued. "This appalling event has captured the attention of the entire nation. It is being addressed by every major news outlet. The citizens of this City are devastated and worried. I want to assure everyone that this City will spare no effort as it pursues the perpetrator of this heinous crime. I have instructed Police Chief Carmichael, who will speak to you next, to apply all the resources of his department to the effort of solving this crime and to request any help he might need from other City resources. I want to assure him that everyone intends to help. As always, we ask the public to provide any assistance they can. Someone must have seen something. Someone must have heard something. This is too public a crime for no one to know anything. We ask you to think about it and review your lives. Please phone in any information you can provide. Now, as I said, I'll turn this over to Chief Carmichael who will provide more details."

The Mayor turned and took her place in line with the others as the slightly heavy, ruddy-faced, short haired, graying Police Chief approached the microphone. He carried a clipboard. He wanted to impress as a man of action, a working law man. No leather folder for him.

He nodded to the Mayor. "Thank you, Mayor Robbins."

He then looked solemnly at the crowd. Mary took another picture.

"As the Mayor has said, we found the bodies of two babies in the dumpster behind the parking lot of Danny's Barbecue Restaurant south of the city on US 1. The 911 operator received a call yesterday afternoon at four forty-seven from a worker at the barbecue who said he had found a body. The operator immediately informed my office, and we dispatched three cars of police officers, an ambulance, three detectives, and a forensic unit. The area was secured within ten minutes of the 911 call. The medics immediately unwrapped the white bundle that the barbecue worker had left on the ground and verified that the infant inside was dead. The police officers did not touch the scene until the detectives arrived.

"The detectives further secured the area, keeping the uniformed police some distance away from the dumpster. They reconfirmed that the infant was dead. One detective then went to the barbecue restaurant and obtained the names and other data for all persons present, including the gentleman who made the 911 call. He had these people stay in place. When the forensics people arrived, they and the other detectives further explored the dumpster and found another bundle wrapped in white. This bundle was removed from the dumpster and unwrapped.

"Again, the team found the body of a dead infant. The two bodies were secured in pouches, loaded in a police vehicle for transportation to the city morgue by a forensic team member. The rest of the forensic team and the detectives investigated the scene, going through all the trash in the dumpster and attempting to get fingerprints off the door to the dumpster. Numerous prints were found, most of which were associated with workers at the barbecue. The others have been entered on line but have not been identified.

"Potentially, some could belong to the perpetrator of this crime, but others could be from people who used the convenience of the dumpster to dispose of waste. Supporting this idea is the fact that some trash was found, including condoms and pornographic magazines, that did not appear to be associated with a restaurant. Nothing was found that appeared to be associated with the two infants.

"Following the work around the dumpster, the detectives interviewed all individuals at the restaurant. No one had any useful information to provide.

"This morning, the medical examiner performed autopsies on the infants. As you have heard from the news reports, the first infant was Caucasian and the second was Afro-American. Both were male. They had both been suffocated.

"Again, I would like to reiterate what the Mayor said about the public needing to provide help. There will be an information sheet passed out at the door giving information as to what we know. It includes a telephone number that can be called, anonymously, by anyone who has information. We would appreciate the news outlets providing this number to the public.

"Now, I would like to again emphasize that this case is of major concern to my department and the entire Alexandria government, and all appropriate resources will be applied until the case is closed and the perpetrator of the crime behind bars.

"Finally, I will take a few questions. Please speak up so that everyone can hear you."

Hands shot up. Mary could barely see over them. The Police Chief pointed to a woman in the front row. "Has any progress been made on identifying the babies?"

Answer: "No. And again, we would like the public's help."

"As a follow-on to that question, have any babies been reported as missing."

Answer: "Again, the answer is no. We have reviewed all possible reports from within a five-hundred-mile radius."

"Why five hundred miles?"

Answer: "We were considering a reasonable driving distance for such young infants. However, we will look at all national reports."

A man to the left of the room spoke up. "Was there anything peculiar about the bodies?"

The Police Chief looked hard at the man asking the question. "What do you mean by 'peculiar?'"

The man looked hesitant. "What I meant was, were they deformed in any way?"

"And why do you ask that?"

"I—I just heard a rumor."

"And who did you hear that from? I'd like to know. Maybe that person has some more interesting information. I would like the opportunity to talk to you some more after the meeting, if you'd please stay around." The Chief nodded to a policeman at the door.

A woman in the front row was standing. "But you didn't answer the question."

The Chief was annoyed. "I'm not going to at this time."

The room was alert. Everyone could smell a story. Many hands were up; reporters were shouting over one another. "It sounds like there was something 'peculiar.'" "Why can't you address the question?" "What's the deal?"

The Chief held up his hand for silence. "I would appreciate your patience. There were some anomalies that are being investigated through appropriate areas of expertise. I think it is inappropriate to discuss or conjecture about this until we know more. I assure you that details will be provided when the time is appropriate. I'll allow a couple more questions, in other areas, if you have them."

Mary tried to get the Police Chief's attention.

Someone else asked, "How long had the infants been dead?"

Answer: "Now there's question I can answer. A day or two."

"As a related question, how long had they been in the dumpster?"

Answer: "We wish we knew. It would narrow things some. The restaurant only serves lunch and dinner. All the trash the night before had been placed in the dumpster after the restaurant closed, Sunday night, around ten thirty. The fellow, who reported finding the babies, was, at that time, taking out the afternoon trash. No trash had been taken out between those two times according to all the restaurant employees. Therefore, the bodies were placed there sometime between ten thirty the night before and four forty-seven yesterday afternoon when they were discovered. The dumpster is not under direct observation from the restaurant. As you would expect, the owner doesn't want his customers looking out the window at a dumpster. Therefore, you wouldn't expect him or his employees to see anything, except possibly when they were arriving or leaving, and they say they didn't. Therefore, the only times we can exclude are the times the employees arrived and left, especially since they park beside the dumpster. Last night, we had an unmarked car patrolling the area and police asking people who were out late at night if they had been there the night before and if they had seen anything. Today, we have detectives asking questions of everyone working in the area. So far, we have learned nothing."

Mary stood on her chair and waved her hand.

She Chief half smiled and pointed at Mary. "Question from the lady standing on the chair in the back."

"Yes, huh, were the infants clothed in any way other than the sheeting they were wrapped in?"

The Chief's smile vanished. "How did you know it was sheeting?"

Mary was surprised at the question. "Well, that's what it looked like when they unwrapped the babies."

"You were there?"

Mary had the interest of the room.

"Yes. Didn't you see the pictures in the paper this morning? I was hoping you might have traced the source of any clothing or the sheeting."

The Chief bit his lip and thought a moment. "There was no clothing. Only the sheeting. And it was a brand sold at Bed Bath & Beyond and all kinds of other places. It is currently being checked for any chemical residue and anything else we can find. Again, we'll make you aware of anything we find, unless we think it will prejudice the case. Thank you for your attendance. We'll keep you informed."

With that, the Mayor and Police Chief turned and left the room with the others following.

Mary tried to get to the guy who had asked the question about the babies being "peculiar," but the policeman from the door already had him by the arm, extracting him from reporters who had gathered around him and leading him to the door where the Police Chief had just exited.

The reporters then turned to Mary. They knew who she was now. Questions came from all sides. She lowered her head and pushed through, saying she knew nothing they didn't already know. Out on the sidewalk, a couple of reporters still followed her but finally broke off when she headed across the plaza. She guessed they had hoped she would go to a bar with them and discuss the case. *No way.* What she knew she considered hers and hers alone until she published.

As she started walking back to the office, she remembered the kid who had followed her earlier. She looked back, and he was there. He had stopped, just as she had. She decided it was a good public place. *Let's get this over with,* she thought and headed back toward him.

She challenged him, looking as fierce as she could. He was already half a foot taller than she was, and she felt a little dread. "Why are you following me?"

He was clutching something in his hand. "You the lady reporter?"

"Yes, I'm a reporter."

He held a folded, wrinkled piece of paper out to her. "My sista tole me to give this to yuh."

Mary took it and started to ask who he was, but he had turned and begun running away. There was no way she was going to catch him.

She unfolded the paper. It looked like someone had been printing with a stubby pencil. It was an address, a street address.

Chapter Nine

TUESDAY - MARY MURPHY

Mary folded the paper back up and put it in her pocketbook. She couldn't think about it now.

She entered the newspaper building and headed for her desk. She sat down and turned on the computer.

Dan came over. "Anything new?"

"Yeah, maybe. Like a headline that would read 'Open Question at Baby Murder Press Conference.' Most of the briefing was routine. Only things new were that the babies were murdered by being suffocated. They were newborns, and they were unclothed. That's enough to make an article. The interesting thing was that one of the reporters asked if there was anything 'peculiar' about the babies. Were they deformed? It sounded like he had some inside information. I was going to talk to him after the meeting, but the police hustled him into a side room. The Police Chief seemed upset by the question but wouldn't discuss it. It left a void in the meeting, enough of a mystery to make everyone wonder. I think I can write it into a good article."

Dan looked interested and nodded. "Write it up and let me see it when you're done."

Mary went to work, wanting to write a good report, wanting to get her name back on the front page. At the same time, she kept thinking about the paper in her pocket. Should she mention it to Dan? No, it was hers. *If it meant something, it could be big.* She liked being on the front page. She knew she was still at the bottom of the totem pole of the newspaper staff. She knew that tomorrow she would be back to the old assignments. She wanted more.

She worked on the article most of the rest of the afternoon, polishing it as best as she could, knowing Dan would still make changes. He had to do his job. Even, make work.

She gave the report to him and waited while he made a couple of changes. "It's good, Mary. The facts are important to get out, and the unanswered question adds some interest, especially with the fact that the reporter was led away after the meeting. Unfortunately, we have two problems. One is that the news anchors are going to have this all out tonight, and the reporter who was led away probably has a scoop. He played it for a reaction, and I think he got it. We'll hope it's not out before tomorrow."

Mary packed up and left.

She sat in her car and turned on the air-conditioning. Then she took out the paper the boy had given her and read it. 227 N. Pearson Street. She checked the maps on her iPhone. There was a Pearson Lane and a Pearson Street. The street was a few of blocks down King Street. Okay, she would check it out.

She drove over to King Street and headed toward the river, found Pearson Street, and turned left. She crossed Cameron Street and began looking for a parking space. She disliked parallel parking, but there was no choice. Fortunately, no one was behind her. She hated having someone behind her. It made her hurry, and she always went into the spot too deep. She wished she could afford one of those new cars that parks itself. *Someday?*

She sat in the car. Two houses ahead on her side of the street was 227. It was two stories with a roof sloping to the rear, painted brick, with brick lintels over its door and windows. The double door was on the right with a six-over-six window to the left. Upstairs, there were two four-over-four windows over the door and downstairs window. The door was brown with a five-light transom. A brick frieze extended across the building under the cornice with a pattern that ran across a couple of feet, down a foot, across two feet, and back up. Mary wondered what the pattern was called. The steps were brick with an iron rail turned sideways so as not to block the sidewalk. She thought it must make it hard to move furniture in and out. She wondered if there was a back entrance. *Probably an alley back there,* she thought.

The whole building couldn't have been more than fifteen or sixteen feet wide. Maybe wide enough for a hallway and living room in front. She wondered where the stairs were located.

She got out of the car, cut across the street, and used the large brass knocker on the door to knock. She tried to knock lightly so everyone on the block wouldn't hear. No one came to the door. The house looked empty. There were no draperies at the windows. Shades were drawn down. She knocked again, louder this time. There was still no answer.

She looked around. There was a yellow house to the right, an unpainted brick one to the left. She decided to try the yellow house.

A woman came to the door. She looked wary.

Mary needed a story to tell. "Hi." She flicked her head to the left. "I noticed the house next door looks empty. I'm looking for a rental. Do you know if it's for rent and who I should contact about it?"

The woman studied Mary as if evaluating her as a potential neighbor. "It might be. One of the guys, who visits there, and two Mexicans moved everything out yesterday. Mostly took metal beds, tables, trays, and straight chairs. Looked like hospital stuff. Loaded it in one of those new Mercedes vans, like the kind FedEx is using."

Mary considered this. "That sounds strange, if a couple was living there."

"No, there wasn't any couple, just some men who came now and then, mostly at night and on weekends. Liked to enter through the rear door. Saw some women now and then. Looked pregnant. It was all kind of strange. Don't like to poke my nose in other people's business, but I kind of hope they're gone."

Hey, Mary thought. *This is kind of interesting. Pregnant, huh?* "I don't see any 'for rent' sign or anything. Do you know who I might phone about the house?"

"No, I'm afraid not. Must be some kind of agency that can tell you."

"No, well, I'm glad to meet you. We might be neighbors." *Not likely*, Mary thought. "Incidentally, my name is Lucy Coggins." She put out her hand.

The woman shook Mary's hand. "Sandra Bizzolli."

"I'm pleased to meet you. I appreciate the help."

As she left, Mary thought, *Now I know what I'm doing tomorrow.*

CHAPTER TEN

TUESDAY - LINDA NEALE

Linda spent the day fretting. What was happening to David? Certainly, nothing ordinary. He was angry and sullen, all at the same time. At least he wasn't threatening. That wouldn't be like David. But he wasn't talking to her either. They always discussed things. They met problems head on and tried to solve them. Now he was going his own way without her. Didn't need her or couldn't involve her? She was afraid of the latter. If he was in trouble, it could affect the whole family.

She couldn't call Brenda. She had shared too much already.

She hated to call her mother. She hated whining to her. Her parents didn't much like David anyway. Her father said David had wasted too much of Linda's life with all those years of graduate school, years that only produced a government job. He insisted that David wasn't ever going to be important or make money with a job like that.

But she finally did call. Surprisingly, her mother tried to offer support, said it was probably just temporary. Marriages had problems. Linda would just have to ride it out.

Linda went through the day in a kind of stupor. She did her job taking care of the children. How she wished they were old enough for school. Just a few hours of freedom would save her.

She paced. Then she sat, depressed, at the kitchen table, her arms stretched in front of her. She lay her head down. Her eyes watered with tears of hopelessness. She hated crying. She drew in a breath and held back the tears. She felt her world was imploding. It wasn't great. One way or another, it had been that way since college. At least, during the five years of graduate school, it was mostly boredom. Now it was boredom with responsibility for two children. Initially, that had been shared but not much anymore. What was happening to her life? Did she have a life?

She gave Billy more toys in his playpen. She absentmindedly rocked Little Dave in a small swing set on the table. She fed them according to schedule and put them down for their naps. She leaned against the bedroom doorway and watched them sleep. Time passed. She shook herself and went back downstairs.

She tried to read a magazine but only turned pages and finally threw it at the wall.

She waited for the day to end for David to come home. She had gotten over the anger. She just wanted to learn what was wrong, to somehow solve the problem, whatever it was.

But David didn't come home.

She called her mother again. This time, she didn't get the stiff-upper-lip routine. Her mother asked if David was dangerous and said she and her father had talked, and they were concerned. She asked if Linda wanted to come home and let David get whatever it was out of his system.

At first, Linda resisted and said that she would somehow handle it.

But as time passed, Linda called again. She said maybe it would be better to come home and said she didn't know where David was anyway. She felt abandoned, no longer part of her husband's life. She'd come in the morning. Seymour, Virginia, was only ninety minutes away.

She thought, *What did I say? To come home? Where was* home? *It should be here. I've paid seven years for this* home.

She heard a car in the driveway. It was late but still daylight. It was just past the longest day of the year. July Fourth was next week. She had bought sparklers to perform for the kids. She'd take them to Seymour with her.

David opened the front door and came in. He looked like he thought Linda was going to beat him, certainly berate him. She just sat at the table.

"David, I don't know what's wrong. You vanish, and I don't know where you are."

Awkwardly, he said, "I was looking for Seth and Doc Gill."

"You were looking for your lab partners at night? Something happened at the lab? Have they been lost for two days while you act strange? Couldn't you have phoned? What the hell is going on?"

"Look, I've just got some problems at the lab. I need Seth and Doc Gill to help me work them out."

"Are you telling me NIH is doing secret work you can't talk about? When did that start?"

"No. No. It's just something I have to work out."

Linda stared at him for a minute and drew in a breath. "Well, you're obviously working it out alone. Since you don't need me, I'm taking the children to my parents. When you work it out, let me know."

She waited for him to protest. He looked down at his hands. "Well, maybe that would be for the best."

She was dumbfounded. Had he really said that? He was going to let her go with no protest.

She could barely find her voice. "Okay, I'll go pack."

David could see the hurt in her eyes in the wilting of her body.

He tried to lessen the hurt. "I love you. Always know that. But your leaving is probably for the best."

She gaped at him and thought, *He doesn't care. What could be so bad?*

She wondered if she would ever be back.

CHAPTER ELEVEN

WEDNESDAY - DAVID NEALE

David helped Linda with the loading of the suitcases, the children's toys, the stroller, the playpen, the bags of food, and all the children's other paraphernalia. It filled the back of the SUV. They had bought the car used. They couldn't afford two new cars when he left graduate school. But it had worked well.

He carried Little Dave out and buckled him in the car seat. Linda loaded up Billy. He kissed Little Dave goodbye and then went around the car and kissed Billy. "Love you, Billy."

"Luv you, Dada." He was just beginning to talk.

He went to kiss Linda, but she turned her head. He stood back. "Drive safely. I'll call you."

"Yeah. You do that," she replied coldly.

He stood in the driveway as Linda drove off. As he turned to go back in the house, Brenda came out of her house next door, acting casual, as she picked up the paper. "That was a load in the car, David. Looks like she's leaving for more than a day."

"Really not your business, Brenda." He tried not to look at her.

"Hear you've been putting in long nights."

Christ, Linda talks too much. "That's not your business either."

"Hey, don't be surly. You may need a friendly neighbor to talk to."

He went in, closed the door, and wondered how long it would be before all the neighbors knew. *Damn it, Brenda,* he thought. *You're the last person I want to talk to.*

He dressed for work. He was going to be late. Lourie already thought he was acting strange. This would just add to it.

How long could he keep going to work and pretending life was normal? He looked at himself in the mirror and spoke out loud. "My god, what have you done? What have you gotten yourself into?"

He drove to work in a fog. More of a fog than yesterday. He almost hit a guy backing out in the parking lot as he arrived at NIH. He got a bad look. He saw that guy sometimes in the café. He'd probably get more bad looks.

He passed Lourie on the way in. "Sorry. Just had to take care of a few things."

He closed himself in the lab. Maybe he could get the coffee going. Maybe he was enough of a scientist for that.

The weekly report was due. Seth usually took care of it. Really not much to say. Seth and Doc Gil had now been gone for a week. All he was doing was tracking what they had started before they left. Logs full of notes. He'd just say that. What else could he say? No real results.

He poured his coffee, sat down, and began typing the report on the computer. *What did the world do before they had backspace and delete keys?* He finished it in five minutes. He couldn't face Lourie with it. He set it aside. *What next?*

Check the rodents. He went to work, checking each. He used a checklist for them and entered the notes in the log.

Feed the rodents. No reason they should suffer.

He skipped lunch. He didn't want to see the guy from the parking lot.

He lingered through the day, filling the time. Finally, time to leave. He took the report to Lourie. "Sorry. One-man operation this week. See you tomorrow. Have a good one."

Lourie gave him an uneasy look. "What the hell is going on with your cohorts? Where are they? Boss wants to know."

Dave gave her a poor-innocent-me look. "Wish I knew. I checked their apartments. They weren't there. It's getting lonely."

He turned and walked down the hall, thinking, *I hope she really believes I'm that ingenuous.*

The parking lot was as hot as ever. The inside of the car was hot as hell. He had forgotten to install the sun shield.

He started the car, turned up the air-conditioning, exited the car, stood for a few minutes in the hundred-degree parking lot where it was cooler than in the car, and then got back in. *Wendy's or McDonald's? Maybe Arby's? A little variety in life.*

Chapter Twelve

WEDNESDAY - MARY MURPHY

Mary arrived at work early, knowing she was going to have one of her days. Pre-July Fourth human interest stuff. Dan had left notes on her desk. She looked them over: Alexandria Convention and Visitors Center, Recreational Parks and Cultural Activities, and Historic Alexandria. She picked up the phone and started to dial to make appointments and contacts.

Charlie came in. He was just a few minutes behind her. "Looks like the world is back to normal, sweetheart. Hope it wasn't a once-in-a-lifetime for you." He picked up a paper from his desk. "Looks like I've got parking fee suspensions and transportation schedules. Think I can sit on my butt and do these."

Mary could do most of her work by Internet and phone, but she wanted to get out for other reasons.

She was early with her phone calls and was asked to call back in twenty minutes. So much for the early start. She hit the computer, checking the city government offices. She opened her notebook and began working up the questions she wanted to ask. She wanted to expand on the online information and tie real people to the action. They would remember, and it might help later.

Twenty minutes passed, and she made her phone calls again and got her day scheduled before the contacts had their first cups of coffee.

She had forty minutes before the first appointment. She told Charlie where she was off to. She should check out more formally, but if anyone asked, Charlie would provide the answers. He was the one with the information, and he liked that.

She exited the building and started toward the government area. She checked to see if she was being tailed. No one in sight. *A girl can't get followed every day,* she mused, *but it did make life interesting. Let's go see where the note leads.*

She went by the Office of Housing. If that didn't work, she would go by Real Estate Assessments.

She approached the lady at the front desk. "My name is Sadie Broadneck." *Where did she get that name?* Little Mary certainly didn't look like a Broadneck, but it was too late to change now. "My husband and I are just moving into town from Southwest Virginia and are looking for a house."

The pleasant-looking Afro-American lady behind the desk sat up quickly. "Well, we have some rental lists by the door and postings on the bulletin board over there."

"No. No. We've seen a house we hope is for rent. It's 227 North Pearson Street. Looks empty, and the neighbor says the tenants have moved out. Can you tell me who the landlord is and how to contact him?"

The receptionist leaned back in her chair and shouted over her shoulder, "Margaret!"

A broad lady with a cup of coffee in her hand was just entering an office. "What-cha need, Loretta?"

"Lady needs help finding a landlord."

Margaret waved Mary back and vanished into the office.

Mary entered the office as Margaret was settling into her desk chair. "Have a seat and tell me about this lost landlord?" she asked, chuckling at her own humor.

Mary would play the game. "Well, I hope I'm in the right place. Loretta told me this was the Landlord Lost and Found Bureau."

Margaret laughed. "How about that? Comedy Central right here in Historic Old Town."

She got serious. "Okay, you know I'm Margaret. Name's on the door. Can't hide. Only hope that Loretta can protect me. What's your name?"

"Sadie Broadneck."

"For real?" Mary would have asked the same thing.

"We're moving from Southwest Virginia, coal country."

"Well, Alexandria's own John L. Lewis would have loved you, but he's long gone."

"John L. who?"

"You're too young. Look him up on your computer. Now let's get down to business. Who are you looking for?"

Mary was glad to get through the preliminaries. She had an appointment in twenty-five minutes.

"My husband and I were admiring a house on North Pearson Street, 227. It looked empty, and the neighbor said the tenant moved out day before yesterday. We'd like to ask if it's available and have a look at it."

Margaret wheeled in her chair, tilted her glasses back, and contemplated the map on the wall. "Between Cameron and Queen. Painted brick house with a roof slanting front to back. Nice house. Johnny Swell owns it."

"Johnny Swell?"

Margaret rotated her chair back, tilted the glasses down, and fixed her eyes on Mary. "Well, we are into names today. Yeah, name's Johnny Swell. Seems to enjoy the name. Lives in a high-rise out Duke Street near Shirley Highway."

"Shirley Highway?"

"You're full of short questions, aren't you? It's Interstate 395. Johnny owns several houses. Kind of abstract about it. Think he inherited them. He ought to sell them, but I guess he doesn't need the money. Some people like being landowners. Kind of colonial importance. Anyway, he doesn't concentrate on them very well, and we get complaints. Responds when we jack him up. I'll give him a call for you."

She picked up the phone, looked through a notebook on her desk, found a page, and dialed. She waited a moment. "Hey, Johnny, it's your matchmaker, Margaret Gilson, down at the housing office. Want to fix you up. Johnny Swell, meet Sadie Broadneck." She listened a moment. "Who are you to ask about names? Yeah, she's pretty good looking. I'd say you've got about a fifty-year lead on her. Looks about your fighting weight. Maybe wants to rent your house on North Pearson."

She listened some more, put her hand over the phone, looked at Mary. "He says it's rented."

Mary became alert. "Tell him the people moved out day before yesterday. The house is sitting empty."

Margaret went back to the phone. "She says the people moved out day before yesterday, and the house is empty. Maybe you better check it."

Margaret listened some more. "Yeah. In this job, you never know what to think about renters or *landlords.*" She listened some more. "Yeah, had to poke you a little. Just checking your temperature. Why don't you meet this lady at the house, maybe kill two birds, as the saying goes?"

Margaret listened and looked at Mary. "What time's good for you?"

Mary thought quickly. "I've got a full schedule. Could he do it at five thirty?"

Margaret went back to the phone. "She says five thirty." She listened. "Yes, today. Appreciate it, Johnny. Wear your hearing aid and keep in touch."

She hung up and turned to Mary. "He says he'll be there and to save him a parking space."

"How do I do that?"

Margaret looked pleased. "You can't. The neighbors would kill you. He knows that, and he knows he can park behind the building."

Margaret stood up and put out her hand. They were obviously finished. "Hope you got what you needed, sweetheart. Just watch him. He's smarter than he looks."

Mary thanked Margaret who interjected, "If it was a good experience, put a note in the recommendations box by the door. I've needed a raise for five years."

As Mary left, she tore a sheet of paper out of her notebook, wrote a note, and stuffed it in the box. She waved at the reception desk. "Thanks, Loretta. You guys are jewels."

To which Loretta retorted, "You picked a good day."

Mary left the building, amazed that a visit to a government office had gone so well. No red tape was stuck to her anywhere. Maybe they were normal people after all.

She hoped the rest of her visits would go as well.

CHAPTER THIRTEEN

WEDNESDAY - MARY MURPHY

The rest of the day had gone well. Everyone had packets of information ready to go. Mary only had to ask a few questions to fill in blanks. She found out who to phone if she had other questions and gave them her card to call with any changes that came up. Everyone wanted the free publicity a newspaper offered.

Back at the office, she organized her notes, outlined potential articles, and discussed them with Ben. They finalized what was needed. She returned to her desk and began writing. She wondered if the word *writing* was appropriate anymore. She conceded typing still required hand/mind coordination. She concluded that if Hemingway, pounding on a typewriter, still called it writing, then it was okay. When the hand/mind part went out of it, they'd have to think of a new word.

She finished it up, gave it to Ben, waited for his thoughts, picked the paper up after he waved to her, made some changes, returned it to Ben, waited a while, and got a thumbs-up.

She packed her things, adding a recorder. She was tired. Being out in the heat, going from building to building had wilted her. She was happy in an air-conditioned office. Not much of an athlete. She didn't eat much, sometimes skipping meals completely. She felt she was skinny enough without working at it. She knew she was blessed. She just had to look at the women around her to know that.

Wilted or not, she had a date. Margaret, the matchmaker, had set her up.

Mary repeated yesterday's drive down King Street, turning left onto Pearson and crossing Cameron Street. There were no parking places. She understood that Johnny Swell knew that. She'd try the alley but didn't see an entrance. She drove up to Princess Street, turned left and went around the block, back to Cameron Street, and turned left. She found the alley in the middle of the block. There were no house numbers in the alley, but her house was unique enough. Fortunately, the parking was vertical, without much room to maneuver in and out. Two spaces were all the narrow house could accommodate.

She pulled in her Kia. Happily, its size left room for another car. She was fifteen minutes early. *Where should I wait? In front of the house or behind?* She knew Johnny had to park. Waiting behind was the answer.

She got out of her car and took a camera from her pocketbook. After having only her cell phone at the barbecue, she had added the camera to the pocketbook. She thought it had really been heavy enough without it. But she had learned.

Mary took pictures of the back of the house, of the alley, and of nearby buildings. Later, she would take pictures of the front and up and down the street. She reminded herself to go back to US 1 and take more pictures of the barbecue parking lot and the dumpster. She wanted a complete package.

A dark blue BMW turned into the alley. At first, it didn't look like it had a driver, but then she saw the top of a head. The driver eased the car into the remaining parking place, slowly and methodically. Mary stayed clear, gave him all the room he needed. The door slowly opened, halfway at first, then seemingly, with an effort, opened all the way. A small man shoved out a cane and eased himself carefully to his feet. He closed the door and turned slowly toward her, showing thick white hair, heavy white eyebrows, and vivid blue eyes that defied any need for glasses. He did look like he was about her height and weight.

"You, Sadie Outback? You my date? Okay." He wagged the end of his cane at her. "Spin around. Let me see if you'll do."

Mary felt awkward. She slowly turned around, keeping an eye on the old man.

"Not much of a spin, but you'll do. Have to give Margaret credit."

He still hadn't introduced himself. She stuck out her hand. "I'm Sadie, and it's Broadneck, Sadie Broadneck. Are you Mr. Swell?"

"Broadback? Outback? You don't look like either one. Must be a load to carry. You can call me Johnny because I'm going to skip the Broadneck."

He turned and headed for the back door of the house. He hardly looked like he needed a cane.

"So, Sadie, what's this about the house being empty? Lease runs for another month. Paid up. Be nice to rent it to you but hard to do since it's under lease."

He knocked on the door and didn't wait long for an answer. He stuck a key in the door, opened it, started in, turned to her, and with a twist of his head, said, "Come on."

He stood in the kitchen, leaning lightly on his cane, a frown on his face. "You may be right. Echoes in here. Come on. Let's look in front." Mary followed through what she assumed was a dining room, an electric Victorian-style fixture hanging low over a table that wasn't there. Stairs were to the left. Nice crown molding. Wide baseboards. The living room was more of the same, but a hole in a ceiling medallion was covered, the fixture long gone.

Johnny Swell inquired, "How'd you know they moved out?"

"Asked the lady next door about the house. Said they came Monday with a Mercedes van. One of the tenants and a couple of Mexican fellows to do the labor."

"Well, she'd know." He obviously had no fondness for the neighbor. "Do my old legs a favor. Take a swing through the upstairs. See if anything's left."

"Be glad to." Mary wanted to see it anyway. She climbed the stairs, trying not to look too eager.

She found a hallway next to the stairs with a bathroom opening into it. Footed bathtub, old pedestal sink, and mirror with a metal frame, fixtures all white ceramic. The sink had a couple of chips, black metal showing through. Otherwise, everything looked sparkling white, whistle clean. She bet they'd even cleaned the drains.

She took out her camera, turned off the flash, and took a couple of pictures. She did the same in both bedrooms, front and back. Everything was clean.

"Not a thing left up there," she said as she descended the stairs. "Not even a dust bunny."

"Son of a gun. They haven't given me any notice. Better than moving out in the middle of the night, but it's nice to have time to advertise." He caught a breath. "Margaret said you're interested in the place. You've had the grand tour. Still interested? Bathroom's old, but the kitchen's pretty new, five years old. Two thousand a month, and you pay the utilities. What do you think?"

Mary tried not to blink at the price. She could barely afford her little apartment south of town.

"I think so. I'd have to talk to my husband. Can we get in right away?"

"Don't know. First of August for sure."

Mary tried to look disappointed. "I like the house but don't want to spend a month in a hotel waiting, storing my furniture."

"I understand, but I'm caught in the middle."

"Nothing you can do?"

"Um. Well, maybe you can. I'll let you contact the lessee, see what's up, and maybe we can negotiate something. Save me from running around. But I'd like to know something in the next couple of days."

"That sounds reasonable. I appreciate it very much. Have you got the lessee's name and phone number?"

"Better than that. I even have his address." Johnny pulled out a little notebook and a pen, tore out a sheet of paper, set them on the kitchen counter, and began copying. "It's always been a little weird. He lives in Fairfax. Said he likes the Alexandria address. Prestige. But his rent payments come from a local bank in Fairfax."

Mary thought, *May not make sense to you, but it might to me.*

Johnny handed her the paper and held the door for her. "Anything else we need to talk about now?"

"I don't think so. I appreciate the tour and help. Thank you, Mr. Swell."

"Well, it's been a short date, but the price is right. And again, it's Johnny. Don't answer to the other name. Makes me sound old." He locked the door. "Give me a call soon. Let me know what's going on."

"Hopefully tomorrow, Johnny." She shook his hand. She had a feeling he would have liked to hug her. She started backing. "I'm going around front and take some pictures for my husband."

He held up his free hand in a kind of wave of surrender and nodded as if to say, "Okay, but life could be better."

Mary turned without tripping over herself—an accomplishment—and headed for the entrance to the alley.

After taking the pictures, she returned to her car. Johnny was gone. She sat in her car and got the air-conditioning going. She pulled her wallet from her pocketbook and extracted Johnny's note from where she had carefully stored it. No stubby pencil this time. The name and address were neatly written in ink. The renter's name was David Neale. At least it was, if it was real. She searched the name on her iPhone. The name came up. The address came up. It might be real. Could David Neale be so dumb?

She punched the address into the GPS. Tuscany Lane in Fairfax.

David Neale, here I come!

Chapter Fourteen

WEDNESDAY - DAVID NEALE

David pulled into the driveway, finished the last fried onion ring, balled up the trash, and stuffed it into the Arby's bag. With paper cup and bag in hand, he opened the door and got out, noticing that Brenda was exiting her door.

"Hey, David. How are things going? How do you feel? Linda wants to know."

Annoyed that Linda was phoning Brenda, David replied, "What does she want me to feel like? Tell her I'm not happy. I've survived, what, less than ten hours?"

Brenda glared at him. "She's worried about you, David."

David became contrite. "Yeah, I know. I've got problems I need to fix. Easier on her if she's not here." Not a good answer. "Tell her I'm okay, that I'm thinking about her and the kids and that I will phone her soon."

He turned toward his front door, but Brenda wasn't through.

"Anything you'd like to talk to me about? Or with Eddie? We'll help if we can. Linda's a good girl. I'm worried about you two."

She sounded sincere, but David thought, *Be careful.*

"Thanks, Brenda. It'll shake out."

He left Brenda standing in the driveway.

Inside, he turned on the foyer light and then the kitchen light. The morning dishes were still in the sink and some on the counter. He'd face them in a minute.

He turned on the TV news and got a beer from the refrigerator. He waited to hear about the "Route-One Babies." That's what the radio said they were being called now. David thought, *Better than "Dumpster Babies" or "Barbecue Babies." They were dead babies, whatever you called them. Dead! Dead! Dead!* And he was linked to them. *They were "David's Babies," "Seth's Babies," and "Doc Gill's Babies forever and ever, and that's the way it was.*

He got another beer. The evening news barely mentioned the babies. He guessed there was no progress solving the case. He had no illusions. The time would come. David knew things were going to get a lot worse.

He switched the television to Netflix, flipped through the shows, found *Bloodline* and flipped it on. *Might as well watch some people who are as miserable and culpable as me!*

CHAPTER FIFTEEN

WEDNESDAY - MARY MURPHY

Mary turned onto Tuscany Lane. Somehow, it didn't look like Italy, not even an Italian street scene. Rows of townhouses were built down each side—six units and then another six—before you got to the next street. Window, front door, garage door, garage door, front door, window, window, front door, and so on—ad infinitum. Front doors black, garage doors white. The paired garage doors had two driveways, separated by a one-foot-wide strip full of grass, weeds, and bare spots. A tree was planted on the street corner and more between each pair of windows. The bottom half of the units was a brick veneer, vinyl siding at the top, colors changing from unit to unit. Some windows had curtains. There were lots of shades and Venetian blinds.

Suburbia? Well, maybe low-level suburbia.

There was David Neale's place. Number 7, four units in from the corner. Pale green vinyl. Venetian blinds downstairs, curtains upstairs. Like there was some effort being made.

There was no car in Neale's driveway. A black Mustang convertible sat next door.

Home of a killer? *What does the home of a killer look like?*

Mary parked at the curb across the street and two units closer to the corner. *What's next?* She sat in her little red Kia and tried to look inconspicuous. She didn't even have a newspaper or an iPad to read. She tried to stare at her phone as if there were something important there. *How do the cops do it on TV? Parking inconspicuously up the block so they can blast off in pursuit of the villains whenever they needed to?*

Mary looked up and down the street. There were a mother and two youngsters in the next block riding tricycles on the sidewalk on the left side of the street. Another woman came around the corner behind Mary on the left, walking a dog, a boxer. Mary shuddered. She liked dogs, but boxers always looked like they were going to slobber on her. Nothing against them. She just wondered.

A woman came out of the end unit. Must be number 11. She moved a sprinkler from the side of the building to the front, let the woman and the boxer pass, and turned the sprinkler on. She went back into her unit. She hadn't looked at Mary. Still, there were all those windows with no curtains, no shades or rolled-up shades. Maybe someone behind each. Some little old lady with nothing to do, except keep track of her neighbors and their comings and goings. Mary hadn't seen any "Neighborhood Watch" sign, but you never knew.

She put the car in gear and decided to drive around the block. *How many times can I do this before it looks weird too?*

As she turned back onto Tuscany, a medium-sized dark green car was pulling into Neale's driveway, Malibu maybe? *Am I that lucky?*

Mary pulled to the curb. Same spot as before.

A man got out of the car. Medium-sized, sandy hair, suit coat over his arm, tie loose. Young-looking, fairly attractive, looked like he was still fighting a boyish cowlick.

At the same time, a woman came out of the unit next door and crossed in front of the Mustang. Blond hair, almost white. Good figure. Moved like she knew it.

The two began talking. Nothing intimate. He didn't approach her. In fact, he seemed to want to get away. He turned, turned back to the woman, and then turned again and went into his unit. *Unit* seemed an appropriate description. She wondered if she could call them homes if they had people in them.

The woman stood for a moment, hunched her shoulders, and went back into her house.

Did David Neale have a wife? If so, she didn't meet him at the door. Wasn't that a "wifey" thing? How was Mary to know? Didn't sound like something she'd do. But who knew?

She pulled up a couple of units and tried to look in the window. Venetian blinds were up, so she had hope. She thought she saw the light come on but wasn't sure. It was just past the longest day of the year, and the sun was shining brightly on Neale's unit. Mary couldn't see a thing. It was just past seven fifteen. *What time did it get dark? Nine or nine fifteen. Nearly two hours of daylight were left.*

Should she come back? Was the guy going to load a body in the trunk of his car? Not likely. And what could she see through the window? Guy in his undershirt, making dinner?

She wasn't ready for a stakeout. Besides, she didn't have a partner to shift with her.

And then there was the problem of her being the only car on the block parked at the curb. Mary was sure an old lady was watching.

So what's the plan? She decided to come back in the morning. *Follow him and see where he goes.*

What time would be good? Six thirty or seven? Six thirty in the morning. She hated six thirty in the morning. Seven was bad enough. At least it was daylight this time of year.

She'd be there at seven.

Chapter Sixteen

THURSDAY - DAVID NEALE

David was up early. He didn't know why. There was plenty of time to get to work. He brushed his teeth and went downstairs to make the coffee. Back upstairs, he showered, dressed in his shirt and pants. The tie could wait until later.

The doorbell rang.

Shit, it's only six forty-five.

He padded downstairs in his slippers and opened the door. A man and a woman stood there and held up badges. He opened the storm door so he could talk to them.

The man in a suit said, "Fairfax County Police."

The woman in a white blouse and gray skirt, her gun plainly visible on her hip, said, "Fairfax County Police. Are you Mr. David Neale?"

David stared, mouth agape, and thought, *Oh shit. It's started.* He nodded.

The man in suit continued. "I'm Detective Seldon. This is Detective Hellenbach. May we come in?"

David pushed the door open further and let them in.

They didn't shake hands.

David led them into the kitchen and gestured toward the table for them to sit. "What's this about?"

The detectives sat. Both looked around the kitchen. "Are you by yourself?" asked Hellenbach.

"Yes. My wife is visiting her folks. Out of town."

"Does seem quiet." She scanned the dishes on the counter and in the sink.

David thought, *I'm going to have to keep up with the damn dishes.*

Sheldon addressed him. "We'd like to ask you a few questions. We got a report that two people are missing. A Seth O'Halloran and a Sidney Gill. Kind of strange. Usually, a relative reports the missing. This report came from a woman named Solomon at the National Institutes of Health. Her call came in Tuesday. You know the two guys?"

Seemed like a safe question to David. "Yeah, I work with them. They're my lab partners. Would you all like a cup of coffee?"

Hellenbach shook her head. Seldon said, "Yes, please. Black"

David poured two cups, added sugar to his, and set them on the table.

Hellenbach offered background, "This Solomon said they hadn't been to work Monday or Tuesday and hadn't said a thing about not being there. Said they hadn't been seen since they went on vacation a week ago. She said she thought they each lived alone and that she was concerned. We told her we had to wait a day to start anything. Yesterday, after lunch, Solomon confirmed they still hadn't been seen. Do you know where they live?"

"Yes. Both have apartments in Alexandria."

"That's right. High-rise and an older-type two-story. Out of our territory."

David thought, *Why did she ask if she already knew the answer? Is she trying to trick me?*

Seldon said, "Had to ask the Alexandria Police Department to check them out for us. Both apartments were locked, no answer. You know what they found, both places?"

"Yeah." David sipped his coffee and visualized himself two nights before. "They found notes from me."

Don't look guilty, he told himself. *There's nothing illegal about notes. No way were they incriminating.*

He looked back and forth at the two detectives. "Yeah, I was worried about them too. We've got research going, and we work as a team. It's hard without them."

"You weren't aware that they weren't going to be at your lab?" questioned Hellenbach.

"No. I fully expected them to be there. They both were on vacation Thursday and Friday last week and were due back on Monday."

He thought to himself, *Why did I volunteer that? Just answer the questions.*

"Do you have any idea where they might be?"

"No. That's why I left the notes."

Hellenbach pressed on. "How about relatives, other friends? Do you know any?"

"No. We work together but seldom see each other after work. Just socialize at lunch."

Shit, he thought. *Still more information than I needed to pass out.*

"Did you have lunch with them last Wednesday? Did they say where they were going on vacation?"

"No, they didn't talk about going on vacation."

David sipped his coffee again. *Not a lie but getting close.*

Hellenbach was grappling for questions. "Were they buddies? Did they do things together, maybe go on vacation together?"

David breathed relief. Another easy question. "Not that I'm aware of. They each seemed to have their own lives."

Seldon thought a while. "Well, sorry to get you going so early. And thanks for the coffee." He started to get up. Hellenbach followed his example.

They were going to leave. David wanted to know more. "So where do you go from here? Lab problems are going to get bad soon."

"Up to the captain. Probably ask more help of the Alexandria Police. Maybe search the apartments and survey the neighbors. Not much we can do from here. Should probably turn it over to them."

They shook hands. "Here's my card," Seldon offered. "Call me, if you hear anything."

"Of course."

After they left, David stared at the card. *How the hell did I get away with that? They could have asked so many questions to which I would have had to lie: "Have you seen either one during the period of their absence?" "Did they tell you their plans?"*

David looked at the kitchen sink. *No. Later.*

He put bread in the toaster, finished his coffee, and poured another cup. He wished that he could just sit. The toast popped up, and he started to nibble on it, decided it needed butter. He applied the butter and sat with his little plate. He decided it needed jelly; he looked in the refrigerator and found grape.

He wondered if all children in the world ate grape jelly. *Even the kids allergic to peanut butter could do that.*

David went back upstairs. He absently tied his tie. He didn't check to see if it went with his suit. He didn't check to see if it had catsup spilled on it. It was the same tie he had worn yesterday.

He used the bathroom and left the house.

His mind was in a fog as he backed the Malibu out of the driveway. He noticed Brenda looking out her window, but he didn't notice the little red car parked across the street.

CHAPTER SEVENTEEN

THURSDAY - MARY MURPHY

It was seven-o-five. Mary thought that was pretty good as she turned onto Tuscany.

"Damn it." Neale's car was there, but so was a police car.

Her mind raced. Did this mean they were ahead of her on the story, whatever the story might be? That they were going to foul the whole thing up, foul up her exclusive? Were the police getting the information she needed? If so, how could she get it from them? No way. They only talked through press conferences. Everyone would know about it at the same time.

She parked her car up the block and sat. She fumed and imagined green smoke pouring from her car. She watched in the rearview mirror. She wished she had a cup of coffee. She hadn't had time to stop. She had been afraid she would be late.

Time passed. *Been half an hour, maybe?* She looked at the clock on the dashboard. *No, only ten minutes.*

Neale's door opened. Two people came out. *Man and a woman. The woman looks tough. Must be the cops.*

David Neale shook their hands and closed the door. *Well, they didn't arrest him. Should have had the camera out in case they did.*

Whatever it was, they couldn't have had much on him. Maybe there's hope.

The police turned around in an empty driveway and drove off. Mary drove up to the corner and turned around. She wanted to be pointing the right direction and assumed Neale would leave the same direction as the cops.

Twenty minutes passed. She guessed he was eating, probably drinking coffee. Once again, she wished she had some. Obviously, stakeouts needed planning.

Neale came out the door carrying a suit coat on a hanger. He hung it in the back of his car, got in, removed the sunscreen, and backed out. He headed in her direction and passed her. At least she had gotten the direction right.

Mary noted the blonde woman watching out her window and wondered what kind of gossip the woman would make of the police visit. *What the hell,* Mary thought, *isn't that what I'm doing?* She wished she could talk to the blonde woman, but knew it would let too much of the cat out of the bag.

She followed David on Route 50, Interstate 66, the beltway, and Route 7 through Tysons. It was hard during rush hour. She frequently lost him and had to weave wildly through traffic to catch up. On Routes 50 and 7, she sweated out the red lights, running a couple. She didn't want to be obvious, but she didn't want other cars between them cutting her off. The way she was driving, she knew she really was obvious. *Hopefully,* she thought, *David Neale hasn't been much of a professional criminal up to now, and with luck, he won't notice me.*

Well, past the craziness of Tysons, David turned on his blinker and turned into the large parking lot of an ugly building. Mary passed the entrance and read the sign: *NATIONAL INSTITUES*

OF HEALTH, VIRGINIA ANNEX. There was no indication of what they did in there. She imagined them passing around little vials of infectious diseases. *To each her own,* she thought, *but not me.*

She pulled into the next parking lot, turned around, and drove back to NIH and into the parking lot. David was a hundred feet from the entrance with his coat on. She pulled into the next lane, turning her head so he couldn't see her face. She thought, *Why did I get a red car?* She reminded herself that she had thought he was a misfit as a criminal, but now she realized she was clumsy as hell as a detective. With her budget, the little red car would have to do.

She parked and waited a few minutes. It was a sizable building. It was a good bet he wouldn't hang out in the lobby. *Must be lots of rooms in back and upstairs.*

She locked her car and walked to the entrance, opened one of the side-by-side doors, and entered, wary that she might be spotted. A guard sat at a desk. *Shit, there's a metal detector to go through.* There was a hall with two elevator doors behind the desk. It looked like there was a wall directory opposite the elevators. She needed to see it. She felt it in her bones. *Maybe an answer board.*

She approached the desk. "I don't know if I'm in the right place. Is there any way I could look at the directory? You can watch me." She set her pocketbook on the table next to the metal detector. She didn't want it to go through the detector. She wondered if the camera and mace would set an alarm off if she carried it through. She'd prefer not to know.

The guard looked a little uncertain. "Okay, but stand away from the elevators. There are lots of people coming in this time of day with elevator doors opening and closing. You get too close—I'm going to get nervous."

Mary eyed the gun at the guard's hip. She didn't want him to get nervous. "Thank you."

She walked gingerly through the metal detector. No sound. She always wondered why bras didn't set them off.

She took a notebook and pen from her bag. "I'll leave the pocketbook for ransom."

She walked to the directory, placing herself well away from the elevators. She could see the headlines: Pint-sized Reporter Shot for Invading NIH.

She scanned the directory.

There he was. *David Neale, PhD*. A group of three*:* Seth O'Halloran, PhD; Sidney Gill, MD; and Neale listed under CYNELOGICAL DISEASES. *Oh great. Sounds like lonely work. Wonder what their wives thought of that. How many times a day did they wash their hands?*

All of it under *GENETIC DISEASES*, headed by *DEPARTMENT HEAD, BEVERLY SOLOMON, PhD*.

Mary opened her pad and wrote down the names, being careful of her printing. The names needed to be correct. Then she stood back and scanned the directory some more.

She didn't see anything else.

"Help you find something?"

She turned. It was a good-looking guy in a lab coat, shaved but with a heavy beard that stayed blue all day. *Swarthy—that was the word.*

"No, thank you. Found what I needed."

There was a problem with being alone and looking lost.

Maybe he was being nice, or maybe he was making a move. No way to tell. Anyway, she thought, *Piss off, will you?*

He smiled—nice smile. "Just thought you looked lost."

Mary thought, *Maybe another time, another day.*

She walked back to the metal detector. Her notebook set the alarm off. She felt everyone looking. She set the notebook down and went through again.

She grabbed her pocketbook and thanked the guard. *Always be nice. It usually pays off,* she reminded herself.

Back in her car, she thought, *Started with one name, and now I have four. I need to learn what I can about them.*

But now, I'd better get to work. She would be late. *Have to think of an excuse before I get there.*

Chapter Eighteen

THURSDAY - LINDA NEALE

Linda had been at her parents' home just a little over a day, and already, she was restless. She hadn't been there much in eleven years. She wasn't accustomed to her parents, and they weren't comfortable with her. They certainly weren't prepared for small children. No equipment at all.

She and the kids were in one bedroom. She set up portable beds around the edge of the room. She had to move out a chest of drawers to make room and had taken down the mirror so it wouldn't fall on the crib. She had set them in the hallway. She didn't know where else they could go.

She tied the Venetian blind cords up high.

She'd have to get plastic covers for the electric outlets.

Her parents, Bill and Grace Davis, weren't happy. She had invaded their privacy and torn up their house. The kitchen had become chaotic. Grace tried to pretend the children weren't there. She and Bill hadn't dealt with children since Linda left for college, and that apparently was just the way they liked it.

Linda felt she was going to be thrown out at any minute.

Her mother told her she needed to work at her marriage. They were never easy. Linda told her she didn't know what she was talking about. Their conversations didn't end well.

Her father went into long dissertations on David Neale's inadequacies, his wasting five years on a PhD, while Linda had to live in virtual poverty, followed by showing a lack in real initiative by settling for a government job where the future seemed limited. "He should be out in industry."

Yeah, Linda had thought to herself, *and you were never anything but a mid-level engineer in industry.* But there was no sense in going there. Arguing with her mother was enough.

At night, Bill watched television in the basement. Grace watched it in the bedroom. They couldn't stand each other's programs. Last night, Linda watched with her father. This morning, her mother wasn't happy about that.

"Do you like all that violence? Hope you don't let your kids watch it. TV's just messing up the world."

Linda tried to get off by herself with the kids. She found a playground to go to. Little Dave was in the stroller with a canopy. Billy was really not big enough for most of the equipment. She found a plastic slide and felt it. Metal slides got too hot. This one seemed okay.

The slide was small enough that she was able to pick Billy up and set him at the top. She then stood at the bottom and encouraged him to slide down. He grabbed the sides of the slide and sat there. She told him to let go and slide. He didn't understand. He began to cry.

Linda picked him up and rocked him against her breasts.

Jesus Christ, she thought. *Prayer or profanity? Probably both. How am I going to do this without David? Damn him. What the hell is going on? What if he never settles down? What am I going to do?*

She settled Billy in the other half of the stroller and started pushing. It was too hot to stay out very long anyway.

She thought about her phone call to Brenda yesterday. She shouldn't have called. It made her look like a fool, calling so soon after leaving in a fit of anger. Besides, David had been at work all day, so Brenda didn't know anything. She had just seen him leave. Brenda saw all from her kitchen window.

She pushed the stroller up her parents' driveway, stretching her body and arms out to get enough leverage.

At the front steps, she thought, *It'd be nice if someone would come out to help me.* She picked up Billy and set him on his feet next to the stroller. Then she picked up Little Dave and set him on her hip. *Maybe God made women's hips for that purpose.* She took Billy's hand and half lifted him as he went up the two steps. *It's a wonder we don't pull their shoulders apart at the socket.*

She went to her bedroom and put Little David in the crib and Billy in a playpen. She squeezed between the two and sat on the bed.

God, when can I call Brenda again?

Chapter Nineteen

THURSDAY - MARY MURPHY

Mary arrived at work late. She stayed close to the wall trying to avoid being seen by Ben from his glassed-in office. From the "Command Center," he could watch everything. Fortunately, he was on the phone, feet up on the desk, and turned sideways.

Mary lowered herself quickly into her chair and gave a sigh of relief. Assignments were on the desk—background on parade preparation—special activities at Mount Vernon. She'd have to cover some territory.

She nodded at Charlie. "My sweet ass is here."

"Sorry I ever said that. Don't rub it in. Where you been?"

"Out, snooping. I'll tell you about it some other time."

"Well, save it." He got up and started gathering his things. He looked at her with a half grin. "I've got to go to the police briefing."

Oh shit, she thought. *Has he been assigned because I was late? Shit, shit, shit!* She hoped her pique didn't show.

"Don't look so glum," Charlie chuckled. "I understand from my contact at city hall that they still don't have a thing on the Route-One Babies. This briefing is a missing persons thing.

They probably are opening it to us because they need the public's help."

"Let me know what happens."

"Always, sweet thing."

Charlie left. She wondered what the "thing" was. Hopefully, it was her whole self. Looked like it was replacing her ass. *Moving up or down in the world?*

She made some phone calls, wrote up what she found out, passed the morning, and made an appointment to go to Mount Vernon in the afternoon.

She wanted to hear from Charlie before she went.

She went to the machines and bought a Diet Pepsi and a Baby Ruth. She'd eat real food later.

She sat at her desk and munched.

Charlie returned. He didn't say anything and didn't look at her.

"Okay, you bastard. What'd they say?"

Charlie looked innocent. "Oh yeah, you were interested, weren't you?"

Mary glared at him. "And?"

Charlie sighed. "Nothing about the babies. Didn't even mention them. The briefing was about two missing scientists."

"Scientists?"

"Yeah. Two guys who work together but don't live together. Probably don't even socialize together. Seems weird they would both disappear at the same time."

"Doing classified work? Maybe they were spies?"

"Don't think so. Don't think NIH does classified work." Charlie considered the issue. "No, they work out past Tysons. Can't imagine anything classified out there."

Mary's ears had perked up at the "NIH." She was glad she wasn't a dog. Then it would be obvious. "That's in Fairfax. What's Alexandria got to do with it?"

"Seems both guys live in Alexandria. Fairfax transferred it to our boys." Charlie was starting to lose interest.

She quickly asked, "You got names and pictures?"

"Pete's got the pictures." Charlie scanned his notes. "You think they're friends of yours?"

"Who knows? I know some people at NIH."

Charlie made two checks in his notebook. "Names are Seth O'Halloran with two *l*'s and Sidney Gill with two *l*'s. You know them?"

Mary tried to get the words out. "N-no. Haven't heard of them."

She turned back to her desk and typed a few words on her computer. *Shit, they had to be connected. The babies and the scientists.* She just needed to put it together. And she had better do it quickly. Too many newspeople out there. And the babies had national interest.

Mary looked up the scientists' addresses on the Internet, carefully wrote them in her notebook, and decided to check the places out after work. Background information would help her get to know these guys. Too bad their houses weren't on the way to Mount Vernon.

She got up and looked at Charlie. "If anyone asks, I'm going to Mount Vernon to ask George about the Fourth of July activities."

Charlie didn't look up. "Okay. Give him my best."

Mary left the building and got in her car. She drove down US 1. As she passed the barbecue, some police tape was still hanging from the dumpster. A makeshift memorial had been established by it. Teddy Bears and dead flowers. A couple of crosses. Sad things.

How can I make the connection? She pondered the question. *I know Bizzolli, Sandra Bizzolli with two l's. Everyone has two l's. And who am I? Broadben? Broadneck? No. I used that at housing. Lucy? That was it. Lucy Coggins. I need to write these names down before I screw up.*

She decided to see Sandra before going by the missing persons' homes.

She'd get the scientists' photos from Steve and see if Sandra could identify them.

How was she going to do that? Why would someone new in town who was looking for a house suddenly show up asking about pictures? Mary needed to remember that the pictures would be in tomorrow's newspaper. Anything she said to Sandra might cause her to become wary when she saw the paper, maybe call the cops.

Maybe she could pretend to be a new cop, just hired. Say she was a cop in Southwest Virginia, had gotten hired, and set right to work doing house-to-house footwork.

She could buy a toy badge. Maybe she could pin it in her wallet so she could flash it quickly.

How would she explain why she was canvassing that area? A fishy story could lead to trouble. Besides, she knew that playing a cop was a bad idea. It could get her in real trouble, maybe felony trouble.

Mary almost missed her turn onto Route 235. *Girl, you can't disconnect too much, or you'll be in Fredericksburg wondering what happened.*

She turned and went back to thinking. What about a PI? She could still flash her badge and hope Sandra was gullible and blind. Mary could say the family had hired her, say they had pointed her to North Pearson because one of the family members had heard it mentioned.

Mary thought she could work with that.

CHAPTER TWENTY

THURSDAY - THE HONORABLE J. MADISON CONROY

J. Madison "Mad Dog" Conroy, the United States congressman from the Eighth District of Virginia, sat morosely at his desk in the Longworth Congressional Office Building. He wished he were in the Rayburn Building. He kind of wished he wasn't a Democrat. They couldn't get anything done. Damn Republicans wouldn't let him accomplish a thing. The only way to get anything passed was to amend a Republican bill or make some lousy trades on funding bills. It was hard to get public recognition. He had to send his constituents postage-free letters praising what he had done.

J. Madison, James Madison, or Jay, as close friends called him, had been named at birth to create a political lineage for a career that was planned before he was born. Sadly, the press was happy to inform the public that any imagined connection to President Madison wasn't real. As a result, the "James" had been shortened to an initial.

He had thick almost white hair and a deeply creased face. He could be charming, with Southern style, when dealing with the elites or back-slapping comfortable with the good old boys.

The ladies liked him, and he liked the ladies, professionally of course. Politics were more important than the ladies. Priorities were priorities. Nonetheless, he thoroughly believed he had the best-looking staff on Capitol Hill.

He was married. He didn't know whether Marie understood him and trusted him or just tolerated his ways. He wasn't about to ask.

J. Madison represented Arlington, part of Fairfax, and the independent cities of Alexandria and Falls Church. It was a government, military, and veteran constituency. If they weren't one of those, they most likely worked in some industry that supported the government. J. Madison worked with his constituents' lobbyists. He supported their goals. He had to in order to survive.

Fortunately, he didn't have to fly hundreds or thousands of miles to see his constituents. He didn't have to send staff to meet with them. He lived among them, met with them, and gave talks to their organizations. On the Fourth of July, he was going to give speeches in three different communities, ride in two parades, and eat lunch and dinner at barbecues. He was trying to think about the speeches and come up with something new. But he was getting nowhere. The world of legislation, as it currently existed in the USA, had him down.

He buzzed his admin assistant.

"Yes, boss."

"Audra, will you ask Anais to come in?"

In a few moments, a statuesque brunette came in. She was beautiful. Audra had hired her. Audra hired all the staff. J. Madison was sure Audra liked women too, but Audra was very circumspect.

"Anais, we need to get together our speeches for the Fourth of July."

"I've got last year's in this folder. Already started updating. I assume you want more Veteran's Administration stuff in it. Anything else?"

"No, that sounds about right. You're way ahead of me, as usual. Give me the drafts when they're ready."

"Absolutely, boss."

Good-looking and smart too. J. Madison wondered why he ever worried about the small stuff. So much was repetition from year to year. Amazing how little changed. He just had to make sure things kept percolating.

Still, he needed to get more publicity. Holidays were helpful. His talks and speeches were great. He held town meetings, shook a thousand hands, and ate pounds of greasy chicken.

Still, he needed something new.

He thought about the baby murders. Awful thing. National attention to his district. Not a good kind.

He should have put out a press release exclaiming his horror. Usually, he added his sympathy for the bereaved, but they were unknown. Anyway, that had happened three days ago, and he had let it slip.

Now he had a second chance although a bit of a stretch.

The Mayor of Alexandria had called this morning. She said the Police Chief had another challenge. Two NIH lab workers were missing—worked together but lived apart, both in Alexandria. Since they were government workers from his district and he was the minority guy on the Health and Science Committee, she thought he should know.

He thought, immediately, that he'd have to track it. *But then,* he thought, *I better get ahead of it.* Two guys who worked together in a lab. Sounded weird. He wondered what they did in the lab. Could be sinister.

He buzzed Audra.

She came in. Sandy blond hair, close cropped, just a little shaggy. Slender, no hips, but still attractive.

"I want you to do two things. There are two scientists from NIH who have gone missing. Here are their names." He handed her his notepaper. "Have someone find out who these guys are and what they do. I need the background in case something comes up."

"Second thing is that I want to put out a press release about the murdered babies. Ask Maury to write something."

Maury Caldwell was his chief of staff, a man good with words and good with the public.

"Anything special you want Maury to say?"

"Just brief him on what I just told you. Ask him to express our sadness at the appalling events regarding the two infants and how disconcerting it is to have that horror followed by the disappearance of two government workers. Say that we have great interest in and concern about what is happening and that this office will provide any support it can. Appeal to our constituents to give any help they can and say that our office will take calls if needed but that we look to the police in Alexandria as being the appropriate place to handle whatever tips come forward. Include the police telephone number that they should call."

He didn't really want calls coming here.

After Audra left, he leaned back, satisfied that he had accomplished something.

He studied the staff picture on the wall. Only two men among a staff of women. Maury Caldwell and one intern. The latter had been slipped in past him. Was supposed to have been female. J. Madison always asked for a female. Maybe someone had decided to screw him.

On balance, though, life was okay.

Chapter Twenty-One

THURSDAY - MARY MURPHY

Mary left work as soon as she could.

She swung by Toys "R" Us and bought a toy sheriff's kit with a badge, pistol belt, and toy pistol. She took out the badge and set up her wallet to look as professional as possible.

She drove to North Pearson Street and found a parking space just past the corner. Surprising for this time of day.

She looked down the street at 229, the yellow house. The lights were on, including the outside light by the door. She sat and practiced what she was going to say.

She left the car, went to the door of 229, and rang the doorbell.

There was shuffling inside.

The door opened. It was a chunky man, round face, close-set eyes, neatly parted dark hair. He was wearing slippers, jeans, and a blue shirt. She assumed it was the better half. *Mr. Bizzolli?*

Mary adjusted. "Is the lady of the house home?"

"You mean Sandra. No, ladies' night out. May I help you?"

Mary's mind raced. No need for Lucy Coggins. Better to use another name. Reduce the connection.

"I hope so. My name's Dorothy Doerr." *Better write that down.* "I'm a private investigator." She flashed the badge. "I've been hired by a family to look for a missing man. You'll read about him and another missing man in tomorrow's newspaper. Wonder if I could ask a couple of questions?"

The man didn't move from the doorway. "Why would I know anything about this?"

"You may not, but the family had heard some talk about North Pearson and asked me to canvass the area."

"So what do you need to know?" He still blocked the door, playing it cautious.

"I'd like to show you a couple of pictures. See if you recognize them."

Mary opened her notebook, took out the pictures, and unfolded them. She held them out for the man to look at. "This is the man I'm trying to get information on." She flipped to the second picture. "And this is the other guy who's missing."

He studied the pictures. "Are these guys in trouble?"

"No, just missing. Why do you ask if they're in trouble?"

"Because they act weird."

"So you know them?"

"I wouldn't say that. I recognize them."

"Oh, how's that?"

"They live next door."

"Oh, what side?"

The man nodded toward 227.

Mary looked that way. "I knocked on that door and got no answer. All the Venetian blinds are closed."

The man nodded as if that was expected. "When I say 'live,' I'm using the word pretty loosely. My wife and I talk about it regularly. Three of them are in and out all the time. Sometimes they go a month without being there. Then there are real busy times."

"You said three. There was another one?"

"Yeah, a younger guy, maybe late twenties, and some women, maybe three of them."

"What did the women look like?"

"Heavyset, poorly dressed, one a little slovenly. One black and two white."

"This is good information. I'll pass it on to the police and the family." She didn't want Mr. Bizzolli going to the police. She wanted him to think that was taken care of.

Now the important question. "Have they been around recently?"

"Yeah, they were in and out all weekend. The women too. Started last Thursday. Young guy carrying a lot of takeout. Seemed to be feeding them all."

"So Sunday was the last time you saw them?"

"Yeah, but Sandra saw one of the guys you're looking for on Monday. He and two Mexicans were moving things out."

"Where did she see them?"

"In the alley, behind the house. Kitchen's in the back of the house. She sees most everything that goes on in the alley. Not much privacy back there."

Mary held up the pictures again. "Which man did she see on Monday?"

Bizzolli pointed at the picture of O'Halloran. "That's the one she described."

"Did he have a commercial truck?"

"No, one of those Mercedes vans. Wasn't that much to move."

"You've been very helpful. One last question. Did you ever talk to these men, get to know them?"

"No. They just politely said 'hi' or 'good morning.' Polite but distant. Kind of all business."

"Okay, I'll get this to the police." Mary took back the pictures and closed them in her notebook.

She put out her hand. "Thank you, again, Mr.—?"

"Bizzolli. And you're welcome. Hope you get somewhere."

"Well, I appreciate your talking the time to talk. Good citizenship."

Mr. Bizzolli grinned. "Well, I couldn't close a door on a Doerr."

Mary tried to remember her latest name, forced a smile, and held up her hand in a wave as she turned to leave. She was pleased with herself. *Maybe I should try being a detective after all. I'd just have to get rid of the red Kia.*

Mary had what she needed. Nonetheless, she went next door. She wanted to give credence to her story of canvassing the neighborhood just in case the Bizzollis asked their neighbors about her. The people at 231 were nice.

They let her into their foyer, out of the heat. They gave a lot of the same information.

As Mary left, she wondered if she should canvass everyone on the street. She thought, *When people see the newspaper tomorrow, others may recognize O'Halloran and Gill and phone the police.* Then the story would get around about her. But more canvassing was more than she could do. At least the people she had interviewed didn't have her real name. Even Johnny Swell didn't have her real name. But he did have David Neale's name. Mary needed to move. She needed to change plans.

Mary drove back to her apartment, packed a small suitcase, threw it in her trunk, and drove back to King Street. She headed out of town toward O'Halloran's address, found it, and sat at the curb. She would have liked to have seen the inside of the building, even his apartment door. However, someone might ask questions. She wondered if it was a crime scene. She pictured crisscrossed tape over the door. That would make her nosing around look really suspicious.

Gill's apartment was next. *No,* she deliberated, *it's getting late. Better do Gill another time.*

She pulled away from the curb and headed for I-395 and then the beltway. She was headed for Tuscany Lane.

CHAPTER TWENTY-TWO

THURSDAY - DAVID NEALE
AND MARY MURPHY

David got home a little late—after seven thirty. He had eaten at TGI Fridays and had a beer and steak. He could only eat hamburgers for so long.

He looked at the dishes, got a beer from the refrigerator, went into the living room, and turned on the television. He sat down and watched Access Hollywood. He didn't even know the people they were talking about.

He sat on the sofa. The sheets and pillows from the other night were still there. He decided he'd put them away when he got up.

He turned down the television and picked up the phone. He wanted to listen to his saved messages. Nothing from Linda. He wondered if he should call her and decided against it. *My life is still too screwed up.*

He wondered why he didn't tell Linda what was going on. *Hell, she's my wife. All she could do is leave me. She's already done that.*

He needed to talk to someone. *Hell, a wife can't testify against her husband. Or can she, if she wants to?*

Maybe it didn't matter if she testified. But then maybe they could indict her for abetting a crime. *Then I'm afraid she'd talk.*

The doorbell rang. *Shit. I don't want to talk to Brenda. She makes me feel guiltier than I am. But maybe she has news of Linda.*

He opened the door. A short, pretty woman stood there holding the storm door open. "Hi. I'm Mary Morris." *It had to match the initials on her suitcase.* "I wonder if I could talk to you about the house you rent on North Pearson Street in Alexandria?"

Mary put out her hand. *Oh shit,* she thought. *I hope he's washed his hands.*

It was like a punch to the jaw to Neale. *How did she know about the house in Alexandria? Was she some kind of police person?*

He noticed her hand sticking out and absentmindedly shook it.

"I'm not sure I know what you're talking about," he responded defensively.

Take it easy, Mary. He doesn't want to talk about it. "Are you David Neale?"

Hesitantly, he acknowledged that he was. "Yes, I am."

"Well, I'm just moving to Northern Virginia and looking for a house. I noticed the house on North Pearson was empty, so I phoned the landlord, Mr. Swell. Funny name. Anyway, he said the house was rented, which surprised me, since the house looked empty. He suggested I check with you as the lessee."

He hesitantly replied, "Okay."

Aha, she thought.

She pounced, "So you know the house?"

"Uh yeah. I rent it for a friend."

"Well, it's empty. Mr. Swell took me through it."

Neale was startled. "Empty?"

"Not a stick of furniture. No dishes. Nothing." Mary felt she had his interest. "May I come in? Maybe we can work out something."

Dave wanted to know more. *What had Seth and Doc Gill done? Gotten rid of evidence?*

He opened the door, ushered Mary in and led her to the kitchen. The living room still had the sheets and pillows, along with beer bottles on the coffee table. Then he remembered the dishes. No way to win.

"Sorry for the mess. My wife's away, and I've been kind of lazy. We can sit at the table."

Mary logged in the information: *married, wife away.*

She sat at the table. "Mr. Swell suggested that if you weren't using the place, you might be willing to have someone take over the rent."

David wasn't sure. He'd have to make the decision without his partners. *Hell, why not?* They appeared to have abandoned him anyway.

Mary pushed. "The neighbors said you didn't use it much anyway, just in and out periodically."

David worried. *She knows a hell of a lot. I wonder what else. Damned nosy Bizzollis.*

He sat down. "So what else did they say?"

Make this good, Mary thought, rising to the occasion. "Do you really want to know?"

"Sure, I'd like to know the gossip. See what the nosy neighbors had to say."

Mary got up, opened the dishwasher, and started loading the dirty dishes.

David protested, "Hey, you don't have to do that."

Mary shook it off. "No problem. Makes it easier to talk. I like to keep busy." And keep her foot in the door.

"Well, they talked about you and two other guys coming and going periodically. Said you had some women in now and then. Thought you had a sexual thing going."

"Sexual thing! You got to be kidding?"

"No. That's what they said."

He protested, "Hey, I don't do that kind of thing. I'm married."

"Well, you know, some married guys have their own thing. Doesn't preclude anything."

"Well, it does with me!" He wished he could tell the Bizzollis off, straighten them out.

David got up and started helping with the dishes.

"You think they're talking to their neighbors, saying that kind of thing?"

"Heck, what do you care? Just adds a little cachet to your life."

"I don't want that kind reputation."

"Well, you probably have it now."

"What do you mean?"

Mary grinned at him. "Well, here we are in front of the kitchen window, hip to hip, like man and wife, doing the dishes."

David quickly moved away and sat down, out of sight. He thought quickly. "Listen. There was no sex. My friend used it for poker games. Asked me to rent it for him so his wife wouldn't know. High stakes games. The women came to serve snacks and drinks."

Mary didn't turn from the dishes. She summarized, "Let's see. Only three guys playing poker. Only beds, chairs, and small tables moved out, along with what the Bizzollis thought were medical items, instrument tables, and the like. They didn't mention any poker tables. Did you guys just sit on chairs without a table to play poker?" She looked at Neale. "Sounds strange, Mr. Neale."

David was getting annoyed and defensive. "Why? Why do I have to explain anything to you?"

Mary had to back up a little. She suddenly remembered that this guy might be a murderer.

"You know, you don't. It's your life. But I bet your wife doesn't know about any of it." She couldn't stop egging him on.

She closed the dishwasher and turned around. He grabbed her by the shoulders. "What the hell are you trying to do?"

She forced a smile. "Hey, nothing. Just giving you a hard time." He didn't even look mean when he was angry. Soft face, floppy, brown hair, easing back at the temples. Not bad-looking. Maybe five ten, five eleven. Tall to her.

She gently pushed him away and walked toward the living room. As she went through the doorway, she needled, "Still, you need a better story."

He stood in the doorway and watched her as she picked up the beer bottles, napkins, and a plate of cracker crumbs. She kicked the sofa skirt straight with her foot and brushed past him. She put the plate in the dishwasher. "Where's the trash can?"

He felt rung out. "In the cabinet to the left of the sink."

She opened it and threw in the bottles. Then she opened the cabinet under the sink. The dishwasher detergent was where it should be. She poured it into the receptacle in the dishwasher door and started the wash while he watched in silence.

She turned to him. "I really don't care what you were doing with the house. None of my business. You just seemed so sensitive about it. I'm sorry. It's my carnivorous personality."

David looked a little appeased but still uncertain. And nervous. "Okay, maybe I acted a little strongly. I'm not a bad guy."

"Okay. Let's start again. Is the house for rent? Guaranteed not to have ghosts or dead bodies."

David blanched. "Why would you say that?"

Mary thought, *Oh god, I've done it again.* Still, the reaction was telling.

She quickly replied, "Sorry again. It's just my nature to make jokes and tease."

She sat back down at the table, wondering if she would survive the night.

She decided on small talk. "I see from the paraphernalia around here that you've got kids?"

He wondered if he should keep going on with this. Still, he wanted to know what she knew. "Yeah, two of them. Year and a half and three months.

"You've been a busy boy. They go away with your wife?"

"Yeah."

"It must be quiet and lonely. You miss them or enjoy the peace?"

David thought, W*hat business was it of yours? What was the acceptable, conventional answer?*

"Yes, I miss them."

"Bet you do. Looks like you had two or three days' worth of dishes."

"Two days." Hell, he couldn't stop telling her things.

Mary got up. "I get the feeling you're not ready to talk about the rental tonight, and it's getting late. I probably won't be able to get a motel room. I saw you had linens on the sofa. I'll get my suitcase and sleep there tonight."

Out the door she went, returning shortly with her MM suitcase. She breezed past him into the living room. "We'll talk about the rental in the morning. Where's the bathroom?" She walked into the hallway. "Oh, I see it." She checked it out. "Hey, Mr. Neale. Don't worry. I've got everything I need."

David protested. "What are you doing? I don't know you. You just walked in here and started taking over. I can't have you stay. You know what the neighbors will think. You've got to go someplace else."

She faced him and looked him in the eye. "What are you going to do? Throw a hundred-pound woman out on the street? Do I look dangerous? Give me a break. Besides, if the neighbors are going to think evil thoughts, they already are."

She walked back into the living room and started spreading the sheets.

David felt defenseless. He was. *Damned women. All of them.* A hundred pounds of woman had him on his heels. *What the hell will Brenda think? What will she say to Linda?*

He noted, "You're going to need a new pillowcase."

"That'd be nice. See you in the morning."

David nodded. "I'll throw some down."

He turned and left the room.

Mary took a deep breath. *You've got brass ones, girl.*

CHAPTER TWENTY-THREE

THURSDAY/FRIDAY - MARY MURPHY

Mary tossed and turned. She hated a sofa. At least she was short enough to fit. She just had to bend her legs a little.

Everything went around and around in her head. She needed to start writing as soon as she could.

She woke up with him in the kitchen. She felt awful and thought, *Must have only gotten three hours sleep, four at the most.*

She sat up, pushed her feet into her slippers, and padded to the bathroom. She wanted to get out of his sight. She did the bathroom routine. Time for hair brushing and a little powder, light lipstick. No time to do her eyes.

She looked for her bathrobe. She'd left it by the sofa. She hurried back and looked at the robe. *God, it's old and ugly.* She decided, *What the hell? I'll just go to the kitchen in my pajamas. Maybe it'll distract him.*

"Good morning. Sleep well?"

He glanced at her, quickly up and down, and then turned away as if embarrassed, as if what he'd seen wasn't really there. "Not really. Haven't slept well in a couple of days."

He'd made coffee. She started opening cabinets, found a mug among an eclectic assortment, with university logos. She stretched to reach one and felt him watching her. She poured herself a cup.

"How come you can't sleep? Something worrying you?"

"Oh, it's nothing. Just an experiment that didn't go well."

She set her coffee on the table and opened the refrigerator. "Oh, where do you do experiments? Sounds interesting . . . You like scrambled eggs?"

"Yeah, eggs would be great. . . I work at NIH, uh, that's the National Institutes of Health."

She pulled out milk, eggs, bread, and butter. She'd use butter to cook the eggs. Better than looking all over for oil or PAM. "I know what it is." She pulled a frying pan from the drawer under the stove. "So you do, like research there? Lab technician or something?"

As she dumped a blob of butter into the frying pan, turned on the stove, and stuffed two pieces of bread in the toaster, she felt him bridle.

"No. I've got a PhD. Do important research. I've got a lab tech who works for me."

She cracked four eggs. "Hey, that's impressive. You work on genetics? Genetics seem like the in-thing these days."

"A little bit. Mostly we look at how diseases—cancers mostly—respond to various stimulations and medications. We work with rats and mice."

She stirred the eggs. "Yeah, who's we?"

"Oh, I have a couple of partners."

"They worried about the experiment too?" Mary buttered the toast, put it and the eggs on plates, and set them on the table. "Experiments always scare me. Always worried about it in chemistry. Always worried I'd get hurt or killed. Do you do anything where someone might get killed?"

David's fork hung in the air. He was suddenly careful. "No. Nothing at NIH will kill you."

"Some disease couldn't get loose?"

"Well, maybe. We're pretty careful."

"How do you get volunteers? I'm always hearing advertisements on the radio about doctors wanting people for trials."

"Oh no. We only work on lab animals. The human work is done elsewhere."

"So what do your partners say about the problem you're having?"

He hesitated again. "Well, I've still got to talk to them." He finished his breakfast. "I'm afraid I need to be going and get to work."

He eyed her pajamas with uncertainty.

"You go ahead. I'll use the shower upstairs and get myself ready. I'll turn the lock in the front door and pull it closed when I leave."

David didn't know what to say. This woman was just making herself at home. She didn't even ask permission, just plowed on. Somehow, he couldn't tell her no. "Okay. Pull it tight."

"Don't worry, David. I'll empty the dishwasher and clean up breakfast before I go. The place will be straight for tonight. We'll talk about the lease then."

David stood for a minute, looking uncertain. Had he told her to call him David? He hadn't called her by name. Could someone sleep in your house and you not call them by name?

He turned, walked out of the kitchen, picked up his suit coat off the stair finial, and went out the door. "Goodbye."

"Yeah, see you tonight. We still need to talk about the lease."

Mary cleaned up, waiting to make sure he was really gone.

She checked the kitchen drawers for notes and looked under the telephone. There was an address book sitting on the phone book. She checked it for Gill and O'Halloran. The phone numbers were there but no addresses. She guessed he didn't visit them. She paged through and found a phone number for 227 North Pearson Street. She checked her phone and did a reverse check on the number. Seth O'Halloran. *Well,* she mused. *They didn't stick David with everything.*

She dialed the number and got a recording. The phone had been disconnected. *No surprise there.*

Mary headed upstairs and checked the bedrooms. There was no den, just a desk in the master bedroom. She checked the drawer in the bedside table under the phone. Phone book, tissue, pens, and bobby pins.

She headed for the desk. Clean and neat, not like the kitchen. Here, David was organized. She checked the drawers and found the paid bills and leafed through them. She saw nothing from Johnny Swell. Maybe he didn't bill. She found the checkbook. There were no check stubs that said Johnny Swell. Maybe Johnny has an LLC or something, or maybe the checks were sent automatically from the bank. She went through the book again, but there was nothing that caught her eye. She guessed that was to be expected.

She looked for bank statements and couldn't find any. She felt she had come up empty.

She checked the bureau drawers. The short one had women's stuff and looked like it had been stripped. Some underwear, stockings, jewelry, and hair stuff were left. The tall bureau had men's clothes, men's jewelry, cuff links, tie clips, and studs, and condoms.

She headed for the bathroom and opened the medicine cabinet. Not much women's stuff left. She closed the cabinet and checked the shower. There was no walk-in shower, just a bathtub. She checked around the bathtub. She'd have to use men's shampoo and bodywash. She wondered if it was really any different from women's stuff other than packaging and the perfume.

She figured out how the shower worked, pulling a button down under the faucet. Every bathtub seemed different.

After her shower, she got dressed and looked around the house once more.

Mary found the *Washington Post* on the foyer table. It was unread. She wondered if David knew yet about his missing partners. Maybe that was why the police had been at David's house this morning.

She looked through the newspaper. Small article on the missing men on the third page of the Metro Section. Pretty well buried. *Well, it won't stay that way for long.*

She left her suitcase in the living room but folded the sheets neatly and stacked them and the pillows at the end of the sofa.

She locked the door and left. The heat and humidity were already at work.

As she walked down the driveway, she turned and looked at the next-door apartment. As expected, there was a blond head trying to stand back from the window so as not to be seen. She wondered if David's marriage was going to survive Mary Murphy.

Mary nodded and smiled at the window.

She wanted to give the blond the bird.

Chapter
Twenty-Four

FRIDAY - DAVID NEALE

What am I going to do with this woman? Always asking questions. Seems to know something about the experiment, and I don't even know who she is.

David had gotten up, brushed his teeth, combed his hair—floppy as it was—and gotten dressed, all the time pondering the strange situation.

She acts like she owns the place.

David went downstairs and retrieved the newspaper from the front yard. Brenda was looking out the window. *Shit, Linda's going to know all about this.*

He lay the paper on the foyer table and thought he might be able to read it, if the woman left in time. He wondered if she was still in the living room. He hoped not and took a peak from the kitchen door. She was sitting up, still in her pajamas. He ducked back. He could soon hear her in the downstairs bathroom. *What's next?*

He started the kitchen routine. Coffee first. Old-style coffee maker—ten-cup. He usually only made half a pot but decided that, with his "guest," he'd better make a full one.

She padded into the kitchen, still in her pajamas. *Damn, she's really making herself at home.*

She said, "Good morning."

"Uh, good morning."

They made small talk. He watched as she got a coffee mug from the cabinet, poured a cup, and sat at the table. Then she headed for the refrigerator, offering to make breakfast. He was happy to let her make the breakfast and wait on him. He watched her move and stretch. He knew she didn't have on any underwear. It made him nervous, maybe excited. Maybe aroused. He decided he'd better get to work.

She said she'd stay and clean up. She wanted to get a shower. She called him David like he was an old friend. He was reluctant. Hell, he didn't know her. She might steal him blind. For reasons he couldn't fathom, he couldn't tell her no.

He went into the hall and picked up his suit coat. "Goodbye." She reminded him of the lease. Sure enough, in all this time, they hadn't talked about it. It sank in. *She's coming back.*

David got into his car and removed the sunscreen. He refused to look in Brenda's window.

He drove to work, distracted. Maybe he'd agree to giving her the lease as soon as he got home and get her out of there.

He'd like to know more about her. Her questions didn't seem to come out of the blue. He felt she had some background on him, but how and why? She made him nervous for a lot of reasons. He needed to ask his own questions.

As he entered the NIH building, Anthony Styles, a guy from another lab, was in the hall waiting for the elevator.

"Hi, Tony. Thanks for pushing the button."

As the elevator door opened, Tony looked at David and asked, "So what's happening with Seth and Doc Gill?"

"What do you mean?" So the word was out.

"The newspaper says they're missing."

"Is that right? They haven't been here all week. True enough, I haven't heard from them. Who reported them?"

The elevator door opened, and they got out.

"Your boss did. Didn't she talk to you?"

"Yeah, she asked if I knew where they were. Didn't know she was going to file a report. Do the police have it?"

"Yeah, Alexandria Police. Wonder why not Fairfax?"

"They live in Alexandria."

"Makes sense." Tony turned to walk to his lab. "Take care. I'll leave you to your mystery."

David went to his lab. Lourie stuck her head in the door. "Did you see the newspaper?"

"No, but Tony, down the hall, already told me about it being in the paper."

"Cops talk to you yet?"

"Yeah, Fairfax cops came by the house. Couldn't help much." David wondered if Alexandria Police would come too.

"Solomon's worried about you getting your work done. Thinks she might have to get you help but doesn't know when. Everything's uncertain now."

"I'll be okay for a while. Tell her not to worry."

Lourie closed the door, and he was glad to be alone.

CHAPTER TWENTY-FIVE

FRIDAY - MARY MURPHY

Mary was back at her desk, a little late for work again.

Charlie eyed her. "Still nosing around?"

"Yeah, you might say that."

"Anything you want to talk about?" Charlie was fishing.

Mary was ready. "Don't know enough. Maybe in a little while."

"Okay, get yourself back to garden parties and flower shows."

Mary bridled. He was reminding her of the assignments she had been stuck with in the past. He could be annoying.

She turned away from him without commenting. She knew he felt he had made his dig.

She knew she had work to do, with the Fourth of July coming up. Still, it had to wait while she made her notes:

> There was something "peculiar" about the missing babies the police weren't talking about;
>
> Yes, David Neale did rent the house on North Pearson and hid the rent payment;
>
> David Neale worked at NIH;
>
> David Neale's partners were missing, and he didn't know where they were;

David and his partners had run some kind of experiment that had gone wrong;

David and his partners were in and out of North Pearson on an irregular basis;

Sometimes heavyset, poorly dressed, possibly pregnant women visited there too;

David lied about why the house was being rented;

David's partner had moved beds, chairs, and medical stuff out of the North Pearson house and left it empty and clean the day the babies were found in the dumpster. The house was practically sterilized. David didn't know this had happened;

The phone at North Pearson had been disconnected;

David Neale was on edge, and his wife was not at home. (Had she moved out?);

The Alexandria Police were working the missing persons case.

Did she have enough? No, Mary didn't think so. The link wasn't strong enough yet. She had more work to do.

Back to David's tonight.

She'd swing by Gill's apartment on the way and finish the background work.

Chapter Twenty-Six

FRIDAY - BRENDA DEHAVEN

Brenda saw them both leave, David hurrying and looking worried, the bimbo looking defiant.

Brenda was upset and excited at the same time. All day she fretted. She didn't know whether to call Linda or not. She wasn't anxious to be the bearer of bad news. But the news was too juicy not to tell someone.

She called Marney down the block. "Bet you don't know what's going on at Linda's."

"What's Linda up to?"

"No, it's not Linda. She left David Wednesday. Went home to her parents."

"Yeah, they fighting?"

"Don't know. All I know is that Linda's real worried about something. But that's not what I called about."

"Oh?"

"No. What I'm calling about is that David's had a visitor. Pretty little bimbo. Spent the night there. Gave me a tough-shit smile when she left this morning."

"No kidding. When the cat's away."

"Yeah. It looks that way. You think I should call Linda?"

"Up to you, girl. I'm not getting in the middle of that."

"Don't you think she ought to know?"

"Don't know. The woman might be David's sister."

"No way. They don't look at all alike."

"Still, you need to be careful, until you know more. You might break up a marriage."

"Yeah. You're right. I'll keep an eye on them."

"Know you will, dear. Let me know what happens. Want to be out of the way of any eruption but still want to know."

"Know what you mean. Hey, we're just concerned neighbors."

"Absolutely."

Brenda hung up and went to the kitchen window. The culprits were long gone. She remembered David's guilty face and shook her head.

She went upstairs and did her makeup. She took a half hour each day. She took off her nightgown and admired her figure in the mirror. *Still pretty good, lady.* She got dressed and went back downstairs.

She thought about going out. Maybe have that martini lunch. But she was afraid she'd miss something. The entertainment was next door.

She spent the day watching television, cleaned a little but not much. She hated to spend her time that way.

The day dragged. Finally, when it had been about time for Eddie to come home, she went to the kitchen window to watch for him.

When she looked out, she gasped. The little red car was in Linda's driveway, the woman sitting there reading something. She had missed the arrival. *Brenda, you need to be alert.*

She fiddled around the kitchen counter for ten minutes, checking the driveway constantly.

David pulled in behind the red car. He got out and got his suit coat. As he approached the red car, the woman got out and picked up a grocery bag from her back seat. *Damn, she's moving in.* They went into David's house together. She couldn't see David's front door. *At least they didn't kiss.*

But she wondered what happened when they got in the house.

Then Eddie came home, and she told him about David and the bimbo while periodically checking the front window.

Eddie picked up the newspaper and started reading it. He told her that what David did was none of their business.

Brenda thought, *Men. They wouldn't know anything going on in the world if women didn't tell them. They miss all the fun and the worry and the concern. It was women's responsibility.*

The next time she looked out the window, Eddie asked, "So what do you see?"

He had heard her after all.

"Not a thing. Looks like they're in for the night. His car's behind hers. It'll take some work for her to get out."

Later, Eddie went to bed.

Brenda stayed up.

She didn't want to miss a thing.

CHAPTER TWENTY-SEVEN

FRIDAY - DAVID NEALE AND MARY MURPHY

David hid in his lab all day.

He lost himself in his work. That was the good part about the job. He had decided to work and not fret. He didn't feel like there was anything he could do. He felt he was swinging on a rope that was going to break, but he didn't know when. So he might as well work.

Nonetheless, he was glad when the day ended, or was he? *She* was going to be there again tonight, full of questions. Well, he would ask some of his own. What did *she* do? Where did *she* live? How could *she* afford North Pearson? Why did *she* ask so many questions?

He drove home, the questions going through his head. He wondered if *she* would really be there.

He turned into Tuscany Lane. *Her* car was in the driveway. *Brenda must be having a fit. Bet she's got a camera out. I may be on YouTube tonight.*

David pulled into the driveway behind *her* red car. He picked up his coat out of the backseat. As he walked past *her* car, its ignition turned off, and the car door opened. *She* had been waiting in the car. Of course. *She* didn't have a house key. *She* opened the back door of *her* car and took out a paper grocery bag. "I got us some steaks and salad makings. Didn't know what you had."

She followed him to the door. He unlocked the door and held it for *her*. *She* walked right in as if *she* were home, went in the kitchen, and turned the broiler on to warm. "Didn't know if you had salad dressing, so I bought some of that too."

Mary dug out a pan. She was learning her way around. She unpacked the steaks. She made sure he saw that they were wrapped in butcher paper. She wanted him to know she had gotten good ones.

David, again, felt uncomfortable. "I think I'd like to change before dinner. Get comfortable."

"Good idea. I think I'll change too. Oven has to heat anyway." David realized *she* was dressed professionally. Blouse, skirt, and low heels. Interesting.

He went upstairs, and she went into the living room to open her suitcase and then to the bathroom.

He went into the bathroom to change. *She* had left her hairbrush on the sink. He put on a pullover shirt and jeans and went back downstairs and sat at the kitchen table, setting the hairbrush at *her* place.

She came in. A T-shirt and also jeans. David thought, *Thank goodness, no short shorts.*

He realized *she* was cooking and waiting on him again. That was nice.

Mary put the steaks in the oven. She started looking for a colander and a salad bowl. David didn't know what *she* was looking for and didn't help. She found what she needed and started washing the lettuce. Suddenly, he realized what *she* was doing. He got up and got salad tongs and set the table, knife, fork, and paper napkins.

Mary acknowledged him. "Thanks for the help. David, how do you like your steak?"

She thought to herself, *It's about time you woke up.*

"Medium rare, if you would please?"

"Me too. That makes it easy."

Mary tossed the salad. Lettuce, tomatoes, and cucumber. "I bought blue cheese dressing. Will that do for you?"

"Thanks. I've got Italian in the refrigerator. I'll put it on." He went to the refrigerator, took it out, and got two beers.

"Beer all right with you?"

She would have really preferred iced tea, but she knew that was not likely to be available. "Sure."

She put the plates on the table, and they both sat down. She noticed her hair-brush and thanked him.

David got his thoughts together. "So what do you do for a living?"

Not "So, *Mary,* what do you do for a living?"

So before she responded, she said, "David, I'm Mary. Mary Morris. I have a name. Maybe I mumbled it yesterday, but I do have a name."

David looked chagrined. "Okay, Mary."

She had thought about his question, about making enough money to rent North Pearson, something that fit the way she dressed. It had to be something that he couldn't ask questions about. Not an accountant or veterinarian or an airline pilot or something like that.

"I'm a receptionist at a hotel." She thought she could fake that.

"Oh, what hotel?"

"The Marriott in Rosslyn. Work the day shift." She worried he might call and check, but she hoped she'd be long gone by then.

"So why are you looking for a house?"

"Came from Birmingham. I was doing the same job down there. Wanted a change of scenery. A little adventure." She hoped he had never been to Birmingham. She hoped it was far away and remote enough.

"The job must pay pretty well."

Mary thought about the house on North Pearson and how much it cost. "Not so great, but I don't need to work. Both my parents are dead, and I inherited a good amount. Keep some in annuities but keep some to spend."

That quieted him. Mary had to fill the void. "So . . . have you thought about the lease?"

David nodded, changing gears. "Oh yes. I think we can work that out. You willing to take over the payments immediately? I'll pay utilities up to now."

Mary assented. "Yes, that sounds fine. I'll call Mr. Swell tomorrow and arrange the paperwork. Sound all right to you?"

David nodded. "Sure, fine."

He hoped she'd leave.

Mary picked up the plates and headed for the sink. "How'd your work go today? Rats and mice okay?"

"Sure. I got a lot done."

"Who feeds them on the weekend? They must get lonely."

"Oh, we have a lab tech who comes in. Has to be careful because they have different diets, depending on the experiment."

"Yeah, I can imagine. You know those NIH guys who are missing? Saw it in your paper this morning."

David thought, *Oh, oh. More sensitive questions.*

"I haven't seen the paper. Meant to read it tonight."

Mary looked around and saw the paper where she had left it. She opened the Metro Section, put page three in front of David, and pointed to the article. "Couple of guys named O'Halloran and Gill. Work at the only place in Northern Virginia where NIH has labs. Bet you work there too."

David hesitated. *Hard to lie about that. Too easy to check. Don't want her looking things up.*

"Yeah, way out Route 7. Yes, I know them."

"Know any reason why they might be missing? You must all know each other."

"No, I don't." He read the article carefully.

"Maybe they were doing secret work, and the Russians got them?"

He answered as if her question wasn't a bit ludicrous. "No, we don't do secret work."

"Well, it seems strange that two of them should vanish at the same time. Do they work together?"

A little exasperated, David thought, *Damn it! She's in control again.*

She walked to the sink and started doing the dishes again. She rinsed the plates and loaded them in the dishwasher.

"Yes. But I don't know any more than that."

He wanted to get off the subject.

"So have you found a place to stay yet?"

She eased off the subject of the missing men. "No, but I'll be out of your hair tomorrow."

Mary didn't want to ask permission to stay. She didn't want to give him a chance to say no.

David floundered again. He just nodded.

Mary made sure the evening continued. "Why don't you turn on the television? I'll finish the dishes and be in in a minute."

David went in, sat on the sofa, and turned on the television. The news was just ending. He was glad no newsreader would be talking about the missing men.

Mary came in and sat on the sofa beside him. He leaned slightly away. She clearly was making herself comfortable. He was not.

It's his television, she thought as the Hollywood news came on. "So what do you like to watch?"

"Uh, it varies. Usually Netflix or Amazon Prime."

"Okay, pick something."

He would have liked a mystery or a shoot-um-up but settled on a comedy. He didn't know why he was trying to please Mary.

They sat quietly and watched. She laughed. He thought she had a nice laugh. Finally, he laughed too and began to relax.

Mary got up and went to the kitchen. He stopped the show. She rummaged around in there.

David shouted, "Do you need help?"

"No, I'll be right there."

She came back with cheese and crackers. "I thought some munchies would be nice."

"Good idea. I'll get some drinks."

He went to the kitchen and equivocated. *Water, soda, beer, or wine. Should I ask her? Hell, she drank beer, so why not wine?*

He opened a bottle, poured two glasses, went back to the living room, and handed her the glass, while she munched crackers. She nodded and made a face that looked half-pleased, half questioning.

He sat back down and started the television again. They both sipped their wine and ate crackers. It seemed she laughed less, as if her mind was elsewhere.

He turned his head to look at her.

She looked back and smiled.

He leaned over and kissed her, briefly, quickly. He scared himself and thought, *What the hell am I doing?*

Mary set her glass down, put her hand behind David's head, and kissed him back. This time, there was nothing brief about it.

He put his hand on her leg, held it still, and then began to run it up the inner seam.

She didn't stop him.

Holy shit!

CHAPTER TWENTY-EIGHT

FRIDAY - DAVID NEALE AND MARY MURPHY

Mary lay in David's bed. She couldn't sleep. He snored lightly beside her. *My god, what have I done? Did I prostitute myself for a story? No. I wasn't thinking about that. Just seemed natural.* But David would never believe that. If she published, he would think she used him. Maybe she had. Subconsciously? Certainly not consciously.

She felt uncomfortable. She was in another woman's bed, lying where she had lain. He'd used a condom that was meant for his wife. Mary didn't even know the woman's name. Maybe that was for the best.

Finally, she dozed.

She awoke. The bed was gently shaking. She listened. David was sobbing. His back was to her.

She reached over, took his shoulder in her hand, and pulled herself against him. She reached across and held him.

He stopped sobbing but breathed deeply, almost like he was surfacing from drowning.

"I didn't do it." He buried his head deeper in the pillow. She imagined his eyes closed, his face in anguish.

Did she dare? "Are you talking about the babies?"

He bolted up and turned toward her, leaning on his elbow. "How the hell do you know?"

"Pretty obvious, after looking at the house in Alexandria and talking to its neighbors. They saw a lot." She'd let him think they saw the babies.

"I didn't kill them. I swear I didn't."

She reached up and stroked his face. "I know you didn't."

"How do you know?"

"It's not in you. You're too gentle. My guess is that one of the missing guys did it. I suspect they're your partners."

"Yes, damned them."

"I'm sorry, David. I'm so sorry."

He lay back down, his back to her. "And they've left me. I'm all alone."

She wanted to say he wasn't alone, that she was with him, but it was too big a lie.

She lay back down, her back to him.

Thoughts swirled in her mind. His life was miserable, and she was going to make it worse. Could she do it? She didn't know. He wasn't a bad guy. It was a hell of a story. Was she enough of the bitch to follow through? She didn't know.

CHAPTER
TWENTY-NINE

SATURDAY - DAVID NEALE
AND MARY MURPHY

Mary awoke. Her eyes opened, and she wondered where she was. "Oh shit!"

It was just barely light. "Must be five thirty or so."

She got up, her arms crossed over her breasts, and walked out the bedroom door and down the stairs. Her clothes were still on the floor, next to the sofa, along with his. She put his on the arm of the sofa, tidying up like she lived there. She took hers to the bathroom, did the morning routine, got dressed, and went back to the living room. She picked up the wine glasses and the cracker-and-cheese plate, took them to the kitchen, dumped the wine in the sink, and scraped the plate into the trash. She put them in the dishwasher. She felt like she was getting rid of the evidence.

She made the coffee. She needed coffee, and she now knew her way around.

She sat at the table and wondered if she could face him.

No, I can't run like a coward, even if I am one.

She stared into space, got up, poured a cup of coffee, sat back down, and waited.

She heard him upstairs and wondered what he was thinking. She wondered if he really was a killer. He sure didn't seem like one. *Maybe I should get out of here before he kills me.* The trouble was that his car was parked behind hers.

She looked out the kitchen window. Two cars were parked in the driveway next door, the Mustang and an Explorer. *Must be the blond's husband's car.* There was no way out unless she backed across the lawn.

"Good morning." He came into the kitchen, didn't look at her, poured some coffee, and sat next to her at the table. She decided he didn't look like he was going to kill her.

He had on new clothes. He hadn't bothered to come get yesterday's.

"Good morning." She got up and went to the refrigerator. She got out what she needed and began making cheese toast and bacon.

They said nothing.

She put the plates on the table. She had to get the silverware and napkins herself. He wasn't moving.

She poured herself another cup of coffee and sat down.

They ate in silence, neither one looking at the other.

Finally, without looking at her, he said, "You're not going to tell, are you?"

She couldn't look at him. "No." A small no. She felt liked she had reached the nadir of her life.

You, liar, she thought.

She finished the breakfast, collected the dishes from the table, loaded the dishwasher, and cleaned the sink, her back to him the whole time.

She finally spoke. "I've got to go."

"Okay."

"I'll get my suitcase. I need you to move your car so I can get out."

Without saying anything, he got up, picked up his keys off the table in the foyer, slipped on his shoes, and went out.

She packed her suitcase, making sure she got everything from the bathroom, closed it up, and carried it to the door.

David came back in and took the suitcase from her and carried it out.

She unlocked her car, and he put the suitcase in the back seat as she got in.

"Goodbye."

"Goodbye."

No "Till I see you again." No "I'll call Mr. Swell and straighten things out." No nothing. Final.

She watched David walk back into the house, hands in pockets, shoulders hunched.

She didn't look at the blond in the window. She couldn't. She really was guilty now. The blond's gossip would be real.

Mary thought of David.

"You poor bastard!"

CHAPTER THIRTY

SATURDAY - BRENDA DEHAVEN

Brenda was up early Saturday morning, at least she thought so. It was seven o'clock. She looked out the kitchen window. David was parking his car at the curb. *Boy, I just made it.*

David went back into his house. A moment later, he came out carrying a suitcase and put it in the bimbo's car. She followed and got into the driver's seat. They hardly looked at each other. They certainly didn't look at her. *No smile today, huh, missy?*

David walked back to his house, without looking back, as the red car pulled out of the driveway and drove away.

Brenda looked at her watch. It was too early to call Linda. Maybe around eleven o'clock. Linda was going to need a friend, and Brenda was ready.

CHAPTER THIRTY-ONE

SATURDAY/SUNDAY - DAVID NEALE

After Mary had left, David sat morosely at the table. He couldn't believe what he had done. He'd made love to another woman. The idea hadn't even dawned on him before last night. Yet it had seemed so easy and natural. How had life become so crazy?

Then he had compounded everything by confessing to Mary. How dumb could he be? He didn't even know her. Why had she been so interested? How did she know so much? How naive could he be? Something wasn't right.

He decided to go out and mow his little lawn. It didn't take long, but he needed to do it before it became too hot. While he did so, he eyed Brenda's window. He felt like there was a telescope in there, although Brenda didn't need one. He hoped she didn't have a camera. Would she keep what she had seen to herself? He doubted it. He suspected eyes were watching him from up and down the street. Would Brenda call Linda? He was afraid she would. What could he say to Linda? It was hard to excuse a strange woman staying in our house for two nights.

He put away the lawn mower. He watched the news on television. He watched the Nats' game. He had no emotion when they lost. He watched the news again and then Netflix and went to bed. He couldn't sleep.

He had an untoasted bagel with cream cheese for breakfast. It was all he could manage. *I could have gotten used to Mary making breakfast,* he thought and then chastised himself for such a foolish and insane thought.

He needed to call Linda. He needed to try to repair his life. He didn't know if he could do it with all the guilt he felt. It was too early anyway. He would think about it. He read the paper and drank coffee. He looked at his watch. It was only nine thirty. Life was at a crawl.

He decided to phone Linda. Grace answered. "Hi, Grace. It's David. How are you?"

"Don't know if she wants to talk to you," snapped Grace. No "good morning." No "how are you?" Not a good sign.

"Well, will you please ask her?"

"Linda, do you want to talk to David?" David heard it muffled. He guessed she had her hand over the phone.

Grace was back on the phone. "No, she doesn't want to talk to you. She's in the living room crying. You've got a lot of nerve calling. Think you need to leave her alone."

She hung up.

David looked at the phone. *Damn. Brenda must have gotten to her.*

David was mad, frustrated, guilty, all at the same time. He hated Brenda. He wanted to punch her, bloody her nose, let her know what he thought of her. The trouble was that what she was saying was true, maybe elaborated, heavily dramatized, but true.

He made another pot of coffee. It was going to be a long day. And tomorrow was a holiday. Another long day.

He longed for the lab.

CHAPTER THIRTY-TWO

SUNDAY - MARY MURPHY

Mary went to work Sunday morning. She didn't have to. It was a day off. She didn't have to work until the Fourth of July, but she couldn't stay in her little apartment.

She had paced and agonized all day Saturday. She hadn't known if she could publish the story. She had known she could write it. She would do it today while her memory was still fresh. She had told David she wouldn't tell. It was only half a lie—or maybe three-quarters. She felt guilty. She didn't want to be a traitor. She knew she wouldn't have to face him again. Or did she know that? There would probably be a trial, or who knew what? As a reporter, she might have to cover the next event. If she published, could she look him in the eye and ask questions as if she were some distant, detached person?

She couldn't help being distracted.

Ben asked her why she was there. She told him that she was bored at home and had to get out. He shook his head. "Mary, you need to get a life."

She couldn't agree more. The life she had was a little screwed up. *No, a lot screwed up.*

She got a cup of coffee and drank it. Her mind was still distracted. She got another cup. *Wake up, girl. You've got to work.*

She turned on her computer. It seemed to take forever to start up.

She started to type. The story flowed easily. She finished in less than an hour. She reread it and only made a couple of corrections. She thought of the headline: "Mysteries of the Dead Babies and Missing Persons Linked." No. Too long. "Baby Killers and NIH Workers Linked." She typed that. Ben would change it anyway.

She saved her text and turned off her computer. She studied the screen. There was a phantom in there ready to spring out and wreak havoc. People's lives were hanging on what it did. In those chips of silicone, something was living. It scared her to death.

CHAPTER THIRTY-THREE

TUESDAY - MARY MURPHY

Mary arrived at work on time Tuesday morning. Yesterday had been a long day. She had covered Fourth of July festivities from nine in the morning until ten at night. Parades, barbecues, parties, the mayor and Mad Dog's speeches. It had gone on and on. Late in the afternoon, she had written things up for the morning paper and then gone back to more speeches and the fireworks.

As she approached her desk, she noticed Charlie leaning back, looking smug. "You see the *Post* this morning?"

"No, after yesterday, I got all the sleep I could this morning."

Charlie held it out. The Metro Section. "They're getting ahead of you. You're losing your story."

Charlie had circled the article. "Route-One Babies Were Deformed." Mary scanned it. "Source asked not to be identified." "Babies had exceptionally long arms, low brows, recessed jaws." "They had some toes webbed together." "Baby Neanderthals."

Shit! I didn't know any of that. David didn't say a thing about the condition of the babies. She hadn't known to ask. She was losing her story.

She felt discouraged, annoyed. The world couldn't do this to her.

She turned on her computer. *Come on. Come on*, she thought. It lit up. She brought up her article and left-clicked *print*.

She went to the printer and waited for it to finish. She took the papers back to her desk, stapled them, and took them to Ben's office. He looked up. She put them in the middle of his desk. He eyed her as she walked out. "And good morning to you too."

She sat at her desk. Ben came out of the office and beckoned to her. She went back into his office.

"You're saying this guy Neale confirmed all this?"

"Yes."

"How did you get him to do that?"

She was cryptic. "Doesn't matter. He did."

Ben watched her for a moment, judging. He decided not to ask more about the subject. "Okay. Sit down and tell me all about it."

She settled in and started with the boy handing her the address. She told everything except for the night in David's bed.

Ben looked at her, mouth slightly agape. "Damn, you're a pushy little thing. I'd never tell you my secrets . . . You've got the byline. Can you live with it?"

She hesitated. "Any way to make David Neale a source who asked not to be identified?"

Ben kind of twisted his mouth at her uncertainty. "Don't think so. The police, they might consider it abetting a murderer. I don't think the paper would defend you. This isn't the *New York Times.*"

"Then I can live with it."

CHAPTER THIRTY-FOUR

WEDNESDAY - DAVID NEALE

Tuesday morning had finally come. It had been a long weekend. David had gone to work and hidden in his lab. He had seen Lourie on the way in and the way out. Filipe, his tech, had been in the lab for a while, but they hardly spoke.

On Wednesday, as he drove to work, he realized he missed Mary Morris. He knew he shouldn't. He knew it was better that she was gone.

He missed her more than he missed Linda. He felt guilty admitting it. Was it her cheerful can-do presence? Or was it the sex? He knew what had happened was wrong. He should feel guiltier than he did. Somehow, he couldn't feel bad about it. He knew what had happened was the reason Linda wouldn't talk to him. He wondered how good a story Brenda had told. It really didn't take that much imagination.

Still, it was good Mary had gone. He didn't know what was happening with the lease for 227 North Pearson. Maybe he'd see her again, but he'd be circumspect about it. He already had enough problems.

As he entered the NIH building, he suddenly felt a cold chill. People were looking at him, some whispering. He got on the elevator. Two other people were already on. He nodded to them, but they just stared ahead. He got off and went to his lab.

He started the morning routine. He took off his suit coat and put on a lab coat. Next, he checked that all the rodents were okay and then checked the logs. He fed the animals and filled out the logs for today.

Suddenly, the lab door opened, and Lourie stuck her head in. She looked very serious. No "good morning."

"You're needed in the conference room."

David felt uncertain. "Okay." It was unusual to be summoned anywhere but Solomon's office.

He carefully closed the logs and put the pen in his lab coat pocket. He wondered if he should put his suit coat back on. He decided against it and picked up a notebook.

He walked down the hall, feeling tense and uncertain about what was happening.

He opened the door to the conference room. There were two people standing by the table that he didn't know—a tall, slightly heavyset white guy and a slender, pretty, medium-height black woman.

The man turned toward him. "Are you David Cummings Neale?"

David was startled at the formality. "Yes."

"Please close the door and come in." He motioned toward the table. "Have a seat."

"I'm Detective Metzinger, and this is Detective Givens. We're from the Alexandria Police Department."

Oh shit, David thought. *Here we go.*

There was no offer of a handshake. Detective Givens headed to the far side of the table. Detective Metzinger waited for David.

David hesitated, uncertain, alarmed. Finally, he took a seat. Detective Metzinger walked around to the far side of the table, lay papers and a pen on the table, pulled out a chair, and methodically sat down.

"We'd like to ask you about the article in the paper this morning."

David was puzzled. "What article?"

"You are David Cummings Neale, aren't you?"

"Yes, I said I was. What's this all about?"

"You haven't seen the article?"

David shook his head. "No."

Metzinger turned to Givens and held out his hand. She unfolded a newspaper and handed it to him. Metzinger noted, "It's the Alexandria paper anyway. You probably don't get it in Fairfax."

He studied the paper a moment, slid it across to David, and pointed at an article.

David picked up the paper and began to read.

It was all there, everything he and Mary Morris had talked about, with some added details. He looked at the byline. Mary Murphy, MM, but not Morris. *That little slut*, he swore to himself. *She used me.*

He was angry and hurt. He had liked her. *I must be the most gullible person in the world.* She had even used his name. But the "Cummings" must have come from somewhere else, maybe his driver's license.

David put the paper down and looked at Metzinger but said nothing.

Metzinger inquired, "Do you know Seth O'Halloran and Sidney Gill?"

"Yes."

"Good answer. Dr. Solomon says they're your lab partners." He was a little smug. "Dr. Solomon also said they haven't been around since Wednesday, two weeks ago."

David nodded.

"Do you know where they are?"

David shook his head. "No."

"When was the last time you saw them?"

Oh no, David thought. *Do I lie? That might be trouble. What would they do on the TV shows?*

"I'm not sure I remember."

"You don't, huh? The article seems to indicate you saw them Sunday before last. Does that sound right?"

David was panicked. On TV, the persons being questioned asked for lawyers. That almost admitted guilt.

Nonetheless, he stammered, "I think I'd like to have a lawyer."

Metzinger looked disgusted. "If you didn't do anything, you don't need a lawyer."

David looked down at the table. "I'm innocent, but I want a lawyer. I don't want you to hang things on me."

Givens started stacking her papers and got up.

"Okay," Metzinger summarized. "You want a lawyer. How about you getting yourself that lawyer and the two of you come to the Alexandria Police Department tomorrow at nine in the morning?" He shoved a card across to David. "That's the address. I'll be waiting for you."

Metzinger got up and picked up his papers. "And incidentally, if I were you, I wouldn't think about leaving the area."

Hell, where would I go? David sighed to himself.

*   *   *

David returned to his lab. He made a half pot of coffee. No use wasting any. After all, he was alone. He had never felt so alone.

He retrieved the logs from where he had left them. He started checking the rats and mice, one by one, measuring and recording statistics associated with each.

He couldn't get Mary Murphy out of his mind. She had prostituted herself to get a story. It was amazing. He postulated, *Whores must come in every shape and size, even with sweet personalities.* Life was really shitty.

The door opened. It was Lourie again. "Dr. Solomon wants to see you in her office."

She closed the door, and he stared at it. *Thought you were my friend, Lourie.*

He went down the hallway and knocked on Dr. Solomon's door.

"Come in."

David went in and stood in front of Dr. Solomon's desk. He wasn't invited to sit.

"This is embarrassing as hell to NIH, David. I'm getting calls from higher up. They're going to have us all put on a spit and roasted if this publicity continues."

David was determined not to be timid and cower. "I didn't kill anyone, Dr. Solomon. I don't know what Seth and Doc Gill did."

"But you ran an illegal experiment."

No use denying it. "But it wasn't on government time or using government money."

"But the newspaper has connected it to NIH. We're all being considered guilty."

"As am I. No one has proven I did anything. So what do you want me to do?"

"I think you should stay away from here."

David needed the job. He needed the money. "So are you firing me?"

"No, I can't. You know that. I have no proven grounds."

David knew that. "Look, I'm doing my job. In fact, I'm doing the job of three men. I have no intention of not doing that job. I'll make every effort to be quiet. I'll even stay in the lab all day. Hopefully, people will forget I'm here." David said it, but he knew the outside world wouldn't let him be quiet. He was the only way *they*, all of them, could complete the story. He was alone.

Dr. Solomon acquiesced, defeated. "Okay. Just stay out of sight, here and at home."

"Will do. I would like to ask, however, if I could take leave this afternoon and tomorrow morning. This situation requires me to take care of some personal business."

He needed a lawyer.

CHAPTER THIRTY-FIVE

WEDNESDAY - DAVID NEALE

Where do you look for a lawyer? David didn't have one. He didn't even have a will. He supposed that, with a wife and kids, he should have a will. He'd take care of that after things settled down. Right now, he needed to deal with the matter at hand. He wished he had a friend he could ask about lawyers, but even if he did, there would be too many questions to answer.

He went home, went into the house, and found the phone book in the kitchen drawer. He went to the yellow pages, wondering if anyone did that anymore. Under *Attorneys,* he found a long list, with different categories. After *Attorneys-Bankruptcy Law,* he found *Attorneys-Criminal Law.* Was that what he needed? It made him feel guilty just thinking about it. Yeah, that was probably what he needed. He wanted a lawyer close by. The firms with multiple names scared him. They sounded expensive. Some names he recognized from advertisements on the radio. They sounded like chains. How personal could they be? Finally, he found *Henry Travers* on US 29 in Centreville. It was a little far to drive, but he thought he'd give it a try.

David called Travers and got his secretary. She said she could give him an appointment next week. He told her it was an emergency, that he needed an appointment today. She said she would check with Mr. Travers, came back, and asked if David could be there at five o'clock.

"I'll be there."

David spent the rest of the afternoon going over what he was going to say.

He arrived fifteen minutes early. It was an old house south of Surrey Road, well, below the turmoil of the center of Centreville. It looked like a survivor from early in the twentieth century. A small sign hung in the front yard, *Henry A. Travers, Attorney at Law.* A vacant lot was to one side of the building. Another old house stood on the other side, advertising antiques. Both were frame and needed painting. The driveway had been expanded into a small parking lot. It also ran behind the house. He could see a gray Lincoln sitting back there.

David parked and went in. A bell rang as he opened the door. No one was in the outer office. An old wooden desk supporting two computer screens sat to the left. A large printer sat on the floor next to the desk. Red leather armchairs lined the right wall. Clearly, it was the waiting area for clients.

Evidently, the secretary had gone home. That's why there was only one car in back.

A man came through the door to the rear. He appeared to be in his midfifties with almost white hair, very thick, a little shaggy. His face already showed the creases of age, the kind you would expect of a fisherman who had long been exposed to the elements. He wore a pin-striped suit with a vest and seemed from another era. The vest made David feel hot.

The man stuck out his hand, and David shook it. "David Neale, I presume. I'm Henry Travers. Come on in."

There was a small wooden conference table to one side of the office, a large wooden desk to the other. Four more red leather armchairs sat around the table, two more in front of the desk, and a large black leather desk chair behind the desk. The walls were paneled. Diplomas and large pictures of Travers with other people hung on the walls along with early twentieth-century photographs of what he assumed was Centreville.

Travers motioned toward the conference table. "Have a seat."

David took a seat at the side of the table, Travers at the end. Two yellow legal pads and pens were set on the table.

"Well, Mr. Neale, you seem to be in a rush. What can I do for you?"

David inhaled, made himself speak. "I need your help."

"Most people do."

"Am I correct that we have client-attorney privileges here? That what I say is just between us?"

Travers lowered his shaggy brows at David. "Yes, if you hire me. I'm $125 an hour."

David made a gulp. He'd better talk fast. "Yes, I need to hire you."

"You *need* to. That sounds serious." He waited a moment. David was silent. "Okay, I'm hired. You can talk."

David leaned back in the chair and took a deep breath. Then he leaned forward. "You heard about the two dead babies they found in Alexandria on Route 1?"

Oh my goodness, thought Henry Travers.

"I didn't kill them." David wanted that straight right from the start.

"Good."

"Before I start, let me tell you that I will need you at the police department in Alexandria tomorrow at nine in the morning."

"Boy, you do operate on short notice." Travers got up, went out to the secretary's desk, and came back with a ledger. "Joanne puts the appointments in the computer, but I make her put them in here too so I can get at them. I do have a couple of appointments in the morning, but I can probably move them. Wills and such. If I need to, I'll have Joanne reschedule them in the morning." Travers sat back down. "Let's hear what you have to say."

David began. He was relieved to be able to talk about it. He began by describing where he worked, who he worked with, and then launched into the experiment of gestation.

Travers listened, made notes. "So you were going to circumvent Mother Nature, win a Nobel Prize. Hate to tell you, but I feel in my bones that such manipulation isn't a good idea."

David concurred. "It wasn't, but we had a lot of enthusiasm when we started."

David talked about renting the house on North Pearson Street, Seth's advertising on the Internet for women to serve as surrogate mothers and selecting heavyset women so their pregnancies wouldn't be too obvious when the women entered and left the Pearson Street house and having Doc Gill extract the women's eggs and the insert them in each woman's uterus after the eggs were fertilized. He told about his role in renting the house and manipulating and fertilizing the eggs. He confirmed to an incredulous Travers that his name was on the lease. In answer to Travers' following questions, he confirmed that he had done the egg fertilization in his lab at NIH using glassware and other materials that were there. He was quick to point out that none of the materials were used up in the process. He emphasized that all equipment and glassware were cleaned and returned to stock for future NIH use. Further, he explained that all his work was done after hours and that all funds for the experiment were provided by Seth.

Travers shook his head. "Well, it could be worse." With some trepidation, he said, "Go on."

David told about the babies being born, one naturally, the others induced so they would all come at about the same time. He talked about the elation when the babies were born after only seven months. He described the shock and horror when the babies came out with "anomalies" that frightened him and his partners, leaving the three of them uncertain about what to do, knowing their experiment hadn't worked as they had hoped despite the early deliveries.

Travers asked if they had talked about what to do.

"No, Seth said I wasn't to worry. He and Doc Gill would take care of it. I was so relieved I got out of there."

"So you think the two of them solved the problem by killing the babies?"

"I don't know. Yeah, it looks like they killed two of the babies. But there were three babies. I don't know what happened to the third."

"And you haven't seen or spoken to either Seth or Doc Gill since?"

"No. They've vanished. The police are looking for them as 'missing persons.'"

Then David told him about Linda leaving and then about the arrival of Mary Murphy. He told him about everything but the sex. He told him about Mary saying the neighbors had seen

Seth and two Mexicans taking the furniture, beds, and medical equipment out of the house the day that the babies were found, leaving the house sterilized.

Travers leaned back and sighed. "Okay, let's sum it up. The Feds can probably get you for misusing government property. They may not be able to prove that, if nothing's missing. I don't think embarrassing the NIH is a crime. Just doesn't make you popular. Besides, they probably won't bother with you unless you get tried for murder."

"Tried for murder? I didn't kill anyone."

"Worse case. You're the only one whose name is associated with the house in Alexandria. Hopefully, the neighbors can identify the other two. Are there pictures of them?"

"Yes. There were pictures of them in the newspaper when they were reported as missing."

Travers mulled over the situation. "Did the neighbors see the babies being moved?"

"I don't know. Mary Murphy didn't say anything about that."

"Well, we'll need to do some snooping. Unless they find the surrogate mothers, maybe there's no proof the babies were ever there. Did you tell this Mary Murphy that the babies were born there?"

David thought about it. "I don't think so."

"You don't think so? That's not good enough. You either did or you didn't."

David's mind struggled. "I'm sure I didn't."

"Okay, I hope we don't learn the hard way that you did."

Travers went back to the summary. "All right, the Commonwealth's Attorney over there in Alexandria might try to get you for murder or as an accessory, but as best as I can tell from the newspapers, they don't have anything but circumstantial evidence and hearsay. They need to connect the babies to the house that you rented. Again, I don't think they have any evidence or even witnesses. Let's see where it goes from here." Travers sat back. "So what's happening tomorrow?"

David told him about this morning's visit from Detectives Metzinger and Givens.

"Okay. What did you say to them?"

"I admitted that Seth and Doc Gill were my partners and that they had been gone since Wednesday, two weeks ago. They asked me when I had last seen them. I said I didn't remember. Then I said I would like to have a lawyer."

"I wish you hadn't said you didn't remember. From now on, you don't say anything. We wait to find out what they've got. As best as I can tell, this Mary Murphy is the only one with any clue."

"You think she'll talk."

"I bet they've already had her to their office."

"So what do we do next?"

You go to the police department tomorrow and say nothing. You can do it by yourself, or I can come with you. If I go, they won't hassle you as much."

"I'd like you to go."

"Okay, pick me up here at five after eight in the morning. I need five minutes to talk to Joanne."

David got up and left. He looked at his watch. Seven o'clock. Two hundred fifty dollars. He wondered if he was going to be able to afford a lawyer.

Chapter Thirty-Six

WEDNESDAY - MARY MURPHY

Mary should have been flying high. Her story had been distributed through all the national news outlets. She was being given congratulations and high-fives all around the news room. Still, she kept thinking about David. She had given him a royal shafting. It distracted from everything.

She worked halfheartedly at all her new assignments. About eleven, she got a call. It was Detective Givens. Could she come to Givens' office? She didn't need to ask what it was about. She knew. She dreaded it, but she knew, after her discussion with Ben, that it was going to happen. She had hoped it wouldn't be so soon.

"Yes, I can. Where do I go, and whom do I ask for?" She wrote it down.

She got up to leave and told Charlie where she was going.

He counseled, "Just tell them what you know. You'll be all right. Goes with the territory."

She packed up her notes. She'd refer to them so she wouldn't make any mistakes.

At the police department, she found herself facing the glassed-in office of a policewoman. There was one of those round speaker things in the middle of the window; looked like a target.

Mary stretched up to the thing. "My name's Mary Murphy. I'm here to see Detective Givens."

The policewoman acknowledged her. "Let me check."

She picked up the phone and dialed three numbers. "A lady named Mary Murphy is here to see you."

She listened a moment and responded, "Okay."

She turned to the window. "I'll buzz you in. Come through the door and have a seat. Someone will come get you." With that, she swiveled in her chair and hit the buzzer.

Mary hurried through the door, afraid there was a timer she had to beat.

Inside, there were three wooden chairs. They didn't look comfortable. She sat down.

Five minutes passed. Mary was twitching. Ten minutes passed. Finally, a black woman in civilian clothes came down a hallway. She put out her hand and shook Mary's. "Detective Givens. Sorry to keep you waiting. We didn't know you would come so fast."

Mary, a little irritated, thought, *I don't remember your telling me to take my time.*

She followed Detective Givens down the hall.

"The Commonwealth's Attorney wanted to send someone over. We had to phone them. They'll be here in a minute."

They entered a small conference room. A tall, slightly heavy middle-aged man in a suit was sitting at the table.

Givens looked at Mary and gestured toward the man. "Ms. Murphy, this is my partner, Detective Metzinger. He's the lead on this." Metzinger nodded but didn't get up.

Mary looked at Givens. "This, being?"

Metzinger spoke, "Your newspaper article, of course. Have a seat. Someone from the Commonwealth's Attorney's Office will be here in a minute. We won't get started till whoever it is arrives."

They all sat and waited.

After a few minutes, the door opened, and a woman entered. Neatly dressed in a suit, hair professionally coifed, short-heel pumps, panty hose on a hot day, a bit of a hatchet face with no smile. *Professional.*

Metzinger and Givens stood. Mary decided that maybe she should too.

The woman put a folder on the table and turned to Mary. "I assume you're Ms. Murphy from the newspaper." She put out her hand and shook Mary's. "I'm Shannon Jennings from the Commonwealth's Attorney's Office."

"Have a seat."

They all sat, Ms. Jennings at the head of the table. She pulled out a note pad and a couple of pens. "As you know, we're very interested in the murder of the two babies last week down on US 1. Right now, you seem to know more about it than anyone else, and we need to be enlightened. We would like to talk to you about it. This is not a deposition, so you don't need a lawyer. Certainly, you're not accused of anything. We would, however, like to record this meeting so that we can refer back to it in case we miss anything. Is that all right?"

Mary nodded. *What else could she do?*

Ms. Jennings looked at Metzinger. "Is the recorder on?"

Metzinger got up and said, "I'll turn it on." He went to the wall and threw a couple of switches. Lights came on three microphones on the table. Givens pushed one in front of Mary, one in front of Jennings, and one between Metzinger and herself.

Ms. Jennings addressed the microphone. "Today is Wednesday, the Sixth of July 2016. We are here for an informal discussion with Ms. Mary Murphy, a reporter with the Alexandria newspaper, to discuss an article she published in this morning's paper. I am Shannon Jennings from the Alexandria Commonwealth's Attorney's Office. Also present are Detectives Drury Metzinger and Leslie Givens of the Alexandria Police Department."

She turned to Mary. "Ms. Murphy, we would appreciate your discussing how you became knowledgeable of all the information published in the article you wrote for today's Alexandria newspaper, a copy of which we will attach to the written summary of this meeting."

Mary took out her notebook and opened it. She pulled the microphone to her. She described how she had accidentally, on her way home, come across the police response to finding the babies, how she had witnessed and photographed the one baby on the ground and the other being removed from the dumpster, both wrapped in white, and how the babies had been put in plastic bags and loaded in a SUV. She said that, as a result of this firsthand knowledge, she had written the article in Tuesday's paper, a week ago, about the discovery and had her name on the article.

She looked around. Everyone had written notes and was waiting.

Mary continued, stating that the next day, because of her initial involvement, her editor had sent her to the press conference at City Hall. She noted that she walked to and from the conference and mentioned the feeling that she was being followed. She described the black teenager. She then shared that she had challenged him after the conference and how he had put a piece of paper with an address on it in her hand before running away.

Metzinger asked, "How did he know he should give it to you?"

"I don't know that he did. My guess is that he knew a woman had written the article and that he waited outside the newspaper office until a woman came out. He followed me to the conference, maybe still uncertain as to what he should do. After the conference, when I challenged him, I think he panicked and gave me the paper whether I was the right person or not. He said his sister told him to give it to me. When I got back to the office, I realized I still had my press badge on, so he really didn't make a bad guess."

"Okay, go on."

Mary described how she had gone to the address and found no one home, that she had talked to the neighbor and learned about three men using the house on an intermittent basis and how she had called the landlord and gone to see the house.

Jennings asked how she knew who the landlord was, and Mary had to go into the whole episode at the Housing Office, remembering all the details, except the name she had called herself.

Then she went through visiting the house with Johnny Swell, pretending she was a potential renter, and finding it stripped of all furniture and thoroughly clean. She discussed how Mr. Swell had given her David Neale's name as the current lessee and said that she should contact Neale if she wanted to rent the place.

Jennings and the detectives continued to write, but didn't say anything.

Mary described following Neale to work and finding that he worked at NIH, how she had gone into the building and found Neale's name on the directory along with his partners, Seth O'Halloran and Sidney Gill. Then she noted how surprised she was when those two were listed as missing persons and how she had gone back to Pearson Street with photographs of O'Halloran and Gill and shown them to the neighbors, neglecting to mention her pretense at being a private investigator. She summarized that she had learned that the two missing men had been in and out of the house at 227 North Pearson along with a younger man and two or three women, that Seth O'Halloran had moved everything out of the house with the help of two Mexican laborers on the day that the babies were found and that the items removed from the house seemed to include several folding hospital beds, tables, chairs, and some hospital equipment.

Jennings asked for the neighbors' names, and Mary gave them to her.

Then she described how she had boldly gone to David Neale's house, gone in, and started talking, beginning with questions about the availability of the house at 227 North Pearson. She told about the flimsy stories David had provided as to why he was renting a house in Alexandria; how he had said his wife was away; how he was upset an experiment he and his partners were working on had gone wrong; how she had found him sobbing and asked him if it was about the babies, that he had asked her how she knew about them and said he hadn't killed them; how she had asked if his partners had; and how he had said that he thought so.

With that, Mary was finished. There was silence in the room, except for pens writing on paper.

Jennings cleared her throat.

"Okay, so here are some questions. Did the neighbors ever see any babies?"

"They didn't say so."

"Did David Neale describe the experiment that he and his partners were doing that had gone wrong?"

"No."

"Did he say where the experiment was done?"

"No. He only said he worked at NIH."

"When you asked him if he was sobbing about the babies, how did you describe the babies?"

"I just said 'babies.' We knew what babies we were talking about."

"Well, you did, but how do we know that he didn't think you were talking about babies starving in the Sudan?"

"That wouldn't make sense. He denied killing them and said his partners had done it."

"We could argue that, but the link's not as solid as I would like. And we really don't have a link of this 'experiment gone wrong' to the dead babies."

Mary protested, "But the *Post* said the babies were deformed. That would result from an experiment gone wrong."

"It could, but you're making a guess. There's no link, no witnesses, only your word."

"But it all comes together."

"In your mind, yes. Too bad you didn't get all this on a recorder."

Mary suddenly felt very inadequate. A picture of her lying naked in David's bed, holding a recorder, flashed through her mind.

"Don't look so down, Mary. I have no doubt there's some truth in your hypothesis, and it's a starting point. It certainly helps us, and we thank you for it. We need the three women. We need the Mexicans. We need Seth O'Halloran's van. We'll take a look at the house on North Pearson and talk to the neighbors. We need a solid link. We need more than you're quoting a sobbing man."

Mary was dejected. "But I've published it. Everyone thinks it's true. David Neale is living with it."

"That's true, but you reporters have a different standard, and you're going to have to live with it."

Mary was annoyed at that. She wanted to say, *Yeah, and your standards are so solid you need an odd number of judges on all courts so you can get things done.*

CHAPTER THIRTY-SEVEN

WEDNESDAY - DRURY METZINGER AND LELIE GIVENS

Drury Metzinger knew Mary had something. Just not enough.

After Jennings left, he turned to Givens. "Jennings just gave us a job. We knew we had it anyway. We need to track down the kid who gave Murphy the address. How about you running over to city hall and checking the surveillance recordings made by the security cameras outside the building? It's lucky it was such a public place. And the time window is narrow, a few minutes after the news conference ended. Oh, and get yourself something to eat on the way."

"Will do. What're you going to do?"

"Talk to Arley Masterson and Big Gert. They're running the 'missing persons' case. Need to find out what they know."

Givens hurried out. Metzinger sat and made a list:

Check out the homes of the missing men. Get fingerprints, if Masterson hasn't already gotten them.

Find black kid who gave the address to Mary Murphy.

Talk to landlord, Johnny Swell, about 227 North Pearson. Take a look inside.

Talk to Bizzollis at 229 and the people at 231. Maybe some other neighbors.

Get the license plate for O'Halloran's car. Hopefully, it was a Mercedes van. Get the police within a couple of hundred miles looking for it.

Put out a request for the press to help find the Mexicans. (He didn't have much hope there, unless they were legal.)

Lots of leg work.

He got up, went back to the big office, and walked over to Masterson's desk.

"Hey, Arley. How's the wife and kids?"

Masterson leaned back in his chair. He was a skinny guy, deep blue eyes, always looked watery. "What's with the small talk, Dru? I know our cases are overlapping. Figured you'd be coming around."

"I was wondering what you found at the missing guys' apartments and if you took prints." He sat down in Big Gert's chair, looking around to make sure she wasn't nearby. Gertrude Sorenson was six feet two and a presence. She and Arley made a pair.

You didn't call her Big Gert to her face.

"For what it's worth, the wife and kids are fine. No, we didn't take prints. We were looking for clues as to where they might have gone—papers, bank statements, notes in phone books, laptops, etc. Didn't find anything."

"You got the computers here?"

"Yeah, they're down in *Evidence*. Murray went over them pretty good. You might talk to him next."

Masterson picked up his casebook. "You're welcome to look at this, if you'd like."

Metzinger looked through it. "So you have APBs out on their cars. Saves me the trouble."

"Yeah, but we've got no hits. It's like they just vanished."

"Hard to hide a black Mercedes van. Says here it's a Sprinter. Haven't heard much about them."

"Yeah. Doesn't seem to be many around. FedEx has them. Ford's got something similar."

"And the other guy has a tan Malibu. Not very conspicuous. Better shot at the van."

"You'd think so but nothing."

A thought struck Metzinger. "Tell me, when you were in these guys' homes, did you see any hospital beds or cribs?"

"I guess you could call them homes. More like bachelor apartments. But no. I didn't see anything like that. Why do you ask?"

"This guy, O'Halloran, moved them out of a house on North Pearson. Used the black van. If the beds are not at their 'apartments,' they must be somewhere."

"Maybe he stored them in one of those storage places?"

"Maybe he did." Metzinger got up. "I appreciate the help. Let me go talk to Murray."

"Keep me informed?"

"Yeah, I will." Metzinger took two steps and turned back, remembering what he should have checked earlier. "Avery, are the search warrants on the two 'apartments' still valid?"

"Yeah. You want 'em?"

"I do, if you don't mind?"

Masterson took them out of his desk drawer and handed them to Metzinger. "Good luck."

"Thanks."

Metzinger headed for Murray Jacoby's desk.

"Hey, Geek Squad. Have you got a minute?"

"Buddy, don't laugh about it. I can always get a job. Better than an old detective."

Metzinger pulled a chair from across the aisle and sat down. "Sad but true. At least, if no one shoots me, and the state stays solvent, I'll get a pension . . . I'll get you to pull out your notes on the missing NIH guys."

"Okay. You involved with them too. I think Big Gert brought them back." Jacoby thumbed through his file drawer. "Yeah, here they are." He set a file in the middle of his desk and opened it. "What do you need to know?"

"Is there anything in there about advertising for surrogate mothers, research on pregnancies, or ordering hospital beds?"

"Yeah, hospital beds, cribs, medical trays, genealogical tools—that kind of stuff on Gill's computer."

"Not the other stuff?"

"No."

"You don't have to look at your notes?"

"Just to get the name of the medical supply house."

Jacoby fingered through his notes and scribbled on a piece of paper that he handed to Metzinger. "Standard Medical Supply in Bethesda. Here's their e-mail."

Metzinger took the note. He didn't do e-mails if he could help it. Face to face was best, the phone second. "Thanks. Do me a favor. Go back over the computer and make sure there's nothing about looking for surrogate mothers or doing research on pregnancies or babies."

"Okay, but there's not."

As he got up, Metzinger thought, *Shit, he must have done it from a public computer or an NIH computer.* He wondered how you went about getting a search warrant for a government computer. Then he realized that you didn't. You called the FBI.

Back at his desk, Metzinger found Givens waiting for him. She held up a DVD. "We got it, Dan."

"Okay. Let's go to the conference room."

Fortunately, the room was empty. Givens loaded the disc and hit play. "Mary Murphy appeared on the screen, suddenly turning and walking purposefully up to a young black guy, baseball cap, pants low, blue underwear, fancy sneakers, looking uncertain. There was a brief exchange. He handed Murphy something, a little white something. Then he bolted. *Gone in a flash.*

"Okay. See if Murray can blow it up and get some stills. Then go to media liaison and get it out for the news tonight." He wrote some things in a pad, tore out the page, and handed it to Givens. "Also get liaison to put out information that we're looking for two Mexican men who helped a guy move hospital equipment out of a house on North Pearson using a black Mercedes van. Put both in context of their being persons of interest but not suspects in the murder of the babies. While you're doing that, I'll make some phone calls."

He returned to his desk and took the phone book from his desk drawer. He looked in the yellow pages for *STORAGE* and found *STORAGE HOUSEHOLD and COMMERCIAL.*

Metzinger started dialing, starting with storage places closest to North Pearson. He identified himself as a policeman and asked about recent rentals and black Mercedes vans. On his fourth call, he hit pay dirt. Sandler's Mini-Storage Park. The fellow who answered was Jeff Sandler. Metzinger guessed he was the owner or, at the least, a relative. Sandler said a fellow had come in with a black Mercedes van and rented a place last week.

Metzinger inquired, "Did he have two Mexicans with him?"

"No, he was by himself."

"He unloaded everything by himself?"

"No. He rented a large unit and drove the van in there and parked it."

"You get his name and phone number?"

"Hey, I don't think I should be passing out that kind of information. Privacy and such."

"That's okay. I'll see you with a search warrant tomorrow."

A quiet "okay" came from the other end of the line.

Metzinger thought about tomorrow. David Neale was coming at nine. If he came with a lawyer, Metzinger expected that it would be a nonevent. Jennings wanted to be there, but it was probably a waste of her time.

After that, it would be a busy day.

CHAPTER
THIRTY-EIGHT

WEDNESDAY - BRENDA DEHAVEN

Brenda worried about calling Linda again. She hadn't taken the news about the little bimbo's visits at all well. That was to be expected, but now David had really put his foot in it. She didn't get the Alexandria newspaper but had heard the local news this morning and run right out and gotten the paper. She read it several times. *So that's why he was going out late all the time.* She couldn't believe he might be a killer. How could anyone murder two babies, only days old? And living right next door the whole time? Poor Linda. She had really married a piece of work.

Right after lunch, Brenda noticed a television truck pull up. WUSA. She wondered if a reporter would come to the door. She decided she'd better get ready and ran upstairs to dress. She wanted something that would look good on television, something that would show off her figure. In truth, most of her clothing showed off her figure. She wished it wasn't so hot. She would have liked to have worn a sweater. A blouse didn't show enough. T-shirts seemed too casual. Tank tops did too, but what the hell?

She found some white shorts and a green tank top. She switched bras. She didn't want any straps. Benda pulled the tank top over her head and squeezed into the shorts. She admired herself in the full-length mirror on the bedroom door.

Downstairs, she slipped on some sandals and again looked out the kitchen window. Another van had arrived. No big antenna on this one. Maybe a radio station or a newspaper. She wondered if she should wait. Maybe all the channels would send vans. Then again, what did they say? "Strike while the iron's hot?"

Brenda picked up some magazines, casually walked out the front door, opened the trunk of her Mustang, and loaded the magazines in, her back to the trucks. She heard truck doors open and close. She waited a few seconds and then turned to see three people coming up the driveway—a man carrying a television camera and a man and a woman carrying microphones. She stood sideways so the cameraman could take pictures, but he wasn't ready. He waited for the microphones to come up.

Brenda tried to be coy. "Hey, what's going on?"

They held the microphones out. The cameraman positioned himself so that only the woman and Brenda were in his viewer. The woman put the microphone to her mouth. "Is David Neale your next-door neighbor?" Then she held it out to Brenda.

"Yes, but he's not home."

The microphone went back and forth.

"And what's your name?"

Brenda hesitated, pretended to be nervous. "Brenda DeHaven." She didn't want to be one of those people who didn't want to be identified, that had the cameras trained on their legs the whole time they were talking, not that she thought she had bad legs.

"Did you see the article in today's paper about Mr. Neale?" They were asking like they didn't want to identify the paper, didn't want to share the story. Brenda looked at the guy. He just smiled and held his microphone out to her in a steady hand. He'd probably dub over the whole thing later.

The woman wanted Brenda's attention back. "Do you have anything to say about the article?"

Brenda gave the woman her full attention. "Yes. It was a heck of a shock. You live next door to people, and you never know what's going on with them. You read about people making bombs in their basements or meth in their garages, but you never expect things to happen the other side of your living room wall."

"You really didn't know anything? He wasn't doing anything suspicious?"

"Well, yeah. He was out at all kinds of weird hours. Left his wife alone. It drove her crazy."

"His wife didn't know where he was or what he was doing?"

"No." She wondered herself. "Couldn't get him to talk about it."

"Anything else?"

"Yeah, he's been real nervous and upset lately."

"How did he act?"

"Well, I didn't see it. His wife just told me about it before she moved out."

"She moved out?"

"Yeah. She left and went home to her parents in Seymour. Took the kids with her."

"When was this?"

"Last week. Wednesday, I think."

"Where do you think Mr. Neale is now?"

"Probably at work. Comes home at night."

"Works at NIH?"

"Yeah."

"Does he have any visitors to his home? Couple of men?"

"No. Just a young woman."

"The reporter who wrote the article?"

"Maybe. I don't know. She stayed over two nights."

The reporter rolled her eyes.

Chapter Thirty-Nine

WEDNESDAY/THURSDAY - DAVID NEALE

After leaving Henry Travers's office, David stopped at a Burger King. He decided to go in. He picked up old wrappers and cups he had in the car and deposited them in the trash inside the door, mixing Arby's and McDonald's trash with Burger King's. It was America. Rivals could help each other out.

He studied the menu on the wall. He hoped for something new, a limited special. But there was nothing new. He ordered a Whopper and fries. He thought of the last time he had a decent meal. Mary Morris/Murphy had cooked it for him. At least she had some good attributes.

He thought of her body against his and then pushed the thought out of his mind. *Stupid, stupid, stupid,* he chastised himself.

He sat morosely at a table, nibbling on fries and catsup. *Is this my new life?* If it was, it wasn't a very happy one.

David took two bites out of his Whopper, stared at it for a moment, and decided he couldn't eat anymore. He took his tray, dumped more than half his food in the trash, went to his car, and drove home. As he turned into Tuscany Lane, he saw four media vans. He shook his head and decided, *No way am I going to face those guys.* He drove past the vans, past his house with its dark windows, past Brenda looking out her window and turned at the end of the block. He drove to US 50, found a low-cost motel and checked in.

It was an expense he couldn't afford. He was afraid the costs were going to pile up. Still, he had to do it this one night. He had to get away from his new world.

He didn't turn on the TV at all; he didn't want to hear any news. He went straight to bed. It was only eight thirty. What else was there to do?

Remarkably, he slept fairly well, but he was wide awake at 4:00 a.m. Why not? He already had more than seven hours of sleep, about what he normally got.

He suddenly realized that he had no toothbrush or shaving gear. He got dressed. He had hung up his clothes the night before and slept in his underwear. The suit wasn't too bad. The shirt was a little rumpled. They would have to do.

He got dressed and went to the front desk. Fortunately, they had little bags of necessities. He returned to his room and cleaned up.

David checked out, asking the desk attendant where he could get coffee. Down the street, he went to the 7-Eleven that had been recommended. He got coffee and a sweet bun and sat in his car and ate them.

It was five fifteen. What next? He drove to Tuscany Lane. The vans were gone. He wondered if they would be back.

He parked in his driveway. He thought about going in and changing his shirt. He decided not to. The cops would just have to accept him as he was.

He turned on the radio and found a music station. *No news, thank you.* He sat there thinking about nothing in particular.

About seven, Brenda's kitchen light came on. David decided it was time to leave.

David drove to the Henry Travers's office, pulled into the driveway, and parked. There were no cars behind the building.

At 7:55 a.m., Henry Travers's Lincoln turned in the driveway, drove past David, and parked behind the building. Travers got out, took his suit coat and a briefcase out of the back seat, and walked back to David's car.

David rolled the window down. "Good morning."

Travers looked concerned. "My god, how long have you been here?"

"Thirty or forty minutes. Better than driving around."

"Okay. Just give me a few minutes. I need to talk to Joanne and have her reschedule my day."

"I don't think she's here yet."

"No, but she'll be here in a minute. She's always punctual but never early."

Travers unlocked the front door and went in.

A moment later, a Ford Fusion pulled into the driveway and parked behind the building. The woman inside took off sunglasses, put on another pair of glasses, got out of the car, and walked behind the building. A moment later, she returned to the car and got her keys. Travers must have forgotten to unlock the back door.

As Travers had predicted, he was out of the building in five minutes. He put his briefcase in the back seat of David's car and settled in the passenger's seat.

"No use wasting gasoline driving two cars."

David felt that the day had finally begun.

As they drove, Travers asked David if he had thought of anything else.

David said no but talked about the media trucks in front of his house.

Travers admonished him not to talk to anyone. "It's hard to do when they're shoving microphones in your face. It can get to you. Just hurry past them and don't tell them where to go."

Travers tapped his fingers on the dashboard. "Did you see the local news last night?"

David glanced at Travers, thinking it couldn't be good. "No, what's happening?"

"Your next-door neighbor got some press time. Her clothing did nothing to reflect on stature of your neighborhood, but hopefully, it distracted viewers from hearing what she said. The cameraman apparently admired her."

"Yeah, that's Brenda. Knows all and sees all."

"Well, at some time, she must have talked to your wife. Describes you as being uptight lately. Said your wife had left you."

"She's just visiting her parents," David protested.

Travers seemed indifferent. "Just telling you what she said. Also talked about your being away from home a lot."

"Yeah, I told you that."

"Her *coup de grace* was her description of a woman coming and staying overnight for two nights while your wife was away."

David seethed quietly. *Damn Brenda! Damn her to hell!*

To Travers, he said, "Do I have to talk about it?"

"Not unless you want to. I may have to ask you about it later. We'll play it by ear. Anyway, your neighbor didn't do anything to make you seem like a good guy. In fact, I think you can now consider yourself a villain."

David said, under his breath, "The woman who visited was the reporter who wrote the article."

"Oh, I see. Makes me want to emphasize again that you don't want to talk to anyone. Hopefully by now, you know better. Unfortunately, sometimes you have to learn things the hard way."

"I understand."

"That's especially true with this interview we're going to have in a few minutes. They'll try to use anything they know about you. That's why I told you about your neighbor. I didn't want you to be surprised. They'll try to get you to bite on something. They'll probably try to offer you a deal. Don't say anything, don't ask questions, don't do anything unless I tell you to."

They reported to the policewoman behind the window, told her they were here to see Metzinger. A moment later, the door buzzed and opened. Givens stuck her head out and beckoned them to follow her.

Without a word, Givens led them to the conference room.

Metzinger was standing just inside the door. A woman was seated at the head of the table. Travers followed David into the room. He introduced himself to the detectives and turned to the woman, extending his hand. "As I told the detectives, I'm Henry Travers, Mr. Neale's attorney."

The woman shook his hand without rising from the table. "I'm Shannon Jennings from the Commonwealth's Attorney's Office. I think I need to introduce the detectives by name."

Travers smiled. "No need. Mr. Neale has told me who they are. May we have a seat?"

Jennings gestured to the chairs on the door side of the table. Travers and Neale sat. Metzinger and Givens went to the window side of the table and sat.

Jennings smiled at Travers. "I don't remember seeing you in our court, Mr. Travers."

"I haven't been there. Spend my time in Fairfax, sometimes Falls Church. There are a lot of lawyers in Alexandria."

"Well, it's a pleasure to meet my neighbor, Mr. Travers."

Travers looked at Jennings. "Commonwealth's Attorney's Office, huh? I'm a little surprised by the high level of interest. You must know that my client is not required to say anything."

"Yes, I know that very well, Mr. Travers. We already know a great deal about Mr. Neale. We know he rented a house here in Alexandria, that he and his lab partners from NIH visited there many times and that the house was furnished with medical beds and cribs and other medical items. We know that Sidney Gill ordered the equipment and where it came from. We also know Mr. Neale and his lab partners were very active in the house for four days before the murdered babies were found on US 1 and that one of his lab partners, Seth O'Halloran, moved everything out of the house the day the babies were found, using a Mercedes van that we have located and for which we have a warrant to investigate. We suspect that it will provide us with a great deal of additional information. We also learned other interesting things from a television interview a reporter had with Mr. Neale's neighbor yesterday. The neighbor seemed very well informed about Mr. Neale's life, and we intend to talk to her some more today. In other words, we know a great deal about Mr. Neale and are learning more by the minute."

It was all spoken from notes, without addressing anyone other than Travers. But Jennings obviously knew David was listening.

David felt like heavy weights were descending on his shoulders. He wished he were somewhere else, somewhere where they didn't know everything about his life.

Travers continued looking at Jennings. "And?"

Jennings stopped looking at her notes and looked directly at Neale. "And, Mr. Neale, we would like to offer you the opportunity to talk about what this is all about and how it is connected to the murders of two babies found on US 1. If you are willing to do that, we can probably make some agreement about the effect the events will have on your future life."

Travers noted the microphones were not on. They were making the offer off the record. He responded. "Ms. Jennings, it is miss, isn't it?"

Jennings looked annoyed. "It's Mrs."

"Sorry. Mrs. Jennings, we appreciate the offer. I don't believe it is relevant. I understand your interest in solving the mystery of the dead babies, but I can assure you my client had nothing to do with their deaths. I continue to counsel him to say nothing about that or anything else. So if you have nothing else to offer, I would appreciate your excusing us so that we can get on with our lives."

Jennings glared at Travers and reprimanded him. "You're not doing your client any favors, counselor. In the end, he's going to be sorry."

Travers rose and picked up his briefcase from beside his chair. He had never opened it. "I appreciate your advice, Mrs. Jennings. I will keep it in mind."

With that, he left the room, and David followed, feeling like the hangman was right behind him.

Back in the car, David asked, "Do you think we should talk to them?"

Travers looked annoyed. "Absolutely not. They don't know who killed the babies. Hell, they don't even know the babies are connected to you."

David demurred, "But I think . . ."

Travers interrupted, turned, and glared at David. "You don't think! *Thinking* and *knowing* are different, and neither one of them is good. *Thinking* gets you in trouble, and *knowing* gets you in jail. Don't do either."

CHAPTER FORTY

THURSDAY - BILL AND GRACE DAVIS

Virginia Ligon Simmons had lived in Seymour all her life. She was old-time Virginia. Her family had arrived in the 1600s, not real early but early enough. She had attended Mary Baldwin College before it was a university and then come home to marry the president of the local bank, a man who lived in constant fear of having the bank bought out by some national bank. She was Grace Davis's "best friend," had watched Linda Davis grow up, and been to the wedding of Linda and David Neale. She even helped set up the reception. She was a small-town girl who thought of herself as worldly. She went to concerts in Charlottesville and sometimes in DC. She got out into the world, and she subscribed to the *Washington Post.*

The people of Seymour got their news from the Charlottesville television channels and so were not aware of the travails of David Neale. Further, the Northern Virginia edition of the *Washington Post* was one day behind the Alexandria paper and thus buried Mary Murphy's report deep in the Metro Section. But the Metro and Style Sections were what Virginia Ligon Simmons read.

David Neale's name was buried deep in the article, but Virginia found it. She couldn't wait to call Grace Davis.

Grace heard the news with shock. It would soon be all over town. The first thing she did was cancel her beauty parlor appointment and bridge club meeting for the day. Maybe they would still have time to find a fourth. She couldn't face the ladies.

Grace hesitated to tell Bill. She knew he would carry on about it with "I told you so's" for the rest of the week, maybe the month. Nonetheless, she had to start somewhere, if nothing else, just to give him a warning.

She was right. Bill didn't take it well.

Bill was horrified. "First, he drives her out of the house, and we get stuck with her and the kids. Now he's humiliated us. He was bad enough. Now he's a criminal."

"Bill, it's a mess. What's it going to do to Linda?"

"Just like us, she's got to live with it. I'm going to be embarrassed to walk down the street."

"Bill, you don't walk the street. You watch television."

"I get haircuts, go to the hardware store."

"Okay, but what do we tell Linda? She's already staying in her bedroom most of the day, crying half the time."

"You tell her the truth. Tell her what that busybody Virginia Ligon Simmons told you."

Grace sighed. "Me. Why me?"

Bill hunched his shoulders and looked annoyed. "You're the mother."

"And you're the father," Grace said with disgust.

Grace went to the kitchen and finished the morning dishes. She knew Linda would be down soon to organize the children's food. With children crowding the kitchen, she knew Linda would be distracted. Probably the best time to tell her. Maybe it wouldn't sink in until later.

CHAPTER FORTY-ONE

THURSDAY - DRURY METZINGER AND LESLIE GIVENS

Shannon Jennings stood up. "Detectives, they're going to fold. We would have gotten Neale today if he hadn't had the lawyer. We just need a little more to finish them off."

Metzinger nodded, knowing who "we" were.

After Jennings left, Metzinger turned to Givens. "We're going to start at the missing guys' apartments. Hope we can get fingerprints so we have something to work with in the future. I'll get you to track down a lab tech to go with us. We'll hit the house on North Pearson next and then go black-van hunting. While you find the tech, I'll see if Masterson and Big Gert will go talk to Neale's brassy neighbor. If she has anything else to say, Big Gert should be able to keep her focused."

Metzinger made sure that Masterson notified the Fairfax Police that they were coming and sent him and Gert on their way. He then checked in with his lieutenant. He needed to keep him informed.

Givens came in with the tech, Jimmy Prothro, and they all headed for Seminary Road. Metzinger had Masterson phone ahead so someone would let them in. He had the contact names from Masterson's previous visits.

They parked right in front of the high-rise, blocking the spot where people could drop spouses and friends off before they headed to the parking lot. Although the car was unmarked, it had light bars inside the windows and government plates. It was obviously a police car.

They found the apartment rather sterile. O'Halloran had tried for a contemporary style, but Masterson thought everything just looked hard and uncomfortable. The tech went to work, finding plenty of prints in the kitchen and bathroom. He bagged O'Halloran's toothbrush, bathroom glass, and hair comb in case they needed DNA. He was surprised the toothbrush and comb were still there. It appeared that O'Halloran had left in a hurry and maybe hadn't come back after whatever he was doing on the Monday he was last seen.

Givens and Metzinger went through drawers, looked at papers, and checked the closets. It appeared that O'Halloran hadn't taken much with him.

Givens commented on empty animal cages she found in the closet and wondered what they were for.

Metzinger looked at the spot where the computer had sat, noting the pattern of dust around it. He wondered if O'Halloran had any kind of cleaning service. If he did, they hadn't been there in a while. That was good. They hadn't disturbed anything.

Givens commented that O'Halloran must have been a lonely guy.

"Why's that?" Metzinger inquired.

"There are no photographs, like he doesn't have any family. Not any selfies in front of the Statue of Liberty or Niagara Falls. Nothing."

"You got selfies in front of Niagara Falls?"

"No, but I've got family."

Next, they went to Gill's apartment. It was in a two-story building that looked like it was built in the forties or fifties. It had mature trees around it.

The apartment had old furniture. Looked like hand-me-downs or Salvation Army. It had been there a while.

They repeated their search.

Givens commented, "At least he has pictures. Looks more human."

Metzinger looked at the pictures. There were some old pictures of a man and woman. It looked like they were taken in the fifties—all black and white. Maybe Gill's parents. There was also a colored portrait of a young woman, maybe from the eighties. Metzinger wondered who she was. Finally, there were a couple of pictures of Gill, one of him leaning on a fence, watching black angus cows, and another of him in a rocking chair, sitting on the porch of a white frame house. From Gill's age, they looked like they were taken in the last few years.

Metzinger's thought process came back to the moment. "We've got to get going. We're meeting Johnny Swell at two."

Givens looked up from searching the desk drawer. "Hope we've got time for a hamburger."

There were no parking places on North Pearson, so they double-parked.

Johnny Swell was waiting for them in the house. Metzinger thought, *Funny-looking little guy.*

Mr. Swell was plainly upset. "First, they vanish in the middle of the night. Then I find out something sinister was going on here. Going to be hard as hell to rent this place if it keeps getting publicity. Thankfully, I have a young woman looking at it."

Givens looked at Metzinger and then at Mr. Swell. "Hate to disillusion you, Mr. Swell, but the young woman was a reporter looking for a story, not a rental."

Johnny Swell's mouth gaped. "She seemed like such a nice young woman."

"She may be nice, but she's not looking for a rental . . . and what's worse is that this is now a crime scene, until we say it isn't. Hope the rent's paid up."

Johnny was alarmed. "Rent's only paid till the end of the month. You mean I can't even show it."

"I'm afraid not, but I suspect we'll have it released by then." Metzinger turned away from Mr. Swell. "We'll look around and set you free as soon as we can."

There wasn't much to look at. Metzinger noticed some marks on the floors where beds might have stood. It appeared that there had been no rugs or cups for the beds' rollers. There had been a bed in the upstairs front bedroom and two in the living room. The back bedroom had the marks closer together. Metzinger studied them carefully. The marks looked like they came from smaller beds, maybe cribs. Three of them. *Why three beds and three cribs? There were only two dead babies.*

Johnny Swell became upset as the tech powdered surfaces for fingerprints. He would have to have them cleaned up.

The tech shook his head. "I can't find much. Maybe signs of a little blood in the sinks, but I can't get anything from them. No fingerprints."

Metzinger turned to Johnny Swell. "Mr. Swell, we appreciate your help and taking your time to meet us here. May I ask you a couple of questions before we leave?"

"Sure, anything to hurry this along."

"We understand that you rented this house to a David Neale."

"That's right."

Metzinger pulled pictures from a folder he was carrying. He showed Mr. Swell a picture of David Neale. "Is this the man you rented it to?"

"Yes, that's him."

Next, Metzinger showed pictures of O'Halloran and Gill. "Do you recognize either of these men?"

Johnny Swell studied the pictures. "No. I've never seen them."

Metzinger put the pictures away. "Did Mr. Neale say why he was renting the house?"

"Something about parents or in-laws visiting a lot. Said they needed a place to stay."

"Did you stop by periodically to check on the house?"

Johnny Swell looked a little guilty. "No, I don't get out much. Came by a couple of times, but no one was home. Hate to go in people's homes when they're not there. If something's missing or damaged, they'd blame it on me."

"So you haven't been in the house or seen Mr. Neale since he rented the place."

"I'm afraid that's right. I was only in when I showed it to the reporter."

Metzinger and Givens left North Pearson feeling very disappointed.

Givens asked if they shouldn't interview the neighbors while they were there.

Metzinger had hurried to the car. "No, I want to get to the storage bin before the guy who runs it leaves. I'll ask Masterson and Big Gert to canvass the street tomorrow, see if they can get some positive identities from the pictures."

They found Sandler's Mini-Storage Park. Metzinger noted, "I don't see the 'park.'"

There were the usual rows of storage units, metal siding and roofs, beige with blue doors. A chain link fence surrounded the place, a square lot cut out the corner for a small office building and parking. There was a sliding gate in the fence near the office building, probably requiring a code to get in.

They parked their car and went into the office. A man sat behind the desk, maybe forty, pot-belied, unshaven for two or three days.

"You the cops?"

"Yes, I'm Detective Metzinger, and this is Detective Givens, and the guy in the lab coat is our lab tech, Jimmy Prothro. Are you Mr. Sandler?"

"I am. You got the warrant?"

Metzinger showed it to Sandler.

"Good. That gets this off my back." He picked up a large bolt cutter and handed it to Metzinger. "You can do the honors."

Metzinger handed the bolt cutter to Prothro and followed Sandler out the back door of his office and onto the asphalt drive that covered all the space around the storage bins.

Sandler stopped in front of number 327. "This is it."

Metzinger motioned to Prothro. "Cut the lock off."

It was a good-sized lock. Prothro struggled a little bit, and Sandler, with disgust, took the bolt cutter and snapped the lock off. He stood back. "I've had a lot of practice."

Prothro slid the latch and pulled up the bin's door.

There sat a black Mercedes van. The doorway must have almost skimmed its top.

Metzinger checked the license plate. It was O'Halloran's. He put on some gloves and checked the van's doors. They were locked.

There were no side windows or back windows. He squeezed in front of the van and tried to look into the back of the van. With the van facing away from the door, it was dark inside. He couldn't see much, but it looked like it was loaded.

Metzinger checked around the van. He didn't see anything.

He walked back to the asphalt, took out his cell phone, and called the towing service.

It had been a long day.

CHAPTER FORTY-TWO

THURSDAY - THE HONORABLE J. MADISON CONROY

J. Madison was headed for lunch in the Congressional Dining Room. He had gone over to the Rayburn Building for variety.

As he entered, he looked for someone to sit with. There had to be some Democrats with an empty seat. It was a way to get to know them.

He spotted Lyle Reninger sitting alone. He was the Republican chair of J. Madison's House and Science Committee.

J. Madison asked if he could join Reninger for lunch.

Reninger looked up, surprised. "If you don't mind sitting with the enemy."

"If it doesn't embarrass you, I'll sit with the enemy."

J. Madison pulled out the seat and sat down. "Haven't seen you in a while. The committee's been kind of quiet."

"Yeah, well, this building's foreign territory for you. You must be lost."

"No. Just looking for variety. Looks like I found it."

"Well, I can certainly give you guidance to the right side of life."

"Thanks, just the same. I've already seen the light."

"Seems like it blinded you a little."

"Guided me like a laser beam."

"So the laser brought you to Rayburn."

"Right into the aura of Lyle Reninger."

"You are a lucky man. So what's going on?"

"Have you heard about the baby murders in my district?"

"Of course. I read the *Washington Post* right after the *Wall Street Journal*. It's been made front page news."

"From what's being reported, it sounds like it involves some renegade scientists from NIH. Maybe something to keep an eye on for a committee inquiry. Guys in lab coats running free with government resources."

Reninger looked doubtful. "Sounds like you know more than I've heard. I read the article. Didn't see anything about the use of government property."

"Just think it's something we should keep an eye on."

"Sounds to me like you're seeking C-Span time."

"What's good for the goose is good for the gander."

"Okay. I'll keep an eye on it."

CHAPTER FORTY-THREE

THURSDAY - LINDA NEALE

Linda couldn't believe what was happening.

First, her husband had become distraught and short tempered. She had thought that if she left him for a few days, things would get better.

Then he had a woman spend two nights at her house. She wondered if he had been trying to force her out of the house so that he could have a new lover over. Was that why he had been away so much? Had he abandoned her for another woman? When he had made love to her, had he been thinking of another woman?

Then the *Washington Post* had published an article implying he was a criminal involved in the deaths of two babies. Was that why he had been so upset when the newscast discussed those deaths the day the babies were found?

It was horrible.

She might be married to a murderer, but that was hard to imagine.

What was supposed to be a couple of days at her parents had become more than a week.

Her father was clearly unhappy with her being there. Now he was raving about her being married to a criminal, saying the marriage needed to be ended.

Her mother was hiding from her and everyone in town.

Linda wished she could leave, but what would she do? Two small kids, no income, and no place to live.

David had called, but her father had answered, told David not to call again, and hung up.

Her father said a reporter had come to the door. Bill said he told the guy off and told him not to come again. Other reporters had phoned. Bill had told them off. Grace had simply hung up.

Her parents didn't want to face Linda, and she didn't want to face them. The house seemed to shrink, crowding in from all sides. She desperately needed to escape, but there was no place to go.

She stayed in her bedroom and watched television most of the time. When the children slept, she tried to read, but that required a mind that wasn't distracted. Often, she slept when the children slept.

When she had to feed the children, they crept downstairs. If Grace was in the kitchen, she gave her daughter a look of pity and left. Linda didn't know if it was because her mother didn't want to talk about David or if she was tired of having Linda and the children in her house. Probably both.

Linda decided this way of life could not go on. Tonight, she would call David.

CHAPTER FORTY-FOUR

THURSDAY - DAVID NEALE

After work, David went to Applebee's. He didn't want fast food. He wanted slow food for as long as Applebee's would allow him stay. He couldn't face reporters, but he couldn't continue to pay for motel rooms either.

When he finally turned into Tuscany Lane, he was relieved to see only one media van. He thought he could handle that.

He turned quickly into the driveway, got out of the car, and bolted for the door, leaving his coat and briefcase behind. The reporter yelled at him and ran up the driveway. David fumbled with his keys, finally got the key in the door, and pushed it open, banging it against the door stop just as the reporter, still shouting, reached the steps. David slammed the door. "Leave me alone!" he yelled and thought he should have been saying, "No comment."

He turned the door lock and pictured the ten o'clock news showing him bolting for the door, the reporter chasing behind him, and then standing in front of his door reporting on David's not being willing to speak while the camera recorded the situation.

David wanted to look out the kitchen window and see what the reporter was doing, but he was afraid to. He didn't want to be caught on camera. He was afraid to even turn on the kitchen light.

His only regret about the incident was that he hadn't had time to glare at Brenda. *What a bitch!*

He checked the phone. The caller ID was full of calls from reporters. The last call was from the Davis's. He wondered if it was Bill or Linda. Bill was the last person he wanted to talk to right behind the reporters. He dialed the answering service, erasing one message after another, until he got to Linda's call. She wanted to talk to him. She would call back. That was good because there was no way he was going to call her and end up talking with Bill.

He went to the kitchen window and checked on the media van. Its headlights were on, and it was pulling away from the curb. David waited until it was out of sight and then turned on the kitchen lights. He got a beer from the refrigerator and went back to the living room, turned on the television, and settled on the sofa to wait for Linda to call.

He thought, *When was the last time I sat on the sofa to watch TV?* He remembered Mary Morris/Murphy and glanced at the seat to see if there was still an impression of her having been there. He looked quickly back at the television, a sense of guilt whirling through his mind.

He took a draft of his beer and waited, his eyes and mind unfocused on his surroundings.

Right at nine o'clock, the phone rang. Caller ID said it was Davis's phone.

He picked it up. "Linda?"

"David, I need—"

He cut her off. "Linda, I didn't kill anyone. You've got to believe me. I'd never do that."

"What about the woman?" Linda made it sound like the murdered babies were secondary.

"She was a reporter. She pretended to be someone who just moved to town. Said she didn't have a place to stay. Wouldn't leave and slept on the sofa."

Linda was doubtful. "And you just let her in?"

"It's a long story. We need to talk about it."

"Maybe someday. Right now, I don't know. Everyone is saying such terrible things about you. But that's not why I called. I need to come home, David. I can't stand it here."

"Sure, come home."

"David, I don't want you there."

"Oh . . . okay. I'll have to find somewhere to stay."

"How long will that take?"

"I don't know, but I don't think you want to come home yet anyway. There are all kinds of reporters out in the street waiting for me to come home every night. Why don't you call me Monday night, and I'll let you know if it's all clear?"

"You really think I have to wait?"

"Yes. Things are not much fun here."

"All right, I'll call Monday night."

She hung up. There was no goodbye and certainly not an "I love you."

CHAPTER FORTY-FIVE

FRIDAY - DRURY METZINGER AND LESLIE GIVENS

Metzinger awoke to a rainy Friday. It was going to be a lousy day for canvassing the North Pearson Street neighbors. Thank goodness, he had decided to have Masterson and Big Gert do it. The "missing persons" were their job anyway.

When he got to the office, Givens was waiting for him. "We've got two hits on the kid who gave Mary Murphy the address. Name's Tyrone Bradbury. Lives with his sister, Venessia Jarvis. She lives a couple of blocks from me."

"What else?"

"Prothro worked late on the van. He got some interesting fingerprints off the beds."

"From O'Halloran, Gill, and Neale?"

"None from Neale, but the other two, yes. But there were some others too. One showed up in the database. A Nancy Mulholland. She has a record for shoplifting. Lives in South Alexandria."

Metzinger sighed. He was going to have to do legwork after all. "Okay, here's what I'd like you to do. Go find Prothro. Hopefully, he's not still at the garage. Tell him to work up the

DNA on the two dead babies, Neale, O'Halloran, and Gill. Tell him we may be bringing in swabs on two women. He'll need to run them too. While you're doing that, I'll talk to Masterson and Big Gert. I need to know if they learned anything from Neale's neighbor."

He left Givens writing notes.

Masterson wasn't at his desk, but Big Gert was. "Gert, did you and Arley learn anything yesterday?"

"You mean from Mrs. Doxie DeHaven?"

"I hope your report's more dignified."

"Yeah. Two uniforms from Fairfax were waiting for us. When four of us showed up at the door, she nearly crapped. Caught her in a robe and nightgown. Filmy thing. She ran upstairs to get dressed while Rome burned. Came down in conservative duds, much more reserved than her appearance on the news. Basically, she said the same things she told the reporter. Neale was away a lot at night and on weekends, hardly there the weekend before the Fourth of July and acted weird and up tight. Said Neale's wife left him because he was acting so unpleasant. Moved in with her parents down in Seymour, north of Charlottesville."

"She said 'north of Charlottesville?'"

"No, I did. Looked it up on Google Earth."

"So nothing new."

"No, just about the woman visitor that we now know was this Murphy woman. DeHaven referred to her as 'the little slut" and later, as 'the bimbo'. Said the woman showed up last Thursday night, left Friday morning, returned Friday night, and left very early Saturday morning. Neale saw the woman off, and DeHaven says they both looked guilty as hell. Then she said Neale mowed the lawn like it was a normal day, but she didn't see him come out the rest of the weekend. I suspect she watches everything from her kitchen window."

"Well, that's not much new. Murphy must not have gotten all she wanted the first night and had to come back for a second round."

"Sounds like it."

"I've got another job for you and Arley. Need you to go out and interview the neighbors on North Pearson, a couple on each side of the house at 227 and maybe a couple across the street." Metzinger pulled a sheet of paper out of a folder he was carrying. "Here's the questions I'd like you to ask. Please take it from there."

"Damn, Dru. It's a miserable day."

"It's what you get paid for, darling. I've got places to go too."

Metzinger returned to his desk. He wished he had brought a raincoat. He hadn't thought he'd have to go walking around in the rain. He'd borrow a police slicker. It made him look scarier anyway.

Givens was back. "Fortunately, Prothro was at his desk. He'd already started the DNA. Said the van had three beds, three cribs, mattresses with plastic covers, some metal straight chairs, medical tray tables, and gynecological medical instruments, including stirrups. The same stuff that Sidney Gill rented. There were also green plastic bags of trash, bloody linens, and lab coats. Also, three plastic tubs that Prothro says are afterbirth."

"Three of them?"

"Yes."

"Three beds, three cribs, three of everything. So where's the third baby?"

Metzinger got a slicker, some swabs, and plastic bags. Givens had a raincoat. They headed out to see Venessia Jarvis.

Jarvis lived in a row house in Northwest Alexandria in poor condition in a poor neighborhood. The metal railing was broken off the porch. Metal stubs stuck out of the wood. The porch needed painting. The green paint that was left was peeling.

Givens knocked on the door with authority.

A teenage boy answered. Not in summer school and not working. "What're you knocking so loud for?"

Metzinger gave the boy a hard look and held up his badge. "Hello, Tyrone. Detectives Metzinger and Givens from the Police Department. May we come in?"

Tyrone looked back into the room as if seeking guidance. Givens brushed by him.

A large woman sat at a table. Dark skin, broad face, flat features. Hair short. Her face showed obvious alarm. She was well over two hundred pounds but didn't seem terribly fat. She looked like she could handle Metzinger and Givens combined.

A little boy, four or five, sat on the floor. A young girl, maybe two, was in a playpen. Wide eyes.

The room was neat as a pin. Metzinger was impressed.

Tyrone closed the door. He looked guilty and annoyed.

Metzinger spoke first. "Ms. Jarvis . . ."

"Mrs. Jarvis."

"Okay, Mrs. Jarvis, we need to ask you some questions."

"I don't want to be involved with anything."

Givens piped in. "I'm afraid you already are. Your husband here?"

"No. Haven't seen him since the second baby was born."

Metzinger pulled a picture of Tyrone and Mary Murphy from his file. He held it for Mrs. Jarvis to see."

"I want to ask you about Tyrone giving a message to this lady."

"Don't see any message."

"It's small, but it's there."

"Don't know anything about a message."

"Did you write it?"

She looked at him.

Metzinger pressed, "Maybe Tyrone wrote it."

She didn't say anything.

"So what do you know about 227 North Pearson Street? You thought it was important enough to write it on paper and give it to a reporter. You may not have wanted to be involved, but you wanted the reporter to look into it. I think you wanted someone to be punished."

Mrs. Jarvis sat and wouldn't look at him.

Givens interjected, "Maybe you want Tyrone to leave so you can talk?"

Mrs. Jarvis looked down and shook her head.

Metzinger continued. "Well, I'll tell you what we do know, and it's all because you wrote that address on a piece of paper. We know you were hired to be a surrogate mother, and we know you had a baby and that you had the baby at 227 North Pearson Street. We know the names of the men who were involved. We also know that two other women also had babies there. We've probably got your fingerprints off one of the beds. We can get a warrant to check."

Mrs. Jarvis looked like she was about to cry.

Metzinger regretted it, but he had to play hardball. "Mrs. Jarvis, if you don't talk to us, we're going to have to take you down to our office, get warrants to have you examined to see if you just had a baby, and get warrants for fingerprints and DNA swabs."

"Can't leave my children."

Givens intervened, "If Tyrone can't stay with them, we'll get someone."

Venessia Jarvis continued to stare at the floor, blinking back tears. In a small voice, she finally said, "They killed my baby."

A thought went through Metzinger's mind. *One was black.*

Metzinger put his hand on the woman's shoulder. "I know they did, Venessia, and we need to do something about it."

Mrs. Jarvis looked up at Metzinger and then looked at Givens as if hoping for more sympathy. "They were going to pay me twenty-five thousand dollars. I got no husband. I needed the money."

Givens sympathized, "We completely understand. No one blames you. You're the victim."

"They never did pay me the last five thousand. Just picked me up at seven months, induced the baby, let me spend a night, stuck me in a cab, and sent me home. I asked for the money, but they said they'd send it to me."

Givens interrupted. "What do you mean by 'at seven months?' Was the baby premature?"

Venessia gave her a slightly bewildered look. "I told them it was too soon, but they said it was all right. Said the baby was ready. I felt like it was ready, but it should have been too soon."

"I understand, but did the baby look premature?"

"I didn't see it. They wouldn't let me see it. They were anxious to get it away. Real nervous about it. Said they didn't want a surrogate mother getting attached to the baby. Said it was bad for everyone."

Metzinger tried to be less harsh. "Mrs. Jarvis, we very much appreciate your talking to us. It's been very helpful. I'm sorry I was so rough on you. We need to close this thing out. We'll involve you as little as possible, but I can't guarantee anything."

Mrs. Jarvis looked down and nodded. "I understand."

The softness had ended. It was business again.

"Mrs. Jarvis, how did they contact you? How did you become a surrogate mother? How did they meet you?"

"I answered an ad on Angie's List. Called a telephone number. A man came here and checked me out. Then he picked me up and drove me to the house."

"The house at 227 North Pearson Street?"

"Yes."

Metzinger pulled out the pictures of O'Halloran and Gill. "Is one of these the man?"

"Yes." She pointed to the picture of O'Halloran. "And the other guy is the doctor."

"Okay, Mrs. Jarvis. We need one more thing. We need to get DNA from you so we can know for sure the baby was yours."

"I know it was mine."

"I know, but we've got to be able to prove it."

"You mean you want to swab my mouth like they do on TV?"

"Yes, and then we'll get out of your way."

Metzinger pulled out the swab and plastic bag. He looked at Givens. "Leslie, will you do it?"

Givens understood. It would be easier on the woman if a black woman did it. She thought, *Sometimes, Metzinger's not so bad.*

She took the swab and bag that was handed to her and took the sample.

Metzinger stuck out his hand, and Mrs. Jarvis shook it. He thanked her again, and the two detectives left.

They got in the car.

Metzinger said, "Poor woman."

"Seven months," Givens said, and she shook her head.

They headed for South Alexandria. Nancy Mulholland's apartment looked as bad, if not worse, than had Venessia Jarvis's. It looked like it had been built in the thirties or forties and hadn't been touched since. It looked like welfare housing gone bad. Maybe it was.

Givens did the knocking again. She liked the feeling of authority. They waited. Givens knocked again. A voice came from within. "For Christ's sake. Hold your horses. I'm coming." They heard it pretty well. It was a thin door.

A woman opened the door. She was, maybe, two hundred pounds; but unlike Venessia Jarvis, this woman was soft, looked like there wasn't a muscle in her body. She was probably in her thirties but looked much older. She had a cigarette in her hand. "Yeah?" she asked and put the cigarette in her mouth.

A stench hit Metzinger's nostrils as he held out his badge. "Detectives Metzinger and Givens. We'd like to ask you some questions?"

He glanced past her. Newspaper and trash were piled everywhere. Two plastic bags of trash sat just inside the door.

Metzinger noticed Givens make a face and decided to stay on the porch. Fortunately, the rain had let up.

Mulholland challenged. "About what?"

"About the baby you just had. About your answering an ad on Angie's List."

Now she looked suspicious. "How'd you know about that?"

"We got fingerprints off the bed where the baby was born."

Mulholland looked disgusted. "Yeah, and they're on file, aren't they? I'm a criminal for life. All I took was some underwear. Might as well have a tattoo in the middle of my forehead."

"We're not interested in the underwear or anything you did in your past. We just need to know about the baby."

"How come? Did I break a law or something?"

Metzinger thought quickly. "No. There's just some question about how the baby was handled."

She drew on her cigarette. "Well, they paid me money to have it. Surrogate mother. Don't know who'd want a baby from me, but they offered money for it, so I said okay. Still owe me money."

"Can you tell me if the birth took place at 227 North Pearson Street?"

"Yeah. North Pearson. Don't know the number. Usually went in the back door."

"And they induced the birth?"

"No." She was resolute. "I went into labor. Wednesday night, two weeks ago. Called the doctor, and he came and got me."

Givens interjected, "How many months pregnant were you?"

Mulholland grinned. "Funny you should ask. Just seven months. But I can tell you I was big and ready."

She dropped the cigarette on the porch floor, put it out with her foot, and kicked it off the porch.

Givens asked, "Did you see the baby?"

"No, they wouldn't let me. Took it right away. Don't know what they did with it. Didn't figure that was my business. Poor kid was probably born with a nicotine cough. May have been hard to get rid of." She made an *oh well* motion with her eyes and head.

Metzinger decided she hadn't connected her child to the murdered babies. He would tell her if she gave him a hard time about the DNA swab.

"Thank you. I appreciate the information. Wonder if we could ask you one more thing. We need to definitively connect you to the baby. Nothing that will affect you, but it might affect how we handle the doctor. We need to get a swab from your mouth."

"Oh shit. You're making a complete file on me like I'm going to lift more panties. Yeah, go ahead. You've already got the fingerprints."

Metzinger took the swab and thanked Mulholland for her help. He and Givens headed back to the car while Nancy Mulholland stood on the porch and lit another cigarette. Inside the car, they breathed deeply, relieved to get away from Mulholland's apartment.

They went by a 7-Eleven. Each got a hotdog and a drink. While they sat in the car, chewing on the hotdogs, a thought struck Metzinger. He thought about the photographs in Gill's apartment. He stuffed the last third of his hotdog in an extra plastic bag he hadn't used for DNA, threw it in the back seat, and put the car in gear. "Let's get back to the office."

* * *

As they drove, Metzinger explained what he was going to do.

"It's those country pictures in Gill's apartment. Rocking on a porch and looking over the fence at the cattle. Maybe Gill has a second house on a farm or something. If so, he would have to pay property tax. I'm going to call the Commissioners of the Revenue in different counties. I'll start with reasonably close rural counties. If I can't succeed in Virginia, I'll try Maryland.

"While I'm doing that, I want you to do something we should have done already. If O'Halloran left his van in a storage unit, he must have found some other way to get around. First, check and see if he has a second car. If he doesn't, then start calling car rental agencies. If he rented a car, he would have had to use his own name because they'd ask for a driver's license. I don't think he's sophisticated enough to have a fake license.

"Second, please go see Murray and have him find the ad that was on Angie's list. Find out where it came from and get the telephone number that was called in reply."

Back in the office, Metzinger and Givens settled into their tasks.

Metzinger pulled up a Virginia County Map on the Internet and printed it as a reference. He then went to each county's Web site and found the telephone number of the Commissioner of the Revenue. He started in the south—Stafford, Spotsylvania, and Orange—skipping Fredericksburg City as unlikely. Some offices were quick and efficient. Some wanted to talk to find out what was going on. He tried to be brief, but they were nosy and made him want to scream. He struck out in all three counties. For variety, he decided to go west and then work down. He tried Clarke, Warren, and Page without luck.

In Fauquier, he hit pay dirt. It was a big county. The clerk said Gill's property was up in the northwest part of the county, other side of I-66, on Tucker Lane, which was off Maidenstone Road. She gave him the address and told him that he hopefully would find the number on the mailbox. She further warned him that mailboxes for small lanes off Maidenstone might be at the lane's corner on Maidenstone, in which case he would have to drive down the lane to find the house he was looking for. All houses had a number for 911.

He pulled up a map of Virginia. Since the Commissioner of the Revenue's office was in Warrenton, he assumed "the other side of I-66" meant north of I-66. He panned out so that he could see all of I-66, but the small roads weren't named. He panned back in and moved west. The counties weren't identified, but he found Maidenstone Road just above the exit north on US 17 to Delaplaine. The map showed some stub streets off Maidenstone but didn't identify them by name.

Metzinger updated his lieutenant and got approval to continue with his plan.

He phoned the Fauquier Sheriff's Office and explained what was going on. He arranged to meet a Fauquier County deputy at the corner of US 17 and Maidenstone at eight thirty the next morning. His Saturday was falling apart.

He repeated the process with the state police and arranged for a trooper to meet them at the same corner.

He looked at Givens. She was waiting to interrupt him. "I found the car. A 2006 purple Taurus from Rent-a-Wreck out on Duke Street. I put out an APB. Also, Murray's working on the Angie's List ad."

"Great work. Here's the good news. I found Gill's second house. The bad news is that you need to cancel any plans you have for tomorrow."

*   *   *

Before he left for the day, he checked in with Masterson. They had only found three people home. "Two of them didn't help much. The other was this Sandra Bizzolli that you had notes on. She had lots more to say."

Metzinger pulled out his notepad and pen. "Okay, let me hear it."

"First, I showed her the pictures. She recognized all three of the men. Said they had been there all weekend the weekend before the Fourth of July. She even recognized the mug shot of Nancy Mulholland. She said Mulholland had been there before the weekend and had left in a cab on Friday. She said two other women left in cabs on Sunday. I asked her when the men left. She said the young guy, Neale, left first, around six thirty or seven Sunday evening. The older guy, Gill, left just after it got dark, maybe nine thirty. They didn't turn the light on in back of the house, but she thought he was carrying something, holding it up to his chest. Put it in the back seat of his car. O'Halloran was still there when she went to bed, but his purple Taurus was gone in the morning. He came back later with a black van and moved things out of the house with two Mexicans from about ten until two. Really full of information. Must live a boring life and spends her time at the window."

Metzinger looked at Masterson, his mouth agape, his mind gyrating.

Masterson looked at him, suddenly worried. "What's wrong, Dru?"

Metzinger focused but didn't look at Masterson. "I asked people on US 1, around the barbecue joint, if they had seen a black Mercedes van. I've been asking about the wrong car. It should have been a purple Taurus."

CHAPTER FORTY-SIX

FRIDAY/SATURDAY - MARY MURPHY

Mary Murphy was relaxing in her apartment Friday night eating a hot dog and drinking iced tea. About seven, the phone rang. It was Dan Jenkins. "I know you're supposed to have tomorrow off, but it's your case, and I need you to cover it."

The editor of the Fauquier newspaper had called him about five, just as he was about to leave work. It seems that a clerk from the Commissioner of the Revenue's office had called him asking questions about the murders of the babies in Alexandria. The clerk was good about giving him leads on stories, wanted to stay anonymous, but when the stories panned out, it made her feel important. Apparently, the Alexandria Police Department had called that afternoon and asked the clerk if a Sidney Gill owned property in Fauquier. She had confirmed that he did and had asked more questions in return. She had found out that the inquiry was relative to the murder of the Route-One Babies.

Dan had immediately become interested and explained who Gill was and that it might be a good story. He asked where Gill had the property and got directions. He wanted Mary to go out in the morning and check the place out. He warned her to be careful and said that if she felt uncomfortable about anything, she was to come home.

That night, Mary didn't sleep well. She wasn't sure she still wanted to be involved in the case. She continued to feel guilty about the article on David Neale. She knew that she had been doing her job, but she still felt like a traitor.

Since she couldn't sleep, she was up early Saturday morning and on I-66 by seven. She found the US 17 exit and then Maidenstone. It turned out to be a kind of long lonely road. *Roads are always long when you don't know where you're going.* She finally found Turner Lane, with three mailboxes at the corner. The numbers didn't match the order of the numbers she had seen for Maidenstone. These were 101, 107, and 115. That left room for development. She had been told 115 was Gill's. 101 and 107 turned out to be small, one-story houses with vinyl siding, maybe two or three rooms with a bath. As she drove along Turner Lane, the road quickly turned to gravel, at least what used to be gravel. Most of it had long since been ground in, and ruts were beginning to form. A patch of grass and weeds extended down the center of the road.

She saw a white frame house in the distance with a couple of outer sheds and a car parked next to it. Another car was stopped a couple of hundred yards from the house, facing toward her. A man standing next to it waved her down.

She rolled down her window, and he stuck his head in. "You better not go any further. An old guy is in there. Yelled at me through a bullhorn when I drove up and got out of my car. He said if I didn't leave, he was going to blow us all up. I thought it best to get clear of the house and think over what I was going to do. Are you a friend of his?"

Mary decided she was in the right place but wasn't sure what to do. "He's not a friend. In fact, I've never met him, but I know who he is."

"My editor says he's someone connected to the baby murders in Alexandria."

"Did you say your editor said that?"

"Yeah, I'm a reporter from Warrenton."

Mary nodded. "Well, your editor called my editor, and that's why I'm here. I'm from Alexandria and have been writing about the case for two weeks."

"Oh, then maybe you can fill me in. Are you going up to the house?"

"I don't think so. My editor said to come home if I didn't feel comfortable. Well, I don't feel comfortable, but I think I'll sit for a while and see if anything happens. I have a feeling it might."

"Okay. My name is Matt Harris. Mind if I sit in your car with you while we wait?"

Mary cleared her papers off the passenger's seat. "Sure. I'm Mary Murphy. I'll fill you in while we sit."

Chapter Forty-Seven

Saturday - Drury Metzinger and Leslie Givens

Metzinger and Givens met at their office at seven thirty. They stopped at Starbucks for coffee. Metzinger warned that it might be the last coffee they could get before they hit the country. They took US 1 to I-495 and then on to I-66. Once on I-66, traffic wasn't too bad. They were going the right direction, away from DC.

At Gainesville, construction started to become a problem. For years, the Virginia Department of Transportation worked on widening I-66, moving away from DC section by section, and then starting all over again. They squeezed extra lanes through overpasses that weren't wide enough. If you followed the joints in the pavement, you'd quickly be in the wrong lane. You had to follow the painted lines. However hard they tried, VDOT was always behind.

Beyond Gainesville, the country began to lose its population, briefly increasing a little bit as they passed the US 15 exit. Metzinger remarked, "There's a McDonald's here. We may need it when we come back."

As they drove, Metzinger told Givens about the visit Masterson had with Sandra Bizzolli. "If Neale went home after he left 227 and his wife or neighbor will back it up, then it looks like maybe he wasn't the one who left the babies in the dumpster."

They passed the exit for The Plains.

"We need to get photographs of a 2006 Ford Taurus, preferably purple, and the kind of car Sidney Gill drives and go back Monday and recanvas the area around the dumpster."

Givens replied to Metzinger's thoughts a little sarcastically, "It's good to have a plan to start next week. I'd hate to waste time. And for your information, Gill drives a tan Malibu."

"How do you know that?"

"It's the car Masterson put out an APB on."

"Smart ass. Now I remember. I thought all our senior citizens were supposed to drive Buicks."

"Haven't you heard? Buick is changing its image, and not all old people drive them. Heck, my mother drives an old Crown Vic. Gives me a hard time. Says she needs to be able to outrun the cops."

They passed the Marshall exit.

Metzinger nodded. "Yeah, and my old man has a red Camaro. My mother says it's a middle-aged crises. Hate to remind them they're in their sixties."

"It's you who need the reminding, Dru. All the magazines say the fifties and sixties are the new middle age."

"Never saw that in *Sports Illustrated*."

They exited on US 17 north. It was an impressive exit, like the interstate was splitting.

Two marked cars sat on the right at the next intersection. Metzinger pulled in behind them. He and Givens got out while the two other guys got out of a trooper's cruiser. They all shook hands and introduced themselves. Both of the new guys wore hats. One was a state trooper and the other, a sheriff's deputy.

Metzinger knew the trooper's head had a buzz cut. His head was held straight. Metzinger didn't know if that was to hold up the hat or if troopers were trained to do that. The man was square-jawed and intense-looking. He introduced himself as Jarvis Moore.

The Sheriff's Deputy, Jimmy Swain, was baby-faced and looked to be twenty.

Deputy Swain acknowledged that he knew where Tucker Lane was and volunteered to lead the convoy.

Maidenstone Road had a few patches of trees along the way but was mostly rolling hills of cleared farmland with very few houses. Swain turned left. It was Tucker Lane. There were three mailboxes on the corner, just as the clerk in Warrenton had suggested. One was 115, Sidney Gill's number. He noted the two one-story houses and decided that neither was the white- frame farmhouse they were looking for. They followed the road, and just over a rise, he saw a white farmhouse with a front porch. It fit the photograph in Gill's apartment. A tan Malibu was parked to the left of the house. This was definitely the place.

There were two cars parked a fair distance from the house. Swain stopped by a little red car and spoke out the window. Then he pulled over to the other side of the road, got out, and walked back to the trooper's car. Next, the trooper got out, and the two policemen walked back to Metzinger and Givens.

The deputy explained what the woman in the red car had said. Metzinger decided they all needed to talk some more to the people in the little red car.

As the group of four walked up to the little red car, Mary turned her head to the window. "Good morning, detectives. I haven't seen you in a while."

Metzinger was astonished. "Mary Murphy, how the hell did you get here?"

Mary was smugly nonchalant. "We reporters have our sources." She turned to Harris. "Matt, these two people in civilian clothes are Detectives Metzinger and Givens from Alexandria." She turned back to the detectives. "Detectives, this is Matt Harris, a reporter from Warrenton."

Harris leaned forward so that he could see past Mary and said, "Pleased to meet you." He then waved to the deputy. "Hey, Jimmy."

Deputy Swain waved back. "Hi, Matt."

Metzinger looked disgusted and annoyed. "So you're messing in police business?"

Mary protested, "No, I'm just looking for a story. Thought you might be here sometime, but I didn't know when. I wanted to interview Gill."

"So why aren't you?"

"Better part of valor. I'm reticent about being blown up. I was just sitting here trying to decide what to do, when you gallant knights drove up."

Metzinger, frowning, leaned in the window and questioned Harris. "So why are you guys saying he's going to blow you up?"

Harris replied, "The guy inside said he was going to do it. I drove up and was walking toward the house when he stuck a bullhorn out the window and told me to stop and that if I came any closer, he was going to blow the place up. He told me to leave, so I did. Got this far and was thinking when Mary drove up."

Metzinger acknowledged what Harris had said. "Okay, I guess I need to talk to Dr. Gill."

Metzinger looked reluctantly at the house. Gill would see him coming for two hundred yards. If he had explosives, he could time it just right.

Jarvis Moore saw Metzinger's hesitation. "I've got a bullhorn in my trunk. Why don't I try to talk to him with it?"

Metzinger nodded. "It's worth a try."

Moore got the bullhorn out of his trunk, turned it on, and checked the battery. He walked to the front of Deputy Swain's car and leaned against it, holding up the bullhorn. "Dr. Gill, this is State Trooper Jarvis Moore. I'm here with Deputy Swain of the Fauquier Sheriff's Office and Detectives Metzinger and Givens of the Alexandria Police. We would very much like to talk to you. Will you let us come in?"

A window slid open on the porch, and a bullhorn appeared. "I don't want to talk to you. I'm living here quietly and not bothering anyone. Just go away and leave me be."

Moore replied, "We can't do that, Dr. Gill. How about letting a couple of us come in?"

"No one is coming in, and don't try. I've got this house loaded with explosives, and there is no way I'll let you in to bother me. You try to get close, and we're all going to heaven. If you want to talk, we'll talk when we get there."

Moore put down his bullhorn and shook his head.

Metzinger assessed the situation. "He sounds determined. We don't know whether he's faking or not, but none of us want to be blown up. Further, if he blows himself up or if we shoot him, we won't get any answers. The house is sitting there with two old trees, a couple of sheds, and a car around it. Everything else is wide open. There's no way to approach the house without being seen. We need to negotiate."

Moore agreed. "I'll get a professional in. It'll take a little while. I'd like some backup too."

Swain said he'd also like some backup. They both got on their cell phones.

Metzinger thought, *Good. I was afraid cell phones wouldn't work here. We must be close enough to I-66.*

When Swain had finished, Metzinger looked at him. "Will you go back to the two little houses and tell the people living there that police activity is going on up here and that they are to stay in their houses? Trooper Moore and I need to get our cars off the road."

He turned to Mary. "Okay, Missy Murphy. You and Mr. Harris need to move your cars down to the entrance of this road. And keep the cars out of the way."

Mary protested, "But we've been here nearly an hour, with no problems. If the house blows up, we're already far away."

Metzinger glared at her. "Don't give me any crap. You're just going to get in the way up here. Move it."

Matt Harris got out of Mary's car and into his own.

Mary backed her car to where there was a gate in the fence that lined the road, backed in, and turned around. She drove back to the entrance to Tucker Lane followed by Harris. They both parked on the opposite side of the road from the house on the corner at 101. They didn't want to mess up the people's yard. They got out of their cars and walked back toward Gill's house, stopping when they got within a hundred yards of the police officers.

Metzinger observed them and shook his head. He had had an idea. He was on the phone talking to Masterson whom he knew was working on Saturday. He explained the situation and then discussed why he was calling. "Arley, will you get Big Gert to cover for you? I need you to find David Neale and bring him out here. I want him to talk to Gill."

He listened while Arley replied, "There's no sense in my doing that. Gert lives in Fairfax City. By the time she comes in here and I go back there, you'll lose an hour. I'll get Gert to pick Neale up and bring him to you. It'll be a civilian car, but that shouldn't matter. Just keep it away from the explosives."

Metzinger acknowledged that it was a good idea. "Give me a call when you get hold of Gert and have her call me when she finds Neale."

"Will do."

CHAPTER FORTY-EIGHT

SATURDAY - DAVID NEALE

David slept late. There was nothing else to do anyway. He thought about mowing the lawn. There really wasn't much to mow. Except for a little rain yesterday morning, it hadn't rained much in two weeks. The grass was dry. It crackled beneath your feet when you walked on it.

He got in the *Washington Post*, glared at Brenda's window, made coffee and a bowl of cereal, and sat at the table. While he ate the cereal and drank the coffee, he read the newspaper. He concentrated on the Metro Section. There was nothing there about the babies. The Saturday paper was thin, especially after you pulled out the real estate section. He was sure he hadn't missed anything. It was a relief.

When he finished eating, he took his dishes to the kitchen sink and began rinsing and loading them in the dishwasher. Since Mary Murphy had embarrassed him, he had tried to keep up with the dishwashing. While David was standing at the sink, he looked out the window as a Chrysler 300 pulled to his curb. He had always thought of it as a man's car, but a woman got out, one of the biggest women he had ever seen. She walked up the

driveway to his front door. He opened the door and storm door
to meet her.

"May I help you?"

She showed him her badge. "Are you David Neale?"

David was uncertain. "Yes."

"I'm Detective Sorenson from the Alexandria Police. I need
you to come with me."

David thought about protesting, but she looked like she
might pick him up and carry him to the car. "Where are we
going?"

She had already turned her back and was headed to her car.
"To talk to a man named Sidney Gill."

Oh, oh, thought David. *More trouble.*

He shouted after her, "I've got to turn off the coffee pot!"

She turned her head. "Okay, but hurry."

David turned off the coffee pot, checked the kitchen to
see if anything else was on. He locked the door, headed for
Sorenson's car, and got in. As they drove off, he glanced at
Brenda's window. She was watching.

David worked up his nerve. "So where is Doc Gill?"

The answer was brief and unexpected. "Fauquier County."

David thought, *So that's where he's hiding.*

At a stop sign, Detective Sorenson dialed her cell phone. She
waited a moment, and David could hear someone answer. "This
is Gert. I've got him in the car, and we're on the way."

She listened a moment longer and clicked the phone off.

They drove in silence the rest of the way.

As they exited I-66, David became alert and started to look
around.

Sorenson stopped and looked at some notes. Then she drove on and turned on to Maidenstone Road. Soon, David felt he was in the middle of nowhere. They'd been driving less than an hour since leaving his house.

Sorenson turned left. There was a little red car parked near the corner. He had seen it before. They passed two houses and were on a slightly rough, dirt road. Two people were standing by a fence. It hit him, and he thought, *Mary Morris/Murphy! What the hell was she doing here? It can't be good.*

They pulled off the road behind four police cars, an ambulance, and an unmarked car. State troopers and other police personnel were all over the place. Medics sat in the cab of the ambulance. Up front, he saw Metzinger and Givens and thought, *The gang's all here.*

Sorenson got out of the car. "Stay here."

She went over to Metzinger and spoke for a few minutes. Then they started walking back to Sorenson's car. Metzinger put his hand on the back of Sorenson's shoulder as if talking to a subordinate and telling her she had done a good job. It looked odd. Sorenson had at least an inch on Metzinger and probably outweighed him by twenty-five pounds.

Metzinger opened the door and got in the driver's seat. Sorenson got in the back seat. "Gert won't leave, so I'll use her car as my office. She'll be our witness. We would like you to do something for us as a concerned citizen."

David neither said yes nor no. "Like what?"

Metzinger nodded toward the white farmhouse. "Your lab partner, Sidney Gill, is in that house. We would very much like to talk to him. I don't know whether that's in your interest or not. Our problem is that he says he has the house loaded with explosives and that he will set them off if we try to enter the house. We would like you to try to talk some reason into him. I'm making the assumption that if you go up to the house and tell him who you are, he won't blow the house up as long as you stay outside and just talk to him. The bad part for me is that, if you get blown up, I'll be in a lot of trouble for using a civilian this way."

David nodded. "Yeah, and I'll be dead. How about you just packing up and leaving the man alone?"

Metzinger shook his head. "You know I can't do that. I'm working on a murder investigation."

David looked innocently at Metzinger. "And you think he murdered someone?"

Any sign of civility vanished from Metzinger's whole being. "Don't be cute with me, Neale. This is not fun and games. I can't make you do this, but I'd like to see Sidney Gill come out of this alive. If he's guilty, we'll find out. If he's innocent, we'll find that out too."

David became serious and thoughtful. "But you can't make me do this?"

"No."

"I'll tell you my thoughts on all this. You think that Doc Gill and I are connected to the deaths of two babies. You also believe that, if you can talk to him, you can perhaps find out who killed the babies and perhaps implicate me or him or both of us in the murder. If you can do that, I would be insane to talk him into coming out of the house. On the other hand, if I go and talk to him and he then blows himself up, you'll think I talked him into doing it so that he can't be a witness against me. Looks like this is a no-win situation for me."

"But you might save a man's life."

David pondered the situation. "Look, I'm scared to death, but I like Doc Gill, and that's why I'll do it."

That gave Metzinger a lot to think about. Finally, he said, "Okay. Walk slowly. Before you start, I'll get the bullhorn and tell him you're coming. If he doesn't want you, he's got a bullhorn and can say so."

Metzinger went over to the state police car and spoke to the trooper inside. The trooper passed a bullhorn out the window. Metzinger went to the front of the parked cars and spoke into the device. "Dr. Gill, David Neale is here and is going to walk up to your house and speak to you. He will not try to come in. Please talk to him."

Metzinger gave Gill a moment to respond. There was none. He turned and waved David forward.

David swallowed hard and began walking. At about fifty yards, he stopped and turned. He noticed Mary Morris/Murphy had moved up behind the police cars. Metzinger flicked his hand a couple of times to tell David to keep going.

About twenty-five yards from the house, David shouted, "Doc, it's me, David Neale! I'm not coming in. I just want to talk to you."

From behind a partially open porch window, Doc Gill replied, "Come on, David. I won't do anything as long as the cops stay where they are. If they move at all, you'd better run."

"Okay." David sat on the front steps.

Doc's hidden voice encouraged David. "Come on and sit in a rocking chair so I can see you."

David got up and sat in the porch rocker near the window.

"They sent you to talk me into giving up, didn't they?"

David replied, "Of course they did, but I don't want to see you hurt."

Doc answered in a solemn tone, "David, I appreciate that, but I can't."

David heard a sound from in the house, a happy sound, a baby's sound. A sudden understanding enveloped his mind.

"Doc, you've got the third baby in there, don't you?"

"Yes."

David gradually absorbed this new knowledge. "So that's why you won't give up."

Doc's voice sought understanding. "If I give up, they'll take her. I'll lose her. They'll poke her and test her. They'll make her a guinea pig. They'll view her as a freak of nature. She's not, David. She's a child. Dorothy's my child."

"Doc, are you telling me you want a child at your age?"

Doc sighed. "David, I'm sorry I got you into all this. If I had said no that day Seth proposed all this, you wouldn't have gone along, would you?"

David considered what he had done. "No, I probably wouldn't have?"

"I didn't think so. But I wanted a baby. I didn't know things would go so wrong. It wasn't a Nobel Prize I wanted. It was the baby. Seth and I talked. It was my sperm."

"But, Doc, why would you want a child?"

"David, you don't know a thing about me. To you, I'm just an old doctor who doesn't practice medicine and who happened to be on an NIH team you were assigned to. What you don't know is that I was once a member of a very successful OB-GYN practice, associated with a major hospital, the whole thing. I was good at it. I had a wonderful life." He choked. "I fell in love. Her name was Rebecca. We were going to be married. We talked of our future, of having a family. It was the happiest time of my life."

For a while, there was silence. David could feel Doc's tears as if they were running down his own face.

Doc continued, a forced voice. "She was killed two days before the wedding. Her car was hit at an intersection by a guy high on drugs. She was killed instantly." Doc sobbed. "David, she was two months pregnant. For months, I held an image in my mind of my beautiful Rebecca holding our child. It haunts till this day."

The horror of it stunned David's mind. "Doc, I'm sorry. I'm so sorry."

"David, I couldn't do my job anymore. I couldn't face the babies or the mothers. I quit and didn't work at all for a while, but I had to make a living, so I went to work at NIH."

David sat with his head bowed.

"David, this is the child my Rebecca and I should have had. I gave her the name that Rebecca and I talked about. Do you understand why I did it, David?"

David choked, "Yes, Doc, of course I do."

"David, I didn't kill those babies. I should have stayed, but I wanted to protect Dorothy. That was all that was on my mind. I waited until it was dark so that no one could see, and then I got out of there and drove here. I shouldn't have left Seth. He was so distraught over the failure of the experiment. He had such high hopes, spent a fortune for the glory he expected. It was tragic and sad, but I had to protect Dorothy."

David tried to soothe Doc. "Hey, I understand. I'm the guilty one. I left as fast as I could when Seth told me he'd take care of everything. Murdering the babies just never entered my mind. It's not my nature, but maybe I should have thought more."

"Lord, David, I wish we could go back and not have done any of this, but what's done is done."

David stood up. "Doc, there's no way I can tell you how sorry I am. I'll go back and try to explain to the police. I'll try to get them to go away."

"David, you and I both know they won't go away."

"I'll try, Doc. I don't want you and Dorothy to die."

Doc sounded resigned. "We don't want to either."

David made it about fifty yards when the shock wave and sound of the explosion threw him to the ground, facedown. He squeezed his eyes shut and put his arm under his forehead. He spat dirt out of his mouth. He could feel stinging on his back. He knew he had been hit by flying debris.

David opened his eyes. Out of the corners, he could see people running by. He knew they must be shouting. He could hear nothing.

He felt a hand on his shoulder. He looked up. The concerned face of Mary Morris/Murphy was looking down at him. She was speaking, but he couldn't her. Anger raged through him. He blamed her for all that had happened. He shouted, "Get away from me! Go get your story! Go find your body parts!" It was the meanest thing he could think of.

Finally, he forced himself to get up. Mary was still standing there. She offered him her hand. He waved her away and began walking. She followed him, about ten feet behind.

He opened the door of a state police cruiser, sat in the passenger seat, and waited. Mary leaned against the car across the road, looking concerned and guilty.

After a while, Metzinger came back and stood at the window of the cruiser. He was saying something. David couldn't make it out.

David looked up at Metzinger. "He didn't want you to take the baby."

The reality of what David had said seemed to be etching its way into Metzinger's mind. He appeared to be asking a question and then waiting for an answer.

David remembered what his attorney had said. He shook his head back and forth while he spoke, "I don't know a thing, detective."

Metzinger turned away in what seemed like frustration. He waved to someone. A moment later, a medic opened the car door and led David back toward the ambulance.

David mumbled, "I just don't know a damned thing."

CHAPTER FORTY-NINE

SATURDAY - MARY MURPHY

Mary Murphy had leaned against the car across from where David Neale sat in the state police cruiser. She was upset at what he had said about the body parts. She felt guilty too. She wasn't interested in gore. She just wanted a story. That was her job.

She had used her phone with a live stream to capture David's visit to the farmhouse. She had still been streaming when the explosion occurred. She had heard the sound and felt the shock. The phone shook in her hand, but she fought to keep it under control. As she had brought the image back to the scene, she had been appalled to see David lying flat on the ground, his head cradled on his arm. Was he dead? She had started running toward him, the camera wobbling on and off the view of the man.

Finally, she had cut off her phone and reached down to touch David's shoulder. She had been stunned by the venom in his voice when spoke to her. She had felt shocked, hurt, and guilty as she timidly followed him back to the police cars.

She just watched as he sat in the car.

Soon, some of the police walked back from the destroyed house. She figured the investigation of the scene was now up to someone else, some experts.

Metzinger approached the cruiser, leaned down to address David, and spoke the obvious, "So it didn't work, huh?"

David looked into Metzinger's face and said, "He didn't want you to take the baby."

Metzinger seemed to take some time to absorb this. "You mean he had the third baby in there?"

David just mumbled.

Mary thought, *Oh my god! A third baby!*

Metzinger gave up trying to talk to David and waved a medic over. David was led to the ambulance, and the medic worked on him, cleaning his face and the back of his head.

The state police trooper walked up to his car and looked at the passenger's seat. She heard him say, "Shit, he bled all over it."

Mary almost laughed.

Her eyes went back to the ambulance. One medic was walking over to Metzinger. They talked for a moment.

While they were doing that, another medic helped David into the back of the ambulance.

Metzinger spoke to the huge woman cop who had brought David, and she got into her Chrysler.

The ambulance drove off with the Chrysler following.

It looked like David would have a ride home.

Mary went over and thanked the Fauquier reporter. He still seemed to be shaken. She knew she was too.

She walked back to her car. It was a longer walk than she remembered.

*   *   *

When Mary got back to the office, she was the center of attention for the Saturday staff. They had a television on, and her streaming work was playing on CNN. It was national news. Everyone in the office had questions. She waved them off. She had to get to writing.

She was almost finished when Dan Jenkins approached her desk. "Mary, you've got to be the luckiest reporter I've ever known. It's almost like things happen because you're there."

Mary was mortified. "I sure as hell hope not. You sent me there. Maybe you knew something."

"Luck of the draw, Mary. I know it's your day off, but there's more for you to do. They're going to have a press conference. It's at City Hall again. I'd appreciate your covering it, if you would?"

Mary nodded. "Okay." She thought to herself that she certainly didn't feel lucky. She felt battered.

As she approached City Hall, a television reporter and cameraman ran over to her. They were soon followed by others. She realized, suddenly, that she was now the news. Her name was out there on national television.

She tried to be polite. She described what she had seen, insisting that it was all on television already for the world to see. She spoke about David as having been brave and how he had been bloodied and taken off to the hospital.

"What hospital?" they asked.

She said she assumed that it was a hospital in Fauquier County, although she didn't know its name.

She finally got to the door.

A couple of reporters stood outside the door. One spoke up, "How's it that you're always at the scene of the news? You getting inside information?"

The other chimed in, "Who you sleeping with, Mary?"

She hurried past, embarrassed. She thought to herself, *All of a sudden, everyone knows my name. I'm not sure I want to be known."* The scrutiny made her feel uncomfortable. She thought, *I wonder if David Neale feels the same way.*

Mary found a seat. It was in the second row this time, not in the back corner.

The reporter next to her said, "Congratulations. Maybe you should be giving this briefing?"

She acknowledged him, "Thanks. I think we'll learn a little more today."

Finally, a group came through the side door. It was high-powered. Mayor Robbins and the Vice Mayor were there. Even Mad Dog Conroy was there, standing next to the Mayor. This was going to be on national television, and no politician was going to fail to be present for such an event. Everyone stood side by side—a police lieutenant, Metzinger, and Givens at the end nearest the door.

Mayor Robbins approached the lectern.

"I'd like to welcome you all to the City Hall. As you know, this has been a day of major events, all very likely associated with the murder of the two babies who were found south of Alexandria the week before last. I told you at that time that the government of this City would go all out to solve that crime. Working through the Police Chief, we have made considerable headway toward closing this case, much of which has been reported in the media. Through our efforts, today we located one of the missing scientists whom we believe was associated with the murders. The dramatic events involving this man were recorded live on national television. We would like to fill in the details. Before we do that, I would like to acknowledge the presence here today of our congressman, J. Madison Conroy, who has taken a major interest in this case and has offered any help he can provide. And now, I would like to ask Chief Carmichael to provide you information on the case."

Carmichael replaced the Mayor at the lectern, placing a pile of papers before him. He studied them for a moment and then looked up from the documents. "As you are aware, we have been looking for two missing scientists who work at the National Institutes of Health in Fairfax but have their apartments here in Alexandria. I'm sure you know, from articles in the media, that these individuals may be linked to the murder of two babies whose bodies were found a couple of weeks ago in a dumpster on US 1 south of the City. Through the efforts of my office, with the support of the Mayor, and in particular, through the efforts of Lieutenant Ramirez and Detectives Metzinger and Givens, standing here behind me"—and he motioned with his hand toward Metzinger who looked nervous and unhappy, and Givens, who stared straight ahead at the wall in the back of the room—"we were able to identify a second home owned by one of the missing men, Dr. Sidney Gill. This home is on a piece of farmland in Fauquier County.

"With the support of the Virginia State Police and the Fauquier Sheriff's Office, Detectives Metzinger and Givens approached the house today, only to have Dr. Gill use a bullhorn to inform the detectives that if they approached the house, he was prepared to blow the house up using explosives that he had prepared within. Because of the barren landscape around the house, the police were not able to approach it and attempted to negotiate with Dr. Gill. As a last resort, Detectives Metzinger and Givens asked one of Dr. Gill's lab partners at NIH, Mr. David Neale, to approach the house and try to reason with Dr. Gill. Mr. Neale did approach the house, sat on the front porch, and talked to Dr. Gill for several minutes. Unfortunately, he apparently was not successful in talking Dr. Gill into surrendering to the police because, as Mr. Neale walked away from the house, Dr. Gill detonated the explosives, completely destroying the house and killing himself. The remains of the house are now being thoroughly investigated as a crime scene.

"The death of Dr. Gill is extremely unfortunate, not only because of the man's death but also because we have lost a person of interest who might have shed light on the deaths of the two babies. I would note the other missing scientist, Seth O'Halloran, is still at large and remains a person of interest in the deaths of the babies. We believe he is driving a rented purple 2006 Ford Taurus. We have a handout we will provide you at the door which states the car's license plate number. As always, we would appreciate any help the public can give us in finding this individual and car.

"Before I open this briefing for questions, I would like Detective Metzinger to address some of the other things we have learned in the last few days."

Metzinger came forward, holding notes and looking uncomfortable.

He spoke, looking at Mary during his introduction. "Thank you, Chief Carmichael. As you know, from what has been written in the media, there is extreme interest in a house at

227 North Pearson Street that was rented by Mr. David Neale and where Mr. Neale, Dr. Gill, and Mr. O'Halloran were seen on an intermittent basis."

From there, Metzinger discussed talking to two women who had been impregnated at the house and who had given birth to babies the weekend before the July Fourth Holiday weekend, believing they were acting as surrogate mothers. He noted that one gave birth naturally, and one had the birth induced and that both babies had been born about the end of the seventh month of pregnancy. He also discussed successfully locating Mr. O'Halloran's van and finding within it three beds and three cribs. He reminded everyone that Mr. O'Halloran had been seen removing these kinds of items from the house at 227 North Pearson. He did not mention finding placentas from three women. He did note that they had DNA from the two women and from the babies and hoped that it would be determined shortly whether they and the dead babies were, indeed, linked.

Metzinger took his place back in line and was replaced at the lectern by the Police Chief.

"I have several members of my department and several other people from the city government here with me today, and we would be glad to address a few questions."

The Chief recognized a reporter in the first row who asked, "Is it normal for your department to have a civilian member of the community act as a negotiator, and do you know what was said between Mr. Neale and Dr. Gill?"

The Chief looked uncomfortable. "It is not normal to use a civilian. We did not force Mr. Neale to act as negotiator. He indicated that he was willing to do it. The use of a civilian negotiator is a procedure that will be the subject of review in my department in the next few days."

Mary noticed Metzinger look even more uncomfortable.

The Chief continued, evidently glad to get away from the subject of the civilian negotiator. "As to what was discussed between Mr. Neale and Dr. Gill, we do not know. Mr. Neale has declined to discuss it, saying simply that 'he knows nothing.' We suspect he is following the advice of his attorney, but it is certainly not helpful."

Mary waved her hand. The Police Chief pointed at her. "Yes, Ms. Murphy."

Mary stood, while thinking, *Oh god, everyone knows me.*

She addressed the Chief. "Sir, in addition to Dr. Gill, was there a baby in the house, perhaps a third baby related somehow to the two babies who were murdered?"

There was murmuring in the room. Metzinger glared at Mary. The Chief looked confused. "And why would you think that?"

"Because I heard Mr. Neale say to Detective Metzinger after the explosion that Dr. Gill didn't want him to take the baby."

The Chief blinked and turned to Metzinger and asked, "Did he say that?"

Metzinger looked miserable. "Yes, but he was in shock, and we don't know what baby he was talking about."

Mary pounced, "But you said there were three beds and three cribs. That would imply there was a third baby. I assume you're looking for it."

Metzinger stepped forward. "Yes, there is possibly a third baby. In fact, it is probable. And we are looking for it. And yes, after what Mr. Neale said, we are looking through the debris of Dr. Gill's house to see if there is a sign of a baby."

Chief Carmichael looked furious. "Does that answer your question, Ms. Murphy?"

"Yes, and I assume we will be notified about the search."

The Chief looked down. "We have tried to be transparent about this case and will certainly continue to provide information, as long as it doesn't impact our ability to prosecute and close the episode."

Reluctantly, he asked, "Are there any more questions?"

A hand was raised on the other side of the room from Mary, and the reporter was recognized by the chief.

"Chief Carmichael, I was interested to hear from Detective Metzinger that the two women identified gave birth after only seven months of pregnancy. Can you tell me whether the babies who were murdered appeared to be premature or if were they full-term babies?"

The Chief, again, looked uncomfortable, as if he wished he had asked someone else to run the briefing. "I don't know, but I've asked the medical examiner to be here."

He turned to one of the men behind him, a somewhat florid, slightly overweight, balding gentleman, who replied, "They appeared to be full-term babies."

The reporter stuck up his hand again. "I have a follow-up question. Mary Murphy reported in her newspaper that Mr. Neale was upset about a failed experiment. Now we know that the murdered babies were somehow deformed, although we don't know details of the deformation, and that they may have been born as full-term babies after only seven months of pregnancy."

The Chief asked, "Is that a question?"

"Only an observation."

*   *   *

The "observation" was all over the news that night, even outplaying Mary's question about the third baby, although that got significant attention.

Mary watched television in horror.

Although it had never been proven, the link between the NIH researchers and the dead babies was firmly cemented in the media's minds. The conjecture about the babies' births was definitively joined to a failed experiment conducted by the three researchers, as if it were fact. Further, it was firmly noted that the experiment was directly a result of an attempt to defy the natural order of things by changing the human period of gestation from nine months to seven months. As far as everyone was concerned, this was no longer an "observation." It was a fact.

CHAPTER FIFTY

SATURDAY - DAVID NEALE

David watched television, feeling in every way like a beaten man. His body hurt from many cuts and small holes where debris had been extracted from his body. It ached from being belted by the shock of the explosion and being thrown to the ground. And he was mentally beaten by the revelation of the experiment. Although it was conjecture, he knew it was true and that all the world believed it was true.

He went to the refrigerator and took out a bottle of wine. He poured himself a glass and thought about whether or not to leave the bottle out. He, finally, decided to put it away. Getting drunk was not a solution.

He turned on the oven to heat and pulled a frozen pizza from the freezer. He read the directions. Preheat to four fifty, put on the rack, and cook for fourteen minutes. Simple enough, but it took longer than the microwave, which he preferred.

He picked up his glass of wine and started to return to the living room sofa when the phone rang. He thought that it must be a reporter, but it might be Linda. He looked at the caller ID: *Silverstone and Draper LLP*. He hesitated. It sounded like a solicitor or robocall. He finally answered with a noncommittal "hello."

A woman's voice answered, deep and mellow. "Good evening. This is the law office of Aubrey Silverstone and William Draper. Is this Mr. David Neale?"

"Yes, it is."

"I hope you're well, Mr. Neale. Please hold the phone while I page Mr. Silverstone."

David waited a moment.

Silverstone came on the phone. "Mr. Neale?"

"Yes?"

"Good evening, Mr. Neale. I appreciate your speaking to me. I have been reading the newspapers about your case with great interest, and I would be very interested in speaking to you about it."

David felt uncomfortable. "Mr. Silverstone, I was not aware I had a 'case.' No one has ever referred to it that way."

Silverstone seemed unfazed. "Well, I suspect you know what I'm talking about. Let's call it your *situation*. As I suspect you're well aware, there are probably going to be legal ramifications as a result of the activities of yourself and your laboratory associates."

David was hesitant. After all, this wasn't his attorney. Maybe he was someone else's attorney. "I am. I've hired an attorney to help me."

"And may I ask if this is a criminal attorney? And how much does he charge?"

It occurred to David that he had never asked Travers if he was a criminal attorney or what his experience was in that field, although the phone book had listed him that way. He decided only to answer the second part of the question. "He charges $125 an hour."

Silverstone sounded a little incredulous as he proceeded. "You said one hundred and twenty-five dollars an hour?"

"Yes."

"I see." Silverstein seemed to hesitate, as if he were thinking. "Well, that still will add up. How would you feel if you could get the legal services you're going to need at no cost?"

The bill he already owed Travers surfaced in David's mind. It would, indeed, add up. "Well, I guess I would be very interested."

"Good. Why don't we have a talk? Say, at my office at ten on Monday morning?"

David, apprehensively, agreed; and Silverstone gave David his telephone number and an address on E Street NW in Washington.

"I'll see you Monday, David."

"Thank you, Mr. Silverstone. I'll see you then."

Life seemed to be traveling at a speed that David was having a trouble keeping up with.

He settled onto the sofa, and the phone rang again.

This time, it was Linda.

"Hi," he answered tentatively.

"Hello, David." She sounded a little formal. "Are the reporters still camped on your door step?"

"No. They're gone, but they may just have had their hands full today."

"Why's that?"

"It's a long story, but these days, everything is a long story. I gather you haven't watched the news today?"

"No. Should have I?"

"I don't know the right answer to that question. It's up to you."

"That sounds mysterious."

"No, it's not mysterious. It's sad and tragic."

"Then I don't think I want to know." She hesitated. "Just wanted to tell you, David, that I'm coming home Monday, reporters or no reporters. I'll stock up on things on the way and plan to stay in the house."

"Okay. That sounds fine. If you can plan to arrive about five in the afternoon, I'll help you unload the car and get everything into the house. Then I'll vanish, if you wish."

"Yes, David. I'd appreciate that, both the help unloading and the vanishing."

David sighed. "Okay, I'll see you Monday."

"See you Monday."

David hung up and thought, *Where the hell am I going to go Monday night?*

Then he remembered the oven. He checked it, and it was at four fifty. Probably been there a while. He set the pizza on the rack and set the timer. As distracted as he was, he was going to need the reminder.

He returned to the sofa and picked up his glass of wine. It had yet to be touched.

He took a sip, found Netflix on the television, and settled in to watch a movie, trying to position himself so that his pain was minimal. He stopped the movie when the timer went off, put the pizza on a plate, and returned to the sofa to finish the movie and eat his dinner.

Shortly before nine, the phone rang again. He stopped the movie, not knowing if he would ever finish it.

It was a cell phone caller.

He answered, "Hello."

There was silence, and then an uncertain voice said, "David?"

"Seth?"

"Yes, David. I heard about Doc."

Rage engulfed David's mind. "Damn it, Seth. Why'd you kill those babies? Hadn't we already screwed up enough? You left Doc and me hanging. He probably died because of you."

A contrite Seth spoke quietly, seriously. "I know, David. I'm sorry. I panicked. I didn't know what to do. All my hopes and dreams had come crashing down. Everyone left me, and I was alone with those two living reminders of my failure. I killed them in a rage and sat there for three hours horrified by what I had done. My life was over. I tried to fix everything so you guys wouldn't be hurt, but obviously, I failed. I'm sorry."

"Damn it, Seth. If you're sorry, turn yourself in and take the blame. Right now, it's all on me, and I didn't kill anyone."

"No, but you were part of the failure. You didn't stop me. You didn't challenge me. You didn't say it was wrong. You left me. You ran."

Miserably, David knew Seth was right. "Shit, Seth. What are we going to do?"

"I'm going to vanish, David. I have no choice. I just wanted to say I was sorry and wish you well."

He hung up.

For a while, David couldn't move. Then he flicked off the television, painfully climbed the stairs, and lay down on his bed, fully clothed.

CHAPTER FIFTY-ONE

SUNDAY - DAVID NEALE

David woke early on Sunday morning. He hurt more than he had the night before.

Sometime during the night, he had put on his pajamas.

He pulled up another blanket and went back to sleep.

Periodically, he woke and dozed again.

Finally, he made himself get up. He didn't bother to shave or get dressed. He put on his robe and went down to the kitchen. He forced himself to make coffee. He slipped on his shoes and went out to get the paper. He waved to Brenda in her kitchen window. She put her hand up halfway and did a royal wave back.

He sat at the kitchen table and read the paper. He was front-page news. He was a villain and a folk hero at the same time. He decided he was living in a very weird world.

He looked at the time on the oven. It was already twelve twenty-five. He poured himself coffee and put a bagel in the toaster. He wondered what he was going to do today. He decided, nothing. He wondered what the world was going to do to him. He never knew these days.

He read the newspaper from cover to cover but didn't remember much of what he read.

He went into the living room, lay on the sofa, and dozed again.

He got up at two o'clock and went back into the kitchen. He looked out the window.

There were a bunch of people along the road, some in his front yard, carrying signs and marching around. There were two vans, both white with the names of churches on the side. The people were picketing, the signs criticizing him for trying to change the laws of God, committing sacrilege, accusing him of wickedness, and on and on. Another van arrived, and more people joined the crowd.

David poured a cold cup of coffee, heated it in the microwave, and returned to the sofa. He turned on the baseball game and watched it for a while. Halfway through the game, he got up and found a beer in the refrigerator. He looked out the window. There were now four church vans and two television vans. The picketers were being interviewed for the evening news.

David went back to the ball game. When it ended, he switched to the golf channel and watched the end of a tournament.

About five thirty, the doorbell rang. He didn't want to talk to reporters or picketers. He looked out the kitchen window. Several of his neighbors were at his front door.

David pulled his robe tighter around his body and opened the door.

A dozen or so neighbors stood in front of the door. Marney Gross, from up the street, stood in front of the crowd. He saw Brenda behind the group, slightly distancing herself while ensuring she was part of the action. Marney was Brenda's friend and sometimes visited with Linda.

Marney looked like she wanted to be firm but also seemed a little leery. David understood. It was hard to face a neighbor who might be a murderer.

David opened the storm door and asked what he could do for them.

"David, all these news vans and now the church people are upsetting the whole neighborhood. We can't let our children out the door. We don't even like going out ourselves for fear of being accosted by these people. What can you do about it? After all, it's happening because of you."

David replied evenly, "No problem. I'll leave. Be gone by tomorrow night." With that, he gently but firmly closed the door in Marney's face and went back to the television.

Chapter Fifty-Two

MONDAY - DAVID NEALE

David came down to the kitchen on Monday morning and was relieved to find Tuscany Lane empty of vans, picketers, and reporters. He guessed they needed their sleep too. He wondered if they would be back. He suspected the church people had made their Sunday statement, had received the publicity they sought for their cause, and had returned to their places of employment on Monday morning. However, he didn't feel he was necessarily in the clear. He suspected that there were other more professional groups that might descend on Tuscany Lane today, ones that would not be as spontaneous as the groups that had come Sunday following church services and had then returned to their Monday morning jobs.

He wanted to get out of the house before they came. He left quickly and went to McDonald's for breakfast, eating in his car so that he could use his phone.

He phoned Lourie and told her he wouldn't be in until this afternoon and to please have Filipe take care of the animals.

Then he phoned Henry Travers. He didn't like burning bridges. Joanne said that a client was just leaving, and Mr. Travers would be with him in a minute. David took a bite of his biscuit, chewing hard so that he wouldn't be caught with a mouthful. He took the last swallow as Travers answered. He told Travers about Silverstone's call and his offer to work for free.

Travers said he had never heard of Silverstone but said that was nothing against the man. There were lots of attorneys he had never heard of. He understood David wanting to receive legal advice for free, but he was curious why Silverstone would work for free. He said he was hesitant to say it, but he wondered if Silverstone was playing off David's notoriety.

David said that he had never really thought about his having notoriety, that he was not sure he was comfortable with notoriety, and that he would be cautious.

Travers also commented that it was interesting that Silverstone was at his office on Saturday evening and that he had a receptionist—or whatever she was—with him.

David admitted that he had wondered about that too. "Maybe he's just a big-time lawyer who has so much work that five-day weeks aren't enough."

"Well, let's hope he has enough time for you, David. I'm here if you need me." With that, Travers hung up.

David left McDonald's, drove down US 50 and onto to I-66. He got off, parked at the Vienna Metro Station, and took the Orange Line into the District. He switched to the Red Line and got off at the next exit in Chinatown. He walked around, looking in shop windows, killing time, until he eventually walked over the E Street. He entered a fairly large lobby with marble walls and marble floor. He found the directory and took the elevator to the fourth floor.

When the elevator opened, he was faced with an entrance of two glass doors with gold acanthus leaf handles.

The reception area was paneled in a polished red granite. Modern paintings in metallic gold with bits of red and green and black backgrounds with gold frames hung on the walls. The floor was covered with a light gray carpeting in a subtle pattern, as if trying not to distract from the walls. Modern chairs with gold upholstery sat against the walls. In the back center of the room, there was a receptionist desk of etched glass with a gold metal band, five inches wide, running around the top edge. The wall behind the desk was glass, etched with acanthus leaves, which apparently was in front of a second wall colored the same red as the granite walls in the other parts of the room. Open doorways presented themselves at either end of the wall. Above the desk, there was an etched rectangle against which were placed large gold letters that read SILVERSTONE & DRAPER LLP.

David was caught off guard. He had expected dark wood paneling. Wasn't that what venerable law offices were supposed to look like? David thought to himself that maybe this law firm wasn't "venerable." It was obviously new and glitzy, ready for the modern world.

Once he had adapted to the initial shock of the reception area, David was not surprised to find a beautiful black-haired young woman with bright red lipstick sitting behind the reception desk.

She smiled at him, showing perfect teeth, and asked if she could help.

David told her his name and that he had an appointment with Mr. Silverstone.

She responded that he was expected and asked him to have a seat while she contacted Mr. Silverstone.

A young man came to one of the open doorways. He was tanned with a short clipped beard, looking very tired.

"Mr. Neale?"

"Yes," David answered, rising from his chair.

"Martin Windsor," the young man said, shaking David's hand. "Please follow me."

David did so, walking along a hallway of gloss white walls interspersed with more etched glass paneling. Etched glass doors, with black door frames, proclaimed the occupants in bold black letters. More modern paintings hung on the white walls. The carpeting was now gray and black.

Martin Windsor opened a door and ushered David in. He returned to the hallway and closed the door.

A man got up from behind a large antique mahogany desk piled with papers. By this time, David had expected a square-jawed tanned gentleman with thick white hair carefully combed back at the temples. The man who walked around the desk and shook David's hand was a slender, somewhat ascetic man who stood well over six feet in height. He moved with vigor, stood back to look at David, and then waved him to have a seat on a chair that was part of a set of two tufted leather chairs and a tufted leather loveseat that sat at one end of the room around a glass and brass coffee table. A console with a tray of coffee mugs, cream, and sugar and an insulated coffee pitcher sat against the wall behind the loveseat. The walls were a soft, off-white. Diplomas and other documents, in narrow antique gold frames, hung on the wall behind the desk. A few black-and-white photographs of Silverstone with dignitaries hung on other walls, but they were conservative in number. Big windows overlooked E Street. It was what David expected in a law office.

Silverstone sat on the loveseat next to David and spoke in a fatherly tone, "Well, Mr. Neale, you certainly have made a splash, a big wave splash, I might add. All over the place in the Sunday papers and on every news channel known to man." Silverstone looked pleased with his observation. "I'll be frank. We don't know right now what's going to happen to you, don't know what the federal and Alexandria prosecutors are thinking. I don't normally work for free, but I want to be in position to handle a big trial and am gambling that might happen to you. I'm prepared to put all the resources of this firm behind you based on that gamble. It will be a notorious trial, and I like notoriety. That's why I'm making this offer."

David tried to protest, "But, Mr. Silverstone, I didn't kill anyone."

"Doesn't matter whether you did or didn't, and right now, I don't care. What you did or didn't do won't stop some prosecutor who wants a scalp on his or her belt from taking you to court. We've got to be ready."

David was disconcerted. "Do you really think that might happen?"

Silverstone leaned back. "I do, indeed. This case is too big for them to ignore. It will be front page all the way. They just need a few facts. We need to set you up for the worse."

"How do we do that?"

"We work on your image. The television people say you're separated from your wife. You need to do something about that. Do you think you can get back together with her?"

David was pleased to be able to reply. "She's coming home tonight." David didn't say he was being thrown out of the house.

"Good. That's a good start. You need to work on it."

Silverstone appraised him again. "I like the way you're dressed. No glitz. Just an average normal-looking guy. You need to keep dressing like that. We can't dress you up in a uniform and make you look important, so you need to look like a normal guy, young and earnest, but definitely not physical. I like the way you walked to the house that blew up. Cautious but determined. A brave man walking toward danger because you wanted to save a friend. It's an excellent image to build on. What did the paper call you? 'A folk hero?' We definitely need to build on that."

Silverstone continued. "I don't know what you guys were doing, messing with Mother Nature. Crimes against God. That's the bad part. We need to avoid that."

David was willing. "So what do we do?"

Silverstone rose from the loveseat and walked round the coffee table, heading for the door. "I've got some ideas I'm going to pursue. I'll be in touch."

David got up and headed for the door.

Silverstone opened it, turned, and shook David's hand. He then put his hand on David's shoulder and asked, as David winced, "Can you find your way out?" He didn't wait for an answer. "Give your cell phone number and e-mail address to the receptionist if you would?"

With that, David was back in the hallway. It had been less than ten minutes. He hadn't even been offered a cup of coffee. Evidently, free legal advice didn't involve a lot of time. Silverstone hadn't even asked David to tell his story. It seemed almost irrelevant.

David stopped by the receptionist, left the building, and went to the Judiciary Square Metro station to begin his trip to work.

Chapter Fifty-Three

MONDAY - DRURY METZINGER
AND LESLIE GIVENS

Metzinger was a mental mess all weekend. He didn't know why he hadn't told the lieutenant about what Neale had said about the baby. He had told the forensics people. They knew what to look for, but somehow, he had wanted to get confirmation before he began talking about it. He didn't know Mary Murphy had heard. He didn't know he would be blindsided. Now he knew that Monday was going to be hard, and there was no way to avoid it.

Sunday morning, his adrenalin had been flowing. He hadn't been able to sit still. He had confessed to his wife and tried to explain his state of mind. She had told him she was sorry, but he would survive. He hoped she was right. She left for church with the children. He apologized but said he couldn't sit still. A half hour after they left, he wrote his wife a note saying he was going to survey the murder scene. He then spent the afternoon reviewing the scene. He talked to the restaurant people again and was repeatedly assured that they had taken trash out Sunday night at about ten thirty and that, at that time, there had been no bundles in the dumpster. They assured him they had not seen a purple Taurus or a tan Malibu. He called his wife and told her he was going to work late. He talked to people visiting the barbecue restaurant and the local stores and those simply walking the street. He kept at it until nearly one in the morning, hoping to replicate the night the babies were left in the dumpster. He got nowhere.

On Monday morning, he arrived at his office as late as he could, desperate for coffee. As he walked to the coffee machine, no one talked to him. Many tried not to look at him. He got a cup and sat at his desk waiting for the hammer to fall. He noted that the lieutenant wasn't in his office.

Leslie came and sat at her desk. He hadn't told her about the baby either. Nonetheless, she spoke to him. "The lieutenant was called up to the Chief's office. Expect the shit to fly."

He cringed and nodded. "It's on me."

Givens wasn't sympathetic. "You bet it is. But be that as it may, life will go on. I talked to Masterson this morning and asked him to check with Brenda DeHaven to see if she recalls what time Neale came home the Sunday night before the babies were found. He said he'd do it right away. I told him to go out there and see if he could catch her in her nighty again, but he said once was enough, and he would phone this time."

Metzinger looked at Givens, bleary-eyed. "Leslie, I appreciate the attempt at humor, but I don't feel like it today. I'm also glad that one of us is on the job." He turned back to the coffee.

He took a sip and told himself to quit moping. What was going to happen was going to happen. He turned back to Givens and told her about surveying the murder neighborhood until late Sunday night.

Givens listened and acknowledge what he had said. "Things were happening so fast last week. Now it sounds like we're at a standstill."

"Hey, don't be so dejected. We've got DNA reports coming in, and maybe the FBI will come up with something. Maybe Murray has something from the Angie's List ad. Plus, we're still looking for O'Halloran. If we find him, this may all break loose."

Just then, Lieutenant Ramirez returned to the room and swept by Metzinger and Givens's desks. "You two, in my office." He was tight-lipped and looked battered.

Metzinger told Givens to sit tight. In the Lieutenant's office, he said, "It's all on me, sir. Givens didn't know a thing."

"Okay. We'll get her in here in a minute." The Lieutenant sat and left Metzinger standing. "As you no doubt know, I just got my ass reamed by the Chief. I don't like that. He told me that if I didn't know about the baby, then my detectives were screwing me and to get my house in order. Right now, you're the house I have to get in order. What's going on, Dru?"

"I screwed up. I really have no excuse." Metzinger didn't like being rebuked, even if he deserved it, but there was no way to get out of it. He really had no good excuse.

"Fine. Now give me an explanation. I want to know what's going on in that head of yours."

Metzinger took a deep breath. "Well, after I walked back from the demolished house, I found David Neale sitting in the state trooper's cruiser, and I started talking to him about what happened, but he apparently couldn't hear me. I guess the explosion did something to his ears. He looked at me, kind of dazed-looking, and said he didn't want you to take his baby. I thought I was the only one who had heard it and later asked the forensics people to look out for signs of a baby. I wanted some kind of confirmation before I gave the statement a whole lot of credence. I shouldn't have been so cautious."

The lieutenant nodded. "Did Neale say anything else?"

"No, he just started mumbling about not knowing anything. That's all he would say the rest of the time I was with him."

The lieutenant looked hard at Metzinger. "Do I need to tell you that in the future you will keep me informed of every detail of your investigation?"

"No, sir. I will definitely do it."

"Okay. Get Givens in here."

Metzinger paged her with a wave, and she came in looking like she was going to be hit with an axe.

The lieutenant told them to sit and asked for any updates. Metzinger told him about his surveying the area around the barbecue the day before and not learning anything new.

When he finished, Givens said she had received a call a couple of minutes ago from Masterson who had talked to David Neale's neighbor, Brenda DeHaven, about when Neale had returned home on the Sunday night of the murders. DeHaven had said that she didn't see him return but that his car was in the driveway at least an hour before the sun went down, so that would be around eight or eight fifteen. "He could have gotten home earlier, but that's the only time we have. She didn't know if the car left again that night."

The lieutenant reasoned. "Well, that doesn't prove that Neale wasn't the killer, but it certainly weakens any argument that he was. Don't know what the prosecutors will make of it." He looked from Metzinger to Givens. "Anything else?"

The two detectives both murmured, "No."

The lieutenant opened a notebook. "Okay then, I have several items for you. First, the DNA report came back. It links the two babies to Seth O'Halloran and the black baby to Venessia Jarvis. No link between the babies and Mulholland."

Metzinger analyzed the information. "So the other dead baby must have belonged to the third woman, and if Sidney Gill had a baby with him at the farmhouse, it must have been Nancy Mulholland's baby."

The lieutenant continued. "There appears to be no 'if' about Gill having a baby with him at the farmhouse. The forensic people found body parts consistent with a baby. And those parts have been sent for DNA analysis."

Givens interjected, "You really are full of information."

"Yeah, and I've got a couple of other things. First, the FBI didn't find anything on the NIH phones or computers. They did get a call from a monkey institute, Pennsylvania Primate Institute, saying that Seth O'Halloran had gotten some cells from them, requested on NIH stationery. There's no record of it at NIH. My guess is that it had something to do with the experiment in question. Second, O'Halloran returned his car to the rental agency yesterday in Pittsburgh, Pennsylvania. It had over fourteen hundred miles on it, so our man has been driving around. Within an hour after turning the car in, he rented another, this time from Hertz, a Toyota Highlander, light gray. Blends in. He used the same credit card for both rentals. We've been tracking it, but this is the first time he's used the card since the original rental."

Metzinger inquired, "Do you think he's headed for Canada?"

"That's our thought. Everyone is looking for him north of Pittsburgh, and the border people are looking for him. We've put the information out to the Mounties as well."

Metzinger inquired, "Do you think O'Halloran was smart enough to have a passport with him? He left pretty fast."

The lieutenant acknowledged this. "That's a good observation. Maybe he doesn't have a passport, and that's why he's driving around in circles. Maybe he just wants us to think he's headed for Canada when, in reality, he has no place to go."

After Metzinger and Givens left the lieutenant's office, they sat at their desks. Metzinger tasted his coffee. It was cold. He got up and started for the coffee maker. "I guess we start writing now. There's nothing new I can think of that we need to do."

Chapter Fifty-Four

MONDAY - THE HONORABLE J. MADISON CONROY

J. Madison Conroy came to work Monday morning full of energy. He had spent much of the weekend watching MSNBC, repeatedly seeing himself at the Saturday news conference. He had managed to stand almost directly behind the lectern so that he was in the picture the entire time. It was great national exposure.

Now he had to build on it. He was confident he knew what to do. He just had to wait a little while so that he wouldn't seems too eager. So he sat and read a bill he was going to have to vote on this afternoon. He just read the précis and scanned the beginning and the end. Some of these bills were eight hundred, a thousand pages, or even more. There was no way he could read them. He had staff to do that and give him a summary, picking out the issues and the crap that others had sneaked in. Fortunately, the crap was mostly in amendments where it could be quickly identified.

He had planned to wait until ten o'clock to make the call, but his mind was wandering so much he gave in at nine thirty.

He buzzed Audra.

"Yes, boss."

"Audra, will you get Lyle Reninger on the phone?"

"Will do."

Conroy set the phone down and waited for it to ring. He could have phoned directly, but there was a dance that had to be performed.

The phone rang. He picked it up, hit the answering button, and put it to his ear. "Lyle, you there?"

"Of course I am. Your secretary wouldn't have connected you if I wasn't."

"Now, Lyle, let's be correct. Audra's my admin assistant. Haven't had a secretary in years."

"And you know, that's all malarkey. What can I do for you, as if I can't guess? Saw your ugly face all over television yesterday, even on FOX. You need to learn to smile more."

"Hey, it was serious business. Still is," J. Madison protested.

"Okay. Let me guess. You're following up on our almost-lunch the other day. You want to have a hearing."

"Absolutely. It's time, Lyle. These guys were misusing government property right under the noses of the NIH administration. We need to haul them in for gross failure to manage and for permitting probable criminal activity to play out in their labs."

"Hey, do we know it was criminal?"

"The illegal and misguided activities of these three NIH workers resulted in the deaths of two babies. That's criminal in my mind."

"Okay. I hear you, Jay, but if we have a hearing, it can't be a trial. We don't want to be blamed for messing with the legal system."

"Well, Lyle, that's always a problem with hearings. It hasn't stopped us in the past. Besides, what's really important here is that these guys have messed with the natural order of things. They've messed with the Lord's plan for the reproduction of mankind. I'll guarantee that your folks in Texas are unhappy about that. We all need to stand up for what's right and let our constituents know we won't tolerate this kind of thing."

"Jay, I know you're right. It will play well at home. Let's do it."

"Great. I'll have my chief of staff contact your chief of staff, and we'll get it underway. It'll be a great way to show our voters that we're working in their interests."

After he hung up, J. Madison felt pleased with himself. He had known that these guy's violations of God's laws would convince Reninger to get on board. It would play well in Texas.

CHAPTER FIFTY-FIVE

MONDAY - DAVID NEALE

David worked all afternoon and returned home just before five o'clock Monday evening. He turned into Roma Lane, a block before Tuscany Lane, and parked near the end of the block. He got out, locked his car, and walked around the corner heading toward Tuscany Lane. Halfway down the side street, he cut behind the buildings along a narrow swath of trees that shielded one set of buildings from those on the next block and then through his back yard to the back door of his house. The back door opened into David's living room. As he unlocked his door, he felt great relief at having avoided anyone in front of the house. He went to the kitchen window and carefully peaked out at the road in front of the house. Indeed, there were picketers. They had even set up a table at the curb in his front yard where there was a giant thermos of liquid and paper cups. The picketers carried signs, similar to those that had been there the day before, although these appeared to be prepared in more professional formats.

David went to the bedroom and packed a suitcase. He took a suit on its hanger out of the closet. When he needed another, he'd pick it up at the cleaners. He took the suitcase downstairs and set it by the back door, laying the suit over it.

In the kitchen, David got a glass of water and sat at the table to wait for Linda.

At five-twenty, David heard a car honk in front of the house. He stood and went to the window as the car honked again. Outside picketers were scattering as Linda wheeled into the driveway. It looked like she wasn't messing around.

David hurried out the door. Picketers were crowding up the drive behind the car. Linda got out of the car and went to its rear and screamed at the picketers to get off her property. David hurried to the back car door, waving the picketers away with his hand. They were all temporarily cowering. He picked up Billy from his car seat, hugged, and kissed him. He shouted at Linda to get Little Dave and get in the house. She did so.

With the children safe, David went back to the car and started unloading, his back to the picketers. On his second trip, the picketers pushed closer, shouting at him, telling him how evil he was. David picked up a bag of groceries, turned to the nearest picketers, and found one not holding a sign. He shoved the bag into the man's arms and told him to put it on the front porch. The man looked startled. David gave another man a crib. Amazingly, they did what they were told to do. Soon, David had everything on the porch. He thanked the men and shook their hands. He decided they were nice people who just had a different view of life. He quickly got everything in the house, remotely locked the car, and closed and locked the front door.

Linda was unfolding the crib. David hurried to help. Little Dave was in a high chair that Linda had pulled from the wall.

When Billy was in the crib, she sat down heavily at the table. "Is it like this, every day?"

David leaned against the counter. "I'm afraid it changes by the day. At least there are no reporters this evening."

"I'm going to be barricaded in here." She looked up at David, suddenly aghast. "What in the world happened to you?"

David half smiled. "I was blown up a little bit."

Linda weakly acknowledged this. "Yeah, I heard on the news. Are you all right?"

"More or less. Physically, all right. Mentally, I sometimes wonder."

Linda nodded. "David, this is all crazy. What are we going to do with those people out there?"

David started to walk over and touch Linda's shoulder.

She saw him coming. "No, stay away!"

David halted and sighed. "I'm going to leave. I'll go out the back door. My car's on the next block. I'll drive by and tell them I'm leaving. Hopefully, that will encourage them to go away."

Linda looked hopeful and anxious. "Then I think you had better go."

David resisted for a minute. "Linda, we need to talk. I need to talk with you about this whole thing."

Linda shook her head emphatically. "Not now. Maybe someday, but not now."

David looked defeated. He felt like they kept coming, one defeat after another. "All right. You have my cell number if you need me. Please know I want to help."

Linda nodded.

David picked up his suit and suitcase, went out the back door, and walked to his car. He drove around the block coming back by the house. He stopped by the man who had carried the groceries and rolled down the car window. The man looked uncertain but leaned down to hear David.

David waved him closer to the window. "Tell everyone I'm leaving and won't be back. My wife and children are alone in the house. Please take it easy on them."

He rolled up the window and took a last look at the house. Linda and Brenda were at their respective windows.

David drove off.

CHAPTER FIFTY-SIX

TUESDAY - DAVID NEALE

After leaving home, David had no idea where to go. He went to a store that sold outdoor goods and bought an air mattress. He even thought of buying a tent but didn't really want to sleep out in the heat. He then went to a second store and bought linens and a pillow. He should have brought them from home but hadn't thought of it.

Next, he went to a fast-food place for dinner. There he sat and ate slowly, thinking about where to go. He thought of going to a motel, but the credit card bill was mounting up quickly. He wasn't even sure where the balance on the card stood since Linda was using the same card. Finally, the idea came to him. The house at 227 North Pearson was rented through the end of July. Technically, he had the right to go there.

He got into his car and drove to Alexandria. Not wanting to park in the back of the house, since it was so visible to the neighbors, he found a parking place on the street in the next block. It would take two trips to carry his things, but hopefully, the neighbors wouldn't notice him.

When he approached the front door, he found crime scene tape crisscrossed over the door. After carefully peeling it back, he unlocked the door and set his suitcase inside. He then went back to the car. In the trunk, he found some duct tape among the tools he kept there. He threw the tape into the bag of linens and returned to the house with the bag and the air mattress, leaving the extra suit and his current suit coat hanging over the back seat of the car.

At the house, he used small pieces of the duct tape to reattach the crime scene tape, closed the door, and made up his bed while it was still light, thinking that it would be dark soon, and he shouldn't turn on any lights.

He noted, sadly, that the air-conditioning was not working. Probably the power was off. He opened windows in the front and the back of the house to get some circulation.

There was no place to sit, so he went to bed. He had been lying there for a few minutes when his cell phone had rung.

It was the lawyer, Silverstone. David wondered if the man always phoned people at night. At least this was a direct call, not one made by a throaty young woman. Maybe Silverstone was trying to be more personal.

"Yes, David Neale," David answered.

"David," a relieved voice said, "glad I caught you. We need to be on a morning show tomorrow. It will give us a great opportunity to show the public that you're a descent young guy, start creating an image. We need to be at the studio in DC by six thirty. Here's the address."

David listened to the address, writing in on the edge of his bed sheet. Then he protested, "Are you sure this is a good idea? Aren't they going to ask me a lot of questions I might not want to answer?"

"Don't worry. I'll handle the questions. I'll let you know when to speak. Most of the time, just let me handle everything. See you at six thirty."

Silverstone hung up before David could say more.

He had been ready to go to sleep. Now his mind kept tumbling. Travis had said for him not to talk and made it sound like he should maintain a low profile. Now Silverstone wanted a high profile, but he still shouldn't talk. Silverstone wanted to create an image. For what? Was he to be pitiful so that people felt sorry for him? What image was going to be created? He didn't even know if he was to try to play a role.

He finally fell asleep but felt like it was only a moment before the alarm went off. After he remembered where he was, he got up. He found his suitcase and picked out his shaving kit. He felt his way up the stairs to the bathroom. It, fortunately, had no window. He closed the door so no light could get out and threw the light switch. It didn't work. It shouldn't have surprised him because he knew the air-conditioning was not working. Now he wished he had a window. He opened the door again to let in what light he could. He unzipped his shaving kit and pulled out his toothbrush and toothpaste. Brushing his teeth was something he could handle with little light. Next, he found his comb and took a guess as to where his part should be. He thought of trying to shave by touch but, with no hot water, decided against it. He wondered how many people shaved in the morning at McDonald's and decided he would be one more.

He carried his shaving kit back downstairs, found his clothes in the half-light, and got dressed. He went out the front door, slipping through the triangle made by the tape, carrying his tie, and shaving kit in this hands. He felt he looked pretty rumpled. He guessed that would be his image, like it or not.

He ate, shaved, and put on his tie at McDonald's and headed for the city. In the parking lot of the television studio, he spotted a large Lincoln. He pulled in next to it, rolled down the window, and asked the driver if it was Mr. Silverstone's car. The driver said it was. David shook his head and wondered if all lawyers read Michael Connelly's books.

He found Silverstone in the lobby in a suit that must have cost a thousand dollars or more. A diamond cuff link shone from his shirt cuff as he reached out to shake David's hand. He stood back to appraise David. "You look a little rumpled."

David was too tired to care. "I'm afraid that's the image you're going to have to work with."

Silverstone acknowledged the situation. "Okay, we'll do that."

David was surprised. Evidently, Silverstone was hard to fluster.

They were led into a studio and shown some stools to sit on. The morning program was taking place in New York. When the time came, they would be interviewed from there. A makeup man worked on David, but Silverstone refused the service. David looked at him. He was immaculate. David was sure that Silverstone must have felt the makeup man would mess him up. David was grateful for the help.

In front of the stools were television screens, one showing the program going on in New York. David and Silverstone were told the other one would show them here in the studio. They were both fitted with an earpiece and a microphone. They waited about twenty minutes and were told that they would be introduced from New York after a set of commercials. The commercials came on, and they were given a warning.

The commercials ended, and the TV host in New York began to speak. "As you are all aware, two babies were found murdered in a dumpster south of Alexandria, Virginia, two weeks ago. This crime has captured national attention. Over the intervening two weeks, this horrendous crime has been linked to some research workers from the National Institutes of Health who apparently went rogue, running an independent and failed experiment in an attempt to modify the period of human gestation. This, in itself, has resulted in great national concern, perhaps verging on a national panic, sparking special alarm and anger from both the religious and scientific communities.

"Of the three researchers, one is currently a wanted man who has thus far eluded the authorities. A second researcher killed himself, blowing up the house in which he was living, in a dramatic episode that was streamed on the Internet. In that episode, the third researcher was seen on the Internet just before the explosion as he walked away from the house following his attempt to talk his lab partner into surrendering to authorities. Today, we have that gentleman, Mr. David Neale, at our studio in Washington where he has agreed to respond to some of our questions." As he said this, the light came on the television camera in front of David, and his face appeared on the television screen. "Mr. Neale is joined today by his attorney, Mr. Aubrey Silverstone. Good morning, gentlemen."

David nodded. "Good morning."

Silverstone nodded and started talking before the host could say more. "Mr. Neale is pleased to have this opportunity to appear before the public. He is, frankly, being treated very poorly by the press, which has implied that he had something to do with the murders of the two babies to which you referred. Nothing could be further from the truth. He has cooperated with the police in their investigation to the extent that he can without implicating himself in any crimes that might be associated with the other activities of the researchers you discussed. Indeed, he went out of his way to try to help the authorities in their attempts to negotiate with Dr. Sidney Gill, bravely putting himself at risk in approaching Gill's house while knowing it might blow up at an—"

The host interrupted, "Yes, Mr. Silverstone. I appreciate that, but I'd like to ask Mr. Neale some questions. Mr. Neale, it has been suggested that you did not negotiate with Dr. Gill, but actually encouraged him to blow up the house to cover what you have done."

Silverstone started to answer, but David put his hand on the lawyer's shoulder and glared at the camera. "Anyone who has said that doesn't know what he's talking about. I tried to talk Dr. Gill into giving himself up. As we talked, I was surprised to learn that Doc Gill had a baby in the house with him. That baby was born in what you refer to as the 'failed experiment.' Doc Gill told me it was his baby. He named the infant Dorothy, a name he and his fiancée had planned to give their child more than thirty years ago before his fiancée was killed in an automobile accident. He loved Dorothy. He had waited more than thirty years for the child. There was no way he was going to have that child taken from him. He told me that if he surrendered, he knew his child would be poked and measured, passed around from scientist to scientist and then from government agency to government agency. I was pleading with a man resolute in what he was going to do. I resent your saying I would be so selfish as to want him to die. I do not kill people. Period."

David sat back, glad he had said it. He knew he had spoken in anger, but it had to be said. He felt Silverstone fuming beside him.

"So, Mr. Neale, you're saying you had nothing to do with the murders."

Silverstone spoke up, "I think Mr. Neale just said that."

"Well, Mr. Neale, did the three of you conduct an experiment, possibly using government property, that was directed at modifying the gestation period of women?"

Again, Silverstone answered, "I believe that is still under investigation, and I have counseled Mr. Neale not to discuss those activities."

David was seething. He hated Silverstone answering for him. It made him feel guilty. He had never intended to do anything wrong, and he hated to feel guilty, even though in some sense he was.

"So, Mr. Neale, if you didn't kill the two babies found in the dumpster, who do you think did?"

Silverstone responded, "You're still implying that Mr. Neale had some knowledge of these murders. It's an allegation that has no basis."

"Well, one of the reporters at our local station in Washington spoke to some people picketing your home in Fairfax and was told that your wife is living there alone, that you have moved out. If you're as innocent as Mr. Silverstone implies, why are you not living together?"

Silverstone hesitated a moment—but only a moment. David knew he was caught off guard and was surprised how fast he recovered. "As we've already stated, this episode has put Mr. Neale under a great deal of pressure. Further, as you noted, Mr. Neale's house is being picketed. Mr. Neale is trying very hard to divert all this attention and the stress that accompanies it away from his family. He hopes, by not staying at home, the picketers and media attention will also leave so that his family can be at peace. He is a loving husband and parent who wants nothing more than to protect the ones he loves. And with that, Mr. Neale and I would like to thank you for permitting us to appear on your show and to demonstrate to the world that Mr. Neale is a normal human being who is caught in an unfortunate web of events and who has shown extraordinary courage in trying to help resolve the issues involved."

The host did not thank them and said, "And there you have it. Mr. Neale avoided answering most of our questions and left the responses to his attorney. He did give some insight into the death of his partner, Dr. Sidney Gill, which was of great interest, and we appreciate that."

Outside the door to the television station, Silverstone turned to David and said, "Why the hell didn't you tell me you weren't living with your wife?"

David glared back. "Why the hell did you put me on that program, like a monkey on a music grinder?"

"I told you why. To work on your image."

"Well, my image is that I can't answer questions about what happened, and therefore, by natural inference, everyone has found me guilty. That's not an image I want."

"No, the image is that you're an ordinary guy who has acted very bravely."

"No, it isn't. It's that I'm a guilty little shit who's hired a big-named, broad-smiling lawyer to try to bail me out," David fumed.

Silverstone sighed. He looked at David as if he were a nuisance flea. "I told you I like notoriety. It shouldn't be a surprise to you. And yes, I'm a big-named lawyer whom you need to get you through this mess."

David turned and started to walk away. "No, I don't need you. I feel bad enough without your help. You're fired."

Silverstone responded, "You know, you're right. You are a little shit, Neale, and you'll be sorry."

CHAPTER FIFTY-SEVEN

TUESDAY - LINDA NEALE

Linda had watched David speak to the crowd and then drive away. She had had no idea where he was going. Fortunately, he always carried his cell phone with him. She couldn't imagine a time when there were no cell phones.

She worked around the kitchen, straightening things up, and watched, with relief, as the crowd of picketers gradually climbed back into their vehicles and departed.

Linda fed the children, made herself a frozen pizza, and settled down with the children in front of the children's channel on television with simply drawn figures bouncing around the landscape.

David had left the mail. Five letters were on the table in the foyer, all addressed to David. He wasn't there, so she opened them. They were all chastising David, mostly on religious grounds, but one was from a professor at the University of Maryland who said David had violated the ethics of science in doing work on the human genome without an appropriate review. She wondered if this was just the beginning.

While she sat there, the phone rang three times. She checked the caller ID and determined the calls were from no one she knew. Finally, she had unplugged the phone, put the children to bed, and gone to bed herself.

As she awoke Tuesday morning, she was relieved not to have to face her parents. She felt alone, but after nearly two weeks at home with her parents' resentment and disapproval, it was still a relief. She knew it would get old after a while, but being by herself felt good.

Little David had gotten her up only once in the night, and she felt rested.

She wondered what the day would bring.

She fed the children and sat down with coffee and toast.

The doorbell rang, and she thought, *Oh no, they're after me again.*

She looked out the window. It was Brenda, holding the newspaper. The rest of the street was clear.

She opened the door and found that Brenda already had the storm door open.

Brenda handed her the newspaper and pushed past her into the house. "Did you see David on the television this morning? I tried to phone you and let you know he was on."

Linda was surprised and a little bewildered. "No, I had no idea he was going to be on, and I've got the phone unplugged. It wouldn't stop ringing. Why would he be on television?"

Brenda poured herself a cup of coffee and sat down at the table. "For one thing, he's famous, notorious, but still famous. All the networks would like to have him on. He's news. They would probably like to have you on too."

Linda remonstrated, "There's no way that's going to happen. I just want to stay away from everyone and everything. All this has nothing to do with me."

Brenda disagreed. "Gal, it has lots to do with you. David's your husband. That automatically means that you're involved."

Linda shook her head. "So again, why was he on? What was he doing?"

Brenda leaned forward, eager to talk. "He was there with some highfalutin lawyer with pearly whites and a million-dollar suit. In contrast, David was rumpled and looking poor—pitiful. The lawyer did most of the talking. However, the TV host asked a question, kind of accusing David of talking that lab partner of his into blowing himself up. With that, David came alive with anger and defended himself while the lawyer tried to keep him quiet. After that, David just sat quietly, looking pissed off, while the lawyer answered the questions."

"Doesn't sound like the interview did anything for David."

Brenda agreed. "I don't think David thought so either."

"What else was discussed?"

"Well, David did say that he didn't kill the babies. Pretty emphatic about it. And oh, the interviewer asked why you and David weren't living together."

"It's none of their business."

"Darling, right now, everyone thinks your business is their business. Comes with the territory. Anyway, the lawyer answered and said that David was trying to protect you. Does that ring true with you?"

Linda thought. "Maybe, at least in part."

Brenda was interested. "And what's the other part?"

"I think he's under so much stress. He's having trouble facing the reality of life. He's kind of hiding in full sight."

"And you're hiding out of sight."

"As best I can."

Just then, they heard the postman at the mail slot. Some mail hit the floor. And then some more mail hit the floor. Then some more.

Linda went to pick it up. Brenda helped. "What's going on here?"

Linda gave a tired sigh. "It's David's hate mail."

"Are you going to open it?" Brenda inquired with interest.

"Yeah, later. I want another cup of coffee now."

Brenda tried not to look disappointed. "Okay, I'll leave you be. If I can do anything for you, you know where I live."

Linda was relieved when Brenda was gone. She had been interested in the news about David, but there was no way she was going to let Brenda go through their mail.

After she finished her coffee, she got up and got a pen, a sheet of paper, and a butter knife to use as a letter opener. She wrote down three categories: *Criticism on Religious Grounds, Criticism of Ethical Grounds,* and *Criticism Based on a Violation of Scientific Ethics.* She started opening letters and putting marks under each category. Some letters didn't fit the categories.

A group of gamers was fascinated and thought that a game should be invented where, based on different decision points, babies could be created with different defects. A satanic follower congratulated David on work that would eventually show how monsters were created. Two women encouraged David to continue the research to save women from the hell of nine-month pregnancies. One woman said she could have fixed the babies if they had contacted her in time; and three women, who said they hadn't been able to have children, wanted to volunteer for David to get them pregnant, even if the babies were defective.

Linda posted the chart on the refrigerator with two magnets. She would update it tomorrow.

CHAPTER FIFTY-EIGHT

TUESDAY - DRURY METZINGER AND LESLIE GIVENS

When Metzinger arrived at work Tuesday morning, there was almost no one in the big office. He heard noise coming down the hall from the conference room and hurried in that direction. Givens met him at the door.

"David Neale is going to be on the morning show in a few minutes."

They pushed their way into the room. Lieutenant Ramirez spotted them. "You two, take notes."

Givens ran back to their desks and got two pads and pencils. Returning to the room, she passed a set to Metzinger who turned to a couple of guys sitting at the table. "You two, get up and give us room at the table. You're just observers. We've got real work to do."

David and Silverstone came on. Someone said, "Looks like he's got a K-Street lawyer."

Another said, "It's no help. Neale still looks guilty as hell."

Then the TV host asked about David's interaction with Sidney Gill, and David came alive. Someone shouted, "Go get 'em, boy!"

Someone else said, "Now, he just looks pissed."

Another voice chipped in, "Maybe guilty and pissed. What do you think, Dru? Anything of value here?"

Metzinger looked at the group. "Maybe nothing of value but interesting to learn what went on at that house before it blew up. I've been wondering."

About the time Silverstone started answering the question about David's separation from his wife, there was a disturbance at the conference room door, and Lieutenant Ramirez was called out of the room.

Someone said, "I wonder what shit just happened."

The interview ended, and the television was turned off. Everyone started filtering out of the room, the voices developing a consensus that David was a poor, guilty schmuck who was in over his head.

Metzinger and Givens sat finishing their notes. Suddenly, Lieutenant Ramirez returned and sat down. "Another link is gone. All we have now is Neale."

Metzinger looked hesitantly at Ramirez. "What does that mean?"

Ramirez replied, desolately, "O'Halloran's dead."

Givens gaped. "What the shit?"

"The West Virginia State Police spotted him, and he ran. They set up a roadblock where he had to go through an underpass. He tried to go across the median to get to the other underpass, but the median was low in the middle for drainage, and it channeled his car right into the middle bridge pier, probably at seventy miles an hour. A quick and definitive end."

The three sat in silence, thinking about what to do next. Metzinger finally summed it up. "So he wasn't going to Canada.

His heading north was just a ploy. Created a little excitement, but if he didn't have a passport, all he could do is bluff."

Givens concurred, "Yeah, Dru, you called it right. So as the lieutenant says, all we've got is David Neale."

They returned to their desks, got coffee, sat, and pondered their circumstances.

After about twenty minutes, the phone rang. Metzinger picked it up. It was Shannon Jennings asking him and Givens to come to her office.

The two of them checked out with the lieutenant and headed for the offices of the Commonwealth's Attorney.

In Jennings' office, they sat in two chairs in front of her desk, Jennings maintaining her senior position behind the desk. "I assume you two know about O'Halloran's death?"

Metzinger acknowledged that they did.

"Well, we certainly have a conundrum here. We have three dead babies linked to two dead lab workers and to two live surrogate mothers. The latter two seem to know nothing, and the other five are certainly not going to tell us anything. We have one lab worker left. He isn't connected to any of the other seven by DNA or fingerprints, nothing physical, so what do we know about him? We know he was the lab partner of the two dead men. We know he rented the house at 227 North Pearson, and we have witnesses who say he was there off and on with the other two and that all three were there the weekend the babies were born. Although there is no physical connection between him and the babies, we know from this morning's interview that he was aware of the babies."

Metzinger interrupted and flipped open his notes. "What he said was that there was a baby in the house with Sidney Gill, that it was Gill's baby, and that it was born in what the host called an 'illegal experiment.' Actually, I don't think he said 'illegal experiment.' I think the host called it a 'failed experiment,' and Neale used the same words. Neale didn't say he knew about the baby before going to negotiate at Gill's farmhouse, and he didn't acknowledge that he was part of the 'failed experiment.' Further, he didn't say he was connected with the two dead babies. His lawyer denied that Neale had knowledge. Those things we can only guess at."

Jennings surrendered the point. "Okay, we know from the next-door neighbor that on the night before the dead babies were found, Neale left 227 North Pearson at about six thirty or seven and that his car was back at his house by eight o'clock and perhaps earlier. It cannot be confirmed that the car didn't leave the house late at night. Neale's wife could confirm that, but she doesn't have to one way or another and might be considered a biased witness. We know that when he left 227 at six thirty, he wasn't carrying anything. Aside from that, do we know anything about David Neale?"

Metzinger spoke, "Well, we think we know he was having trouble with his marriage, and we heard from a reporter that he was upset about being involved in a failed experiment and that it was connected to 'the babies,' although the exact 'babies' were not specified."

Jennings nodded. "Yeah, those are things with possible implications, but we don't really *know* what they mean. If we were at a trial, we could possibly introduce that information and use it to cross examine Neale, if he chose to testify, but the implications of those things are not things we *know*."

Givens decided to say something. "Look, we know that there were three babies born in the house at 227. They had to leave there some way. We have a witness who saw Sidney Gill carry something out of the house after it got dark. The witness can only say it might have been a baby. We do know, from DNA, that Gill had Mulholland's baby at the farmhouse, so it's fairly safe to say he did take a baby out when he left 227. That seems to mean that two babies, the babies who were later found murdered, were still in the house with O'Halloran. DNA has confirmed definitively that one of the two murdered babies was born in the house and had O'Halloran as the sperm donor and Mrs. Jarvis as the surrogate mother. The other murdered baby also had O'Halloran as the sperm donor. We can't definitely connect it to 227 because we haven't found the mother yet, but our lab computer guy found the Angie's List ad for the surrogate mothers. It asked for applicants, weighing one hundred ninety-five pounds or more, and instructed them to phone O'Halloran at his home phone number in the evening. Phone records say he got four replies. Two we already know about. A third said by phone that she didn't participate. The fourth is out of town, but we'll pursue her."

"What we might guess—or even presume—is that after Neale and Gill left that Sunday night, O'Halloran murdered the two babies and later disposed of them in the dumpster. Certainly, O'Halloran felt guilty because he ran. The major issue is that the medical examiner says that as of 5:00 p.m. the day the babies were found, the babies had been dead between twelve and twenty-four hours, the broad range resulting from the babies baking in a closed dumpster when the temperature outside was ninety-five degrees, feeling like a hundred and five. Like being confined all day in a hot car. Unfortunately, the twenty-four hours at the end of the range means that both Neale and Gill could have still been in the house when the babies were killed. The vagueness of the report doesn't let any of the three men off the hook. If I were to guess, I'd say that the heat accelerated the babies' decomposition, and that O'Halloran was the killer."

Jennings concurred. "Yes, I think we all believe that. It's unfortunate that, when the babies arrived at the medical examiner's office, a little after 5:00 p.m., most of the staff had just left for the day. The one examiner who was on duty was fairly new and had limited experience. His twelve- to twenty-four-hour estimate was done quickly, and the babies were put away in a cooler until the next morning. I would hate to try to use that in court."

Metzinger was baffled. "So why are we here? If we could indict David Neale for something, what would it be? In the worst case, murder or participating in murder. In the second worst case, a knowing accomplice in an activity that resulted in murder. Third, having knowledge of a murder and withholding that knowledge. I don't think the first fits the timeline, despite the medical examiner's report. The second would require that he had knowledge that the babies were going to be killed when he left the night of the murders. I don't know how you would prove that. The third requires that he had knowledge that the murders had been committed after the fact, but unless he had contact with O'Halloran, that would only be conjecture on his part. Hell, we don't even know if he misused government property. I'm sure there are some minor things you could get him on, like, perhaps, the misuse of drugs or some medical thing. I think you have a tough job, Jennings, but I don't know where you go from here."

Jennings agreed with what had been said. "What I need is a plan."

Metzinger protested. "A plan for what? To prove Neale is guilty of one of the foregoing? If he's not guilty, there's no way of proving that he is. Do we have a witness who says he was at the dumpster? Do we have a witness who says he moved the babies from the house? Do we have a witness who says he left his house the night the babies were put in the dumpster? No. I've looked. Do we have a witness as to what went on in the house at 227 Sunday night? No, they're both dead. If Neale was involved, he's got to confess, and this isn't television where suspects always fold. So what do you want us to do?"

Jennings sagged in her chair. "I don't know. I need to close this thing."

"Then gather your evidence and say it all points to O'Halloran. That's what I'm going to do. You can't let these things hang over your head forever. Close the book."

Metzinger got up and signaled Givens to follow.

They left Jennings slumped behind her desk.

CHAPTER FIFTY-NINE

TUESDAY - DRURY METZINGER
AND DAVID NEALE

Metzinger had only been home for ten minutes when the phone rang.

It was the sergeant at the desk at Police Headquarters.

"Sorry to bother you at home, Dru, but it's about your case."

Metzinger leaned back and closed his eyes, as if a headache were coming on. "What?"

"A woman named Sandra Bizzolli called. She lives in the house next to 227 North Pearson."

"Yeah, I know who she is. What did she call about?"

"She says this David Neale is living in the house at 227. Says she became suspicious because all the windows are open. Do you want me to send someone down to get him out?"

Metzinger pounded his fist, lightly, a couple of times on the table. "No, I'll go take care of it."

When he arrived at 227 North Pearson, Metzinger double-parked. He noted that the house didn't have any lights on inside. But it was early. Still daylight. He knocked on the door. No one answered. He knocked harder. The door opened, and David Neale stood there.

Metzinger spoke matter-of-factly. "You know you can't stay here."

David replied, "Why not? The rent's paid through the end of the month."

Metzinger developed his annoyed and impatient look. "Mr. Neale, don't give me a hard time. You know it's a crime scene."

David opened the door further, moved the tape, and stepped out onto the stoop. "Not much of a crime scene. Nothing's in there." He looked at Metzinger. "How'd you know I was here?"

"Your neighbor phoned it in. She saw the windows opened and started looking for you."

David considered what Metzinger had said. "I thought I had been careful. Even parked in the next block so she wouldn't see my car." He again looked at Metzinger. "How come you came? Seems like you could have sent anybody from your department to evict me."

Metzinger looked back. "I wanted a chance to talk to you alone. Haven't ever had a private conversation with anyone as famous as you."

David took a deep breath. "If I'm famous, then being famous is lousy. Why am I famous? I thought I was simply a 'person of interest.'"

"'Persons of interest' don't usually get front-page coverage, coverage in a third of the articles on the editorial pages of the *Washington Post*, and full-page ads from a bunch of concerned scientists. Don't you read your press?"

David sat down on the top step and patted the spot beside him. "Haven't read the paper since Sunday. It's too depressing."

Metzinger hesitated and then sat down. "Saw you on television this morning. You looked pissed."

"Yeah. I was considering killing my now ex-lawyer. Okay, you wanted a chance to talk to my famous self. What about?"

"About the case, what else?"

"I've already told you that I didn't kill the babies. What else do you want to know?"

"Metzinger leaned back on his elbows. "I thought you might tell me who did."

David chuckled softly. "Let me see. On television, the cop asking questions is asked by the perp if he's wired, and then the perp rips off the cop's shirt to make sure he's not. Are you wired?"

Metzinger leaned forward again. "Hardly. I'd just gotten home when they called me. Didn't even have a chance to eat dinner. And please don't tear off my shirt. The police department won't let me write it off as an expense."

David mused, "Well, we can try to make light of what has happened, but you and I know there's nothing funny about it. I expect that you're as tired of the whole thing as I am." He looked at Metzinger. "I expect my lawyer would tell me not to talk to you, but I think you know about as much as I do. I'd like to talk to someone. I'm not a Catholic and don't have a confessor, so maybe you'll do."

David looked thoughtful for a moment and then said, "Seth killed them, the two babies. And I say that with stipulations. I was not present during the murders. I was not aware beforehand that the murders were going to happen or that they were happening when they did, and at no time was the concept of murdering the babies ever discussed. When I learned the two babies had been found dead, I felt as much horror as anyone, maybe more, because I was connected to the events that led to the tragedy."

Metzinger challenged the assertion. "If you weren't there, how do you know O'Halloran, and not Gill, did the killing?"

"Because Seth phoned me Saturday night. I suspect you have my phone records and can verify that. He kind of apologized. He said he had panicked and had done it in anger and desperation."

Again, Metzinger questioned the story. "Yeah, we figured it was O'Halloran. But if he was so panicked, how do you explain his being so methodical in cleaning up the evidence?"

"Because Seth was methodical. It's what made him good in the laboratory. Everything was carefully done, completely documented. It was his nature. And you've got to understand his mental state after the babies were born defective. He had put everything he had into what we were doing, time and over a hundred thousand dollars, no small amount for a government worker. The work in our lab isn't very exciting. This was going to be Seth's Nobel Prize experiment. It was going to make him famous. He put everything he had into it. And it failed, devastatingly so."

"So why didn't you get upset, and why didn't Gill? Didn't you want to kill the babies too?"

"Well, I expect that Doc Gill got what he wanted. He had no dreams of Nobel Prizes. He evidently wanted a baby to replace the child he had lost over thirty years ago. The baby he got wasn't perfect, but he found he could love it just the same. He tried to go off and live peacefully with his child, his Dorothy, but the world wouldn't let him."

Metzinger felt a little guilty. "And you?"

"Me? Yeah, I had dreams. But I wasn't vested in the whole thing the way Seth was. I was kind of just going along. It gave me a chance to do some of the things I had learned in graduate school. But it wasn't my money, and I certainly didn't have the emotional involvement."

Metzinger still had to inquire. "So you just left that night, left your partners and the babies, and never went back. What did you expect to happen?"

"I've asked myself that question over and over again. Seth said he would take care of everything. It never dawned on me that he would kill the babies. I know you're going to say that I couldn't be that naive. But I was. When I was ten or eleven years old, I killed a bird with my BB gun. Shot it over and over again until it fell off a tree limb. I was sick for days afterward. Killing is just not in my system. If it had been up to me, I would have tried to hide the babies, and I probably would have eventually turned myself in. But instead, I took the easy way out and ran. I'm sorry I did, but that doesn't do much good now."

Metzinger had to push a little further. "So you ran an experiment with some fluid from monkeys trying to win the Nobel Prize."

David was quiet for a while. "So you can't quit, can you? Here, I've poured my soul out, and you can't just pat me on the back and say, 'There, there, don't take it so hard.'" He was quiet a little longer. "And it wasn't from monkeys. It was from Gibbons. And I appreciate your listening to me. I'll pack up and get out of here."

They stood up, and Metzinger said, "I'll help."

CHAPTER SIXTY

TUESDAY - MARY MURPHY
AND DAVID NEALE

Mary came straight home from work. She put on a T-shirt and jeans, fed the cat, and heated up leftover Chinese for dinner, rice and beef and peppers. She poured herself a glass of wine and carried it and her dinner to the sofa. She flicked on the television and watched while she ate dinner and sipped her wine.

David's morning show interview was on the local news and then again on the national news. Mostly, they showed him defending what he had said to Dr. Gill and later looking angry at everyone. Mary thought she knew why. There were lots of reasons: he didn't like being there; he didn't like the questions the TV host was asking; and he didn't like his lawyer. Sadly, he just looked surly.

They had all watched the interview in the big office at work. She had been annoyed by the egotistical self-importance of the lawyer. She was glad that the evening news programs concentrated on David and pretty much cut out the lawyer. She figured that the lawyer must be crying in his wine. He certainly wasn't the type to drink beer.

The local news station added in some interviews with people on the street afterward. Some thought David looked mean enough to kill. Others were sympathetic with Dr. Gill and said it was just a tragedy all around. Everyone clearly felt that David was involved in the murder or, at a minimum, an accessory.

After the news, she figured, *What the hell? Another night at home* alone, and she went into her bedroom and put on her pajamas.

Back in the living room/kitchen, she turned the television to Netflix, checked the movies, and found a love story. She settled into the sofa with a refill of her glass of wine.

Around eight thirty, there was a knock at the door. "What the hell? I don't know anybody," she mumbled under her breath.

Mary ran to the bedroom and grabbed her old bathrobe. As she wrapped it around her, she headed for the door as the knock came again. "Hold your damned horses."

She opened the door, and David Neale pushed in past her, carrying a suitcase, a pillow, and sheets.

Mary was initially speechless but soon recovered. "What the hell are you doing here?"

David set down the suitcase and tossed the linens on the sofa. "I've been thrown out of my house by my wife and out of 227 North Pearson by Detective Metzinger, and I can't afford any more motels. I've got no place to go, and you owe me one. I looked up your address on the Internet, and here I am. I figured if you could move in with me, I could move in with you."

Mary was taken aback. "Temporarily, I hope?"

"Temporarily, we both hope." He looked at Mary. "I'm glad you found your bathrobe. It's a different image."

"Yeah, it's an image I'm going to maintain."

"Good idea. Have you got any more wine? Never mind. I see it on the counter. I'll find a glass. You go on with your movie."

David made himself at home. He found some cheese in the refrigerator. He looked at Mary. "Where do you keep your crackers? I haven't eaten dinner."

Mary groaned. She got up, put crackers, cheese, and a knife on a plate, handed it to David, and, without a word, went back to the sofa, tucked her robe around her, and pulled her legs under her.

David sat in a chair across from her, avoiding the sofa. He ate his cheese and crackers, occasionally looking at Mary.

Finally, she said, "Why don't you move into the chair in the corner on this side of the room? That way, I won't have to look at you."

Or me at you, thought David. He got up and moved.

They both sat quietly for a while. David asked, "Where's the bathroom?"

Mary point at the bedroom. "In there."

David looked at the bedroom. "That may be a problem."

"Not if you don't wake me."

"Okay. I'm going to get a shower. I didn't have any hot water at 227." David got up and headed for the bathroom.

Mary shouted after him, "The towels are under the sink!"

David cut through the bedroom, noting a neatly made bed with fabric headboard and decorator pillows covered with an off-white full bed comforter. Full-length drapes hung at the windows over Venetian blinds. It seemed awfully neat for an unmarried young woman. Maybe there was more to Mary than met the eye.

He closed the bathroom door and started to lock it, thinking, *Fat chance that she'll barge in.* He locked it anyway. Bodywash, shampoo, and conditioner were lined up on the back edge of the tub. It was all feminine packaged stuff, but he decided it would do.

The shower felt good. With his nerves going crazy with all the events of the past days and a lack of shower for two days, it was badly needed. He dried himself while standing in the tub. He was afraid to get water on the fluffy white rug spread on the floor. He put all his clothes back on and went back to the living room.

Mary looked up. "You going to sleep that way?"

David was a little embarrassed. "No. I didn't bring a bathrobe with me."

Mary's eyes twinkled. "Well, they're certainly mandatory garments. I don't think one of mine will fit."

"Do you have another one?"

Mary laughed. "Do you think I'd be wearing this robe if I had another? The answer is no, but you'd be welcome to it if I had one. The thought's there."

David smiled. "I appreciate that. I'd hate to expose you to my manly charms."

"I think, Mr. Neale, you already have."

"Not in the light of day."

Mary acknowledged that. "Very true, but it was enough."

David became more serious. "Okay, we've acknowledged that. Let's just say it was a mistake and put it behind us."

"Yeah, I'm sorry. I hope your wife can accept that." Mary wondered if she was really sorry, but it was the thing to say. She was single. There were no repercussions for her.

David considered that. "She doesn't really know. She just suspects."

"I guess we should keep it that way, for what it's worth."

"That's my wish."

Mary became serious. "So what's up next, Mr. Neale?"

"Well, Ms. Mary Morris/Murphy, I think by now you should call me David, and I would like to call you Mary."

"Sounds like a deal, although if we're ever seen in public, I won't recognize you."

"Fair enough. And now that you have started asking questions, do I treat you as a reporter or as someone who is interested and perhaps cares."

"Well, as someone who cares, but if I were you, I wouldn't drop any blockbusters. I like to think I have the soul of a reporter."

David contemplated that. "I don't think there are any blockbusters left. I think everyone knows everything except the details of the experiment, and I won't talk about that."

Mary laughed. "Well, then there's no fun left."

David was serious. "For me, the fun ended a couple of weeks ago."

"Sorry, I know my worldview is different. I'll try to adjust, but you're not going to depress me."

"I'm sorry. I know I'm sharing too much. So what about you, Mary? You've got a lovely apartment in what is, frankly, not a wonderful apartment building. In fact, your apartment's kind of glamorous."

Mary granted that was true. "I grew up with nice things and don't intend to change. My parents think I'm nuts to be doing what I'm doing, but they helped. I'm pretty lucky."

"As pretty as you are, you must have lots of dates? Must keep you busy."

"Yeah, I'm a sexy femme-fatale. I think the word you meant was *cute*."

"You make *cute* sound like a four-letter word."

"Isn't it?"

"Yeah, come to think about it. It is. But you are cute in a very pretty way. Men have got to be attracted to you."

"Thank you, I guess. I haven't lived here very long, and I don't have any women friends, so when I go out, I have to go by myself. And I do get hit on, but I generally don't feel comfortable with the guys who do that. Can't even go to the movies by myself. I let a couple of guys pick me up, but it's always been disappointing. The guys I work with are all old. It's been a little frustrating since I left college. I could better judge the guys I met there because of the environment and the student background. Some nice guys and still a lot of jerks."

"I'm afraid being jerks is what young guys are about, unless they're quiet and don't get noticed."

Mary suddenly sympathized. "Was that you, David, quiet and unnoticed?"

"Kind of, until Linda noticed me."

"You didn't notice her?"

"Yeah, after she noticed me. I think we became convenient to each other. Now we have two kids. Things really change."

Mary decided she didn't like the conversation. She was afraid they were edging into self-pity, David with a wife he wasn't sure he loved and her with her loneliness.

"So as I said when we started this maudlin conversation, what do you do next?"

"Well, I guess I'll temporarily find some cheap place to live, maybe an inexpensive motel with weekly rates. Then if I don't end up in court someplace, I'll start approaching Linda again, probably by telephone at first, and try to figure out where we stand." David wanted the conversation off him. "So, Mary, what's next for you?"

Mary considered the question. "I haven't thought about it, but now that you ask, I don't really know. I work for a small newspaper that doesn't have significant investigative powers. Indeed, it's not very interested in anything but local news. It was serendipity that you happened to me—that is, twice being in the right place at the right time. That resulted in headlines for news that no one else had. I became almost as important in the media as you. I gave interviews to all kinds of people. I was suddenly important. But I always knew it would end, and I'd go back to reporting garden shows, historic celebrations, and such. CNN didn't offer me a job. Maybe my voice didn't translate well to TV. Who knows? So I'll keep working where I am and periodically applying for jobs at big newspapers. At least I have a resume now. I hope it's worth something."

David wanted to encourage her. "Hey, from what I can tell, you were a hell of an investigator on this mess of mine. You certainly had the moxie to force your way into my house."

"And the ability to lie?"

"Definitely the ability to cover yourself."

"Nice way to say it." Mary became pensive. "You know, David, I didn't have sex with you to get a story. I can be a hustler, but I'm not a whore. You were a nice guy."

David considered what she had said. "Yeah, I called you a lot of things after you published your story, 'whore' among them. I didn't have enough ego to think you did it for any other reason. I still thought that when I came here tonight. I figured you used your wiles to get the story, whatever it took. I was really uncertain about coming here tonight, but I was desperate and figured you owed me."

Mary chuckled, "I did use my 'wiles.' I just didn't know how far my 'wiles' would take me."

David grew very serious. "Well, Mary, I said I was sorry about what happened between us. In reality, I'm not. Guilty, yes, but sorry, no. You're something special."

Mary blushed. "There are times I might say thank-you for a complement. I'm not sure this is one of those times."

David smiled. "Take it for what it's worth." He stood up and extended his hand to Mary, "Friends?"

Mary took his hand. "Friends. Now let's get some sleep. You through in the bathroom?"

"I think so."

"I don't have a lock on my bedroom door, so come in when you need to use the bathroom. Just be quiet."

Mary closed the bedroom door. David turned out all but one light, took his pajamas out of the suitcase, and dressed for bed. He looked at his suit, amazed at its rumpled appearance. He was glad he had another in the car and would get it in the morning.

He threw his pillow on the sofa, lay down, wrapped himself in his sheet, and went to bed. He was tired, and, even with his legs pulled up, he went to sleep.

*   *   *

David awoke early. His body hurt. He got up and stretched, willing the pain to go away. He listened to see if there was noise coming from the bedroom. He heard nothing. He got out fresh underwear, set his shorts and undershirt by his trousers, looked at the bedroom door, quickly slipped off his pajamas bottoms, and put on his shorts. He breathed a sigh of relief and put on his trousers. He slipped off his pajama top and put on his undershirt and tucked it in as best he could.

Next, he went to the bedroom door and listened. He then slowly opened the door. When there was no shout to stop, he went in. He noticed Mary lying on her back with the covers up to her waist and looked away. He locked the bathroom door and went about his morning routine. He hesitated to flush the toilet but finally decided he had to.

As he passed back through the bedroom, he noticed Mary's covers were up to her neck, and the back of her head was all he could see. He softly said, "I'm out of the bathroom."

A muffled voice muttered, "In a little while."

David put on the rest of his clothes and went out to his car to get his clean suit. As he came back in, he picked up the *Washington Post*, carried it in, and put it on the kitchen counter. He was afraid to read it. He looked in the cabinets for coffee and filters, finding a jar of peanut butter in the process. He made coffee, put bread in the toaster, and eventually spread the toast with peanut butter for breakfast.

David settled on the sofa with his coffee.

Eventually, the bedroom door opened; and Mary, in her bathrobe, padded in and poured herself a cup of coffee, which she then carried back into the bedroom, closing the door behind her. Nothing was said.

Twenty-five minutes later, she reappeared, dressed in slacks and a blouse with a light jacket over her shoulders.

She asked, "Have you had breakfast?"

David said he had.

She nodded. "I did better for you at your house."

"You had a purpose."

"Yes, but I also like breakfast."

She took a Pop-Tarts out of the freezer and put it in the toaster. "I was up too late last night. I need to get going."

David watched her eat the Pop-Tarts and down another cup of coffee, all while standing.

She picked up her pocketbook from the counter and turned to David. "You ready to go?"

David got up and said, "I need to change my suit first."

Mary appraised David's trousers. "Probably a good idea. You coming back tonight?"

David shook his head. "No, I'll find some place to stay. Thank you for letting me crash."

"You're welcome. As you say, I owe you. I wish you the best of luck"

David replied, "You too. And watch your wiles."

"My what?"

"Your wiles. You don't control them very well."

Mary smirked. "Oh yeah. My wiles. I'll keep my eye on them. Turn the button in the door when you go out."

She closed the door and left.

CHAPTER SIXTY-ONE

WEDNESDAY - LINDA NEALE

Linda Neale was feeling a little bit lonely. David had been part of her life for a long time, and she missed him. Still, she knew he had made a major screwup. She was sure he hadn't killed the babies. She had never believed that he had. He was too quiet and much too gentle a man. When she had seen the repeat of his morning interview on the evening news, she had been happy to see him become angry on television. She knew he had it in him. She had wanted to cheer.

Still, there was the question of the woman that Brenda described as the "little bimbo." Two nights alone in the house with her husband was hard to accept. It didn't take much for her mind to run wild with the possibilities.

To keep her thoughts off that episode in her husband's life, she played with her statistics on letters received. She had the summary in Excel now. Every day's mail was educational. David had been called names she had never heard. She summarized them on a separate page. She was thankful the children were so young. She figured she would delete the data before they got old enough to read and ask questions. For now, the page was educational.

Nearly three hundred letters had come yesterday. It had taken her all afternoon to read and summarize them and get the statistics in the computer.

She also had an Excel page summarizing the editorials and letters to the editor in the *Washington Post* and the *New York Times*, to which she now subscribed. The newspaper comments were more erudite than the letters but were still interesting.

This morning, she had fed the children and settled them down. Right now, they were being good. She was lucky. They had their moments, but they were usually good.

She sat with her coffee and went over the morning's *Post* and *Times*, making notes on a pad of paper. She wondered what the *Wall Street Journal* was saying. Maybe she was being too liberal. She'd have to buy a copy of the *Journal*.

She couldn't wait for the mail to arrive. The mailman was now parking in front of her house so that he didn't have to carry David's mail too far. He usually came midmorning.

Linda was on her third cup of coffee when there was a knock at the door. She opened it to find the mailman standing there, a huge bag over his shoulder. He said there was too much to feed through the mail slot and asked if he could come in and leave it somewhere. She led him to the kitchen, moved her things off the kitchen table, and asked him to dump the mail there. He did so and asked her to sign for one letter, which she did. The mailman was very grateful, thanking her repeatedly as he went out the door. While he was doing this, she noted he was looking around the inside of the house. Linda guessed he needed to be able to describe the den of iniquity.

She closed the door behind him and hurried to the table. It looked like there were more letters today than yesterday.

She quickly picked up the large letter she had signed for. It was from the United States House of Representatives. Linda opened it and read the contents with shock and disbelief. David was being summoned to appear before the Congressional Committee on Health and Sciences . . . in the Rayburn Building . . . at 9:00 a.m. Monday . . . be in Room 3B207 at 8:00 a.m. She whistled and set it aside. She would have to call David later.

Right now, she wanted to get at the pile of letters. She began to sort them into rough stacks: letters from religious organizations; letters from scientific-sounding organizations; letters from what sounded like right wing organizations; letters from what sounded like liberal organizations; letters from organizations supporting eugenics; and letters from individuals or letters that had no return address. As she read them, she would categorize them in a more refined manner.

After sorting, she started with the letters with no return addresses. They were the ones that usually did the most to expand her vocabulary. They, however, were not always easy to read. A few even threatened to take David's life. They were unsettling, and she wondered if she should pass them to the police.

As she picked through the mail, she came to a letter from a company called Johnston Capital Investments. She opened it and scanned several pages. Then she sat back and read it in detail. Some of it sounded like legal mumbo jumbo, but what she got from it was that Symon Johnston ran a company that funded start-up businesses and had an interest in David because of his being a household name in the field of gestation and in vitro fertilization. The letter suggested establishing a business that would help women with problems associated with pregnancy, not just the usual problems of having trouble becoming pregnant but also with the broader aspect of using surrogate mothers for women who wanted children but didn't want to bother with pregnancy because of their professions or simply for other reasons. It further suggested establishing a lab directed at bypassing the surrogate mothers, developing fetuses entirely in the lab to avoid issues with surrogate mothers. Mr. Johnston suggested that there might even be a possibility of expanding the business through franchises.

Mr. Johnston wanted to use David's name for the clinic and build on David's notoriety.

The letter asked David to contact Johnston at a certain telephone number. Linda checked the area code and found that the call was from south of San Francisco.

Linda studied the letter and then phoned Brenda to come over and discuss it. She had shooed Brenda away from the mail yesterday, but this was different, and Linda needed to talk to someone about it, someone who had gutsy ideas.

Brenda read the letter and thought it was a great idea. "You need to meet with this guy and see what he can provide by way of helping set up such a business. You're going to need more than funds. You're going to need doctors, lab people, business people, lawyers, and I don't know what else. Eddie and I have about twenty thousand in the bank. I think we'd like to be in on this."

"You really think this can be done, Brenda? It's a big gamble."

"Hey, if you play it right, it's not going to be your money. Get a good lawyer to go over the contracts before you sign them. Make sure you're protected. Basically, you're giving permission for people to use David's name, although I suspect David will also have to provide a live face."

Linda thought about David. "You know, he's kind of a quiet guy."

"If this guy Johnston is any good, he'll take care of that. After all, it's going to be his money."

Linda was getting excited. "Damn, maybe David will become a big success, and I can stuff it down my father's throat. Maybe it will help us get along."

After Brenda left, Linda sat and thought about what to do. She didn't want David to be frightened about the idea, thinking it was too big a jump and worrying about "putting himself out there." She decided to get a jump on the process. She called the California number, told the person who answered who she was, and asked to speak to Mr. Johnston. She was glad that Johnston's business had someone to answer the phone. At least it was more than a one-person operation.

Symon Johnston came on the phone. "Yes, Mrs. Neale. I appreciate your phoning me. What do you and Mr. Neale think of the ideas in the letter?"

"We think they are very exciting, Mr. Johnston. David's at work, so I had to read your letter to him over the phone. He asked me to call you back."

"That's great. And please call me Sy," he said like he was Linda's new best friend.

"And I'm Linda. What do we need to do next to learn more about your proposal?"

"You're a direct lady, Linda. Right to the point. What I would like to do is to have my associate, Robert Byrne, meet with you when he's in Washington on Friday. Does that sound possible?"

Linda wondered if she was sounding too eager. She wasn't at all sure how to play the game. "I'm sure we can arrange our schedules to manage a meeting."

Johnston sounded pleased. "Good. Bob is staying at the Grand Hyatt Thursday and Friday nights. I'll have him phone you and finalize the meeting."

"That sounds fine, Sy. We'll look forward to meeting Mr. Byrne."

"And eventually, I'll look forward to meeting you and David. I hope we have a great future together."

Linda hung up the phone and took a deep breath, wondering if this was the beginning of the big time. She needed to phone David but had to take a break first. She fed the children and then herself, read a few letters, and put them in the appropriate stacks while making notes. Somehow, it wasn't as fascinating as it had been yesterday. Her mind was too distracted. She decided she should phone David.

She dialed his cell phone, but it went to voicemail. She'd have to phone the NIH number. She dialed it, and Lourie answered it. Lourie used to sound friendly but not today. Her voice had an edge. "I'll page him."

While she waited, she wondered if David felt the same frost.

David answered, "Hi, what's up? You don't usually call me at work."

Linda played it carefully. "Yeah, I hate to phone you at work. I don't want to interrupt anything important. Any chance you can talk now?"

"Good news or bad news? Let me sit down."

Linda thought a moment. "I guess a little bit of both."

David sounded leery. "Well, what do I get first?"

Linda settled down. "Well, let me tell you what I've been doing."

She went into a long discussion of the letters he had been receiving, almost eight hundred so far, summarized their natures, provided some of the interesting quotes, saying most people were mad at him—for a variety of reasons—and a few people thought he was on a noble mission. She also noted that if he wanted a different woman to sleep with every night, he was probably good for nearly a month.

David noted that he might be able to help some of the women.

Linda agreed, saying he had certainly been potent with her the last couple of years.

That left him protesting that he was talking about helping through lab work.

Linda ended that discussion. "David, a lot of this stuff is just noise. These people aren't going to do much to you, even the ones who want to string you up on the cross. What it does mean is that you are going to lose your job."

David objected. "I can't be fired. I'm a government employee, and I do my job. I do it well."

Linda disputed David's assertion. "David, you maybe the best, most thorough, and valuable scientist in the world, but these scientists who are criticizing you mean business. It's just a matter of days to when you're going to be up for review on ethical grounds. They say there are rules for genetic research that most scientists have agreed to and that you have violated them, that you have not followed the protocols that their disciplines require, and that by doing so, you have put the entire scientific community on the defensive and at risk. The only thing left for them to do is to decide exactly what they are going to do to you."

"But we didn't modify any genes."

"Believe me, they think you did. You're working on borrowed time. I think you ought to think about resigning before they fire you and make a big deal of it."

"How can I do that? How would we live? We need the paycheck."

Linda perked up. "And that leads to the next subject. You and I are going into business with an investor in California. He's going to set us up to support women who want to become pregnant and can't and, more importantly, women who want children and don't want to be pregnant. And all he wants to do is use your name."

"Why would he do that? I'm notorious."

"Yeah, but this guy, Symon Johnston, believes it's notoriety with a good essence. He believes you're now known as someone who can help women get pregnant, and you're an expert at finding women to act as surrogates. He knows anyone can do this, but he believes your name now makes you uniquely marketable. In other words, this major screwup you've just gone through may be our path to fame and fortune."

David had to blink and think. "Do you think this is real?"

"Brenda and I have been talking. We have no doubt that, with some help, we can make it real."

David had some of the wind taken out of him. "You've been talking to Brenda about this?"

Don't put her down. She's one of our biggest supporters. Wants to put twenty thousand dollars into our start-up."

"So what do we do next?"

Linda hesitated. "I guess you had better come home tonight so we can talk about it. We have a meeting with Mr. Johnston's associate on Friday."

"Jesus, this is moving fast. I'll come home right after work."

David started to hang up as Linda shouted, "Oh, there's one more thing! You got a subpoena to appear before Congress on Monday."

David almost hyperventilated. "The United States Congress?"

"Yeah, some committee."

"And that's an 'oh, by the way' at the end of a conversation."

Linda blew it off. "Hey, Friday's before Monday. I would have shown the subpoena to you tonight."

CHAPTER SIXTY-TWO

WEDNESDAY - THE HONORABLE J. MADISON CONROY

J. Madison was a happy man. He was looking forward to the hearing on Monday. They were kicking off with this young guy named Neale. He was all over the news and looked like a great target for the lead-in to the hearing. They'd have the Director of NIH and the Secretary of Health and Human Services in as well, but Neale was the star. The big guys from NIH and Health and Human Services probably didn't know who Neale was, but J. Madison's committee would take them over the coals anyway for not having proper control of their employees.

He was pleased that the police had found out that Neale's lab partner had used NIH stationery in obtaining materials from the Pennsylvania Primate Institute. He would push Neale and find out how materials ordered in the name of the U.S. Government were used for nongovernment activities that were not approved by the government and were now condemned by a broad spectrum of the nation's population. Hopefully, he could also show that Neale and his compatriots had used—or misused—government property in whatever experiment they had conducted and be able to link that to poor supervision so that he had grounds to go after the big wheels.

He settled down to make notes for the questions he would ask when Audra buzzed him. "The mayor of Alexandria's on the phone for you."

J. Madison picked up the phone. Maybe there was going to be more ammunition for him to use. "Hey, Dana, how are you? You got everything under control over there? Always like to know it's safe to come home at night."

"Good morning, Jay. Yes, it's all under control. Safest town around. I thought I'd catch you up on the Route-One Baby case. The Commonwealth's Attorney came over this morning. He's concluded that the evidence they have indicates that this Seth O'Halloran killed the babies and acted alone in doing so. Since O'Halloran's dead, they want to close the case and plan to have a press conference on it this afternoon."

"Jesus Christ, Dana! You know I'm having a hearing on this thing next Monday. If you make that announcement, it'll make me an afterthought."

"Yes, but you've got to understand my position too. We've got a national criminal case open over here, and every day that passes without an answer makes me look bad."

J. Madison, painfully distressed, tried not to shout. "Damn it, Dana. You know I give you all kinds of help over there. Push legislation, personally back you in elections, all kinds of shit. You've got to help me. Delay the press conference till next week. Do that for me."

Mayor Robbins remained calm. "I understand your problem, Jay. And oh, by the way, how are you coming on getting funds to help us with the riverfront park development?"

"Damn it, Dana! You're screwing me. I'll make it a major priority. Just help me out."

"Always glad to support you, Jay. I'll watch you on TV Monday, and you can watch me later in the week. Have a great day."

J. Madison hung up. "Bitch."

CHAPTER SIXTY-THREE

WEDNESDAY - DAVID NEALE
AND LINDA NEALE

David was excited about Linda's phone call and frightened too. He didn't know a thing about these people who were offering to create a clinic in his name and knew even less about how it would all be done and what he would expect to get out of it. "Hell, how do you figure out what your name is worth?"

He was terrified at the thought of going before Congress. He had no idea what to expect. He couldn't go alone. He needed a lawyer but didn't know what for. People always had a lawyer.

He phoned Henry Travers' office. Joanne answered. He made his desperate pitch to her, and she worked him in for an appointment during lunchtime on Thursday.

When he got home, he was glad to see that Tuscany Lane appeared to be back to normal. He parked in the driveway behind Linda's car and walked uncertainly to the door.

He found Linda and the children in the kitchen. The children paid no attention to him as he said, "Hi."

Linda was almost jumping up and down. "Hey. Are you as excited as I am? We're going to be rich, David!"

"Excited and nervous. This is a big step, Linda. We really don't know what we're doing. We've got a fast-learning curve coming up. Aren't you a little nervous?" He picked up Billy, kissed, and hugged him. "Missed you, tiger."

Linda wiped her hands on a towel. She made no move to welcome and kiss him. "The way I see it, you screwed up big time, and we have a chance to come out of it smelling like a rose. Yes, I'm nervous, but we're going to damn well do it."

"Just want to make sure you understand we've got work ahead of us."

They sat quietly at dinner. David fed the children and realized he had missed them. After dinner, he bathed them, put them to bed, and read to Billy.

When he came back downstairs, Linda was sitting with two glasses of wine on the table. "Hey, I appreciate your doing that. It's a real break after the last couple of weeks. Maybe I missed you."

David knew he had to say it. "I missed you too." He didn't think he had. Life had been so wild.

Linda got serious. "What do you really think about this offer of Johnston's?"

"As I said, it's exciting and scary too. You talked to this guy Johnston. What did you think of him?"

"It was just over the phone. He seemed all right. Confident, sure of himself, but still he seemed sincere. He had a friendly, nice voice."

"Did he say what we would be doing? What he expected from us?"

"Well, you know he expects to use your name. He'll name the business after you. Says he wants you to run a lab and develop ways to have babies gestate in the lab. I'm sure we'll learn more Friday when we meet Mr. Johnston's associate, Robert Byrne."

"Does this mean we'll be moving to California?"

"We didn't talk about it, but it wouldn't surprise me."

"Would that bother you?"

"No, I don't think so." Linda sipped her wine and smiled. "I guess we'd need earthquake insurance. What about you?"

"I'd be all right. You wouldn't miss being close to your parents?"

"After the last two weeks, a once-a-year visit will be just fine."

"We'll need money to move and buy a house. Maybe some money to carry us over the next few weeks. Do you think Johnston will help with that?"

"We sure need to ask. Brenda says we need a lawyer to go over any contracts. I guess our lawyer might need to negotiate with them too."

"For once, Brenda's right. I'm meeting with my criminal lawyer tomorrow at noon to talk about this congressional thing. I'll see if he can suggest someone."

"Are we paying for this criminal lawyer? I didn't know about him."

"I'm afraid we can't afford to do without him. He's a good guy, old school, and about as cheap as they come."

"Doesn't sound like he's any good."

"Right now, he'll do just fine. He's good counsel, and I need his presence for intimidation, if nothing else."

"Who are you trying to intimidate?"

"I've had cops talk to me three times, and believe me, I've felt better when the lawyer was present."

"I guess I've stopped thinking about that. Are you going to be tried? That might foul this whole thing up."

"I don't think so, but you never know. I think everyone knows that Seth killed the babies and that I had nothing to do with it. But you never know."

"You really didn't have anything to do with it?"

David was appalled. "Do you really think I could kill two babies?"

Linda understood the reaction. She happily backed off. "No, of course not."

David relaxed. "I don't think I'll be tried, but then again, you never know. Right now, I think the world is so ridiculous that I can't even say if a trial would hurt or help a new business."

Linda shook her head. "I'd prefer not to find out."

She became very serious. "David, this is scary. Exciting as hell, but still scary. Do you think we can do it?"

David drained the last half of his glass of wine, turned to Linda, and said, "Damned right we can." He grinned, and then Linda did too.

He got up. "Let's go to bed."

Linda let him sleep in the bed with her, although she turned her back.

CHAPTER SIXTY-FOUR

THURSDAY - DAVID NEALE

David left work early again on Thursday. It seemed like he was hardly there anymore. He was using his vacation time at an alarming rate. Each time he was away, he had to let Lourie know. She was barely talking to him, and the whole thing had become uncomfortable.

He left work a little after eleven. He took the Beltway, I-66, and State 28 to US 29. He stopped and picked up food from McDonald's and headed for Travers's. There were two cars in the driveway. He figured he would have to wait. Joanne signaled him to a chair. She pulled out her own lunch and began to eat. She didn't seem particularly interested in David. He guessed she had seen enough not to get excited about a notorious client.

A couple came out of Travers's office. They didn't seem to be very friendly. The man did hold the door for the woman but didn't join her as she walked away. David figured that explained why there were two cars.

Travers beckoned him into the office. "So the free, high-powered lawyer was not to your taste?"

Travers sat at his conference table and motioned David to sit.

David sighed. "Not only not to my taste but not free." David passed Travers his share of the lunch. "Got you a bottle of water. Didn't know what you drank."

"Thank you. Lunch is much appreciated. I wasn't sure how I was going to handle it. Water's great."

"You are very welcome. I appreciate your seeing me on such short notice. As to the fancy lawyer, my wife phoned and said I received a bill from him in this morning's mail, over $2,000. You think I'm stuck with it?"

Travers spread out his lunch. "Did you sign a contract? Get something in writing saying he would work for free?"

David felt guilty. "No."

Travers made a face. "Then I'm afraid you may have to pay it. Everyone saw you two together on television, so you can't say he didn't work with you."

"If I don't pay, do you think he'll take me to court?"

Travers shook his head. "I doubt it. I expect he'll just turn it over to a collection agency and get it reflected on your credit report."

"Doesn't sound like I'm in good shape?"

"No, I don't think so. But that's not why you came to see me."

David took out the papers from the subpoena and handed them to Travers. "I came to see you about this. I need a lawyer again."

Travers looked over the papers. "You're saying you want me to go to the congressional hearing with you?"

"I'd be grateful if you would?"

Travers studied the papers. "You know I've never done anything like this before. Even representing you before was stepping a little out of my league. I do small-time court stuff,

settlements, uncontested divorces, wills, powers of attorney—
that kind of thing."

"I don't think you'll have to do much."

Travers nodded. "So you're just going to plead the Fifth?"

"No, I'll probably try to answer the questions. I'm tired of
feeling guilty. I believe the police have pretty well concluded
that I didn't kill the babies and was not involved in the killing
in any way. If they are going to get me on something less than
that, I'd like to get it over with."

"You know that's a gamble. If prosecution's determined
enough, they can take things pretty far."

"I don't think they can prove anything. The evidence is not
there."

"Hey, it's your neck. I won't advise you to do what you're
planning, but yeah, I'll hold your hand while you're doing it.
It'll be a new experience for me."

"I appreciate that very much. Now I've got a second item."

David explained the offer from Johnston and his need for an
appropriate attorney to help him with the contracts that would
be involved in the process.

Travers leaned back. "Now you're really getting out of my
league. I don't even work with those kinds of guys. I'll have to
make some phone calls and get back to you. You know, you're
now talking about a big money attorney?"

David acknowledged that. "I know. I don't think I have much
choice. I think that's what my equity line of credit is for."

David pushed back his chair and stood up. "Shall I pick you
up on Monday?"

Travers stood, and they shook hands. "No. I don't like driving in Washington, even with someone else. I'll take the Metro. Eight in the morning, huh? Courts don't even do that."

"Okay, I'll see you there."

"So we're winging it. If I think you're really screwing up, do you want me to tug at your sleeve?"

"Yeah, but only if I'm really screwing up."

CHAPTER SIXTY-FIVE

FRIDAY - DAVID NEALE
AND LINDA NEALE

David and Linda drove up to the entrance of the Grand Hyatt and had the doorman arrange to have their car parked. They had thought about looking for a parking lot, but that didn't seem to fit the moment. Besides, after lunch, they wanted to leave with some style.

Bob Byrne had phoned the night before and said he would meet them in the hotel's restaurant. David approached the hostess and inquired as to whether Mr. Byrne had arrived and had a table. "Oh yes. You must be the Neales?"

David acknowledged that they were, and the hostess led them to Byrne's table. Robert Byrne was an attractive man, probably in his early forties, with dark, almost black hair and eyebrows and a firm jaw, well-tanned. David introduced Linda and himself as Byrne stood and offered a firm, professional handshake and said, "I'm very pleased to meet you. Sy is excited about the potential you offer us, and it's wonderful to have the opportunity to discuss it with you. Please have a seat."

They all sat as Byrne patted a briefcase sitting in the fourth chair and continued. "I've got a lot in here that I want to talk to you about, but I think we should order lunch first."

They studied the menu. Linda ordered a smoked trout salad with iced tea; David, a beef brisket sandwich with water; and Byrne, a panini with a beer. "Would you like a cocktail or a beer?"

Both Linda and David thanked him, but declined. "We need to keep our minds about us," David said while Linda gave him a quick glare, as if to say, "Be a little more sophisticated."

While they waited for their meals, Byrne asked David and Linda where they came from, where they had gone to college, how they met—all the introductory questions they had expected. In the process, they learned that Byrne had a degree in business from Stanford, had worked in investments for Bank of America following graduation, and had later joined Johnston Capital Investments.

While they ate their meals, David asked for information about what Johnston Capital Investments did, and Byrne explained that they didn't just provide funds to businesses but actually worked with entrepreneurs to set up companies, with the purpose of eventually selling the companies or having them go public. Byrne allowed that David wasn't the normal entrepreneur trying to set up a company but was in the position of providing a name on which Sy Johnston visualized setting up a new company, one for which Johnston Capital Investments would provide management, facilities, and labor, not to mention the start-up funding. He withdrew a business plan from his briefcase and handed it to David.

"You'll need to study this. It will give you a detailed understanding of what we want to do. We're already exploring the purchase of an 'in vitro' clinic to provide the initial facility and medical staff. Our management staff will expand that to increase use of surrogate mothers and establish lab facilities for future development of what we call environmentally pure fetal development, which may change, but basically means growing fetuses in the laboratory from zagat to baby. We don't know whether the environment of a surrogate mother influences the development of a fetus, but we could say that a lab process would eliminate that possibility."

As they ordered their dessert, David pointed out that if the woman carrying the baby influenced the baby environmentally during gestation, having a baby grown in the laboratory would also eliminate the real mother's influence.

Byrne acknowledged that but said a mother using a surrogate had already given up her environmental influence during gestation and that no one knew what that influence was anyway. What Byrne and, by inference, Sy Johnston, did believe was that there were numerous women who did not want to carry babies themselves. He acknowledged that many women, perhaps most of them, received an innate satisfaction and fulfillment in participating in the entire maternal spectrum to include pregnancy and giving birth. However, he felt there were some professional women who did not want to take the time for the gestation process, while still wanting children.

In addition, he felt there were women who simply did not want to deal with pregnancy or were just plain afraid of it. Finally, he felt that some women, having had a couple of children, were satisfied that they had had enough and would be happy for another approach. These were in addition to that population of woman who, for medical reasons, cannot carry a pregnancy. What was essential was that this would not be an inexpensive process. It would have some of the appeal of a high-priced spa. He viewed it as a process in which surrogate mothers would be carefully selected and paid on the order of a hundred thousand dollars for carrying the babies, probably two or three times what they would normally earn in a year. By creating a special group of surrogates, highly tested and regulated, he viewed this as being a process that would appeal to an exclusive group of women who could afford it and thus generate a great deal of money.

David commented, "So this is not a plan for the masses. This is the kind of thing where we could sell Hermes in the waiting room."

Byrne smiled. "Well, I don't think we'll go quite that far. I'll mention it to Sy, but he envisions a very clean, luxurious medical atmosphere with professionals responding to our patient's every need."

"And what do you expect me to do?" David inquired.

Byrne pushed his plate away and leaned forward. "We would expect you not only to provide your name but also provide a face for the company. Although you're fairly young, you have a gravitas about you that we want to use. We saw you on television, and even though you looked angry, we liked what we saw. At that time, we had already mailed you the letter with the initial proposal, but your appearance added to what we thought you could do. We would visualize your participating in interviews with the media about what we offer and in sessions with potential patients where you would explain what we can do for them."

Linda spoke up, concerned, "But David's kind of reserved. He's never done that kind of thing."

David put his hand on hers. "I've never done it because I haven't needed to. Don't worry. If I'm talking about science, I can do it."

Linda looked at him as if he was someone she didn't know.

Byrne looked at Linda. "And we'll help him until he gets the process down."

"So now, the next question"—David looked down at the table and then up again into Byrne's eyes—"it appears that you're planning to start this process in California and that you expect me to be there. That's going to require some logistical costs on my part. How do you plan to support this?"

Byrne nodded. "That's an expected question. We would propose providing you with a check for half a million dollars as a down payment for using your name with an additional payment of half a million when the business is up and running. We further propose a base salary of $150,000 a year with a profit-sharing incentive."

David tried not to look incredulous. He could feel Linda looking at him. He knew she was dumbfounded as well. "That sounds very reasonable. I assume the profit-sharing would include any income obtained should we develop franchises."

"Of course. That's covered in our proposed contract." Byrne pulled some papers from the briefcase. "This is the proposed contract. We hope it covers everything."

David accepted the papers. "Of course, I'll need to have my attorney review this."

Byrne closed the briefcase. "We certainly expect you to do that. The contract also addresses what you would receive as compensation should we need to end our association and compensation you would receive if we should sell the business, your rights to continue with a new owner, and what you would receive if the company should go public." He gave David a few business cards. "If there are any questions, have your attorney phone me."

David tried to sound very business-like. "We will do the contract review as expeditiously as possible. Linda and I very much appreciate the opportunity you have provided and look forward to working with you."

They stood and shook hands.

Byrne affirmed all that had been said. "I too look forward to working with you. I hope I have answered all your questions and made the opportunity sound as appealing as it is to us at Johnston Capital Investments. When we finalize the contract, we would like to fly you to California so you can meet our staff and start working on details."

David and Linda said they would look forward to that and thanked Byrne for the meal.

As they walked out the door of the hotel, Linda asked David, "Do we have an attorney?"

David chuckled, "Yes. I haven't met him, but I have an appointment with him next Wednesday. Now, I even have a contract to show him."

Linda laughed and squeezed David's arm.

After their car arrived, Linda got in the driver's seat and took David to Metro Center. Next, she would drive home, and he would take the metro to the National Institutes of Health in Bethesda where he would submit his resignation.

CHAPTER SIXTY-SIX

MONDAY - DAVID NEALE

David didn't sleep much all weekend. He worried about what would happen at the congressional hearing. He wanted to make an introductory statement but didn't know if that was allowed. On the assumption that it would be allowed, he practiced it over and over in his mind.

He and Linda talked some about Johnston's offer, but he leveled with her and told her that Congress was on his mind and that he would probably appear remote until the hearing was over. She wanted to talk about the future but finally accepted things as they were and pretty much left him alone.

He arrived at the Rayburn Building about seven thirty, found the entrance to the underground garage, and turned in. He was immediately stopped and asked to show the pass that had been provided with the subpoena. The guard walked around the car, peered in the widows, and asked David to open the trunk. All David had with him was a single spiral notebook. Finally, he was told where the visitor's parking was located and allowed to proceed.

At the elevators, he was met by another guard and a metal detector he would have to walk through. Again, he showed his pass, put his notebook, watch, keys, and change on a conveyor belt, and walked through the detector. He asked directions to the room where he was supposed to go. He took the elevator to the third floor and found room 3B207, which was locked. *Well, he thought, I'm twenty minutes early.* He stood there and then leaned against the door frame. He could hear noise coming from people around the corner and went to look. There seemed to be a gang of news and television people, some with cameras, gathered in the hallway. He ducked out of sight. He guessed they were early too.

He walked back to his designated room. At ten minutes to eight, Henry Travers rounded the corner and waved to him. "Have you changed your mind? We can still plead the Fifth."

David gave him a sad half smile. "No. I'm pretty much going to tell all . . . Sorry to tell you, we're locked out."

"Maybe they've changed their minds."

"Don't I wish."

At five minutes of eight, a man pushing a cart came down the hall. He was some kind of caterer with coffee, cups, pastries, the works.

He nodded good morning and unlocked the door. David and Travers followed him into the room. There was a conference table surrounded by chairs and more leather chairs against the walls. Obviously, David was small-time. *Some of the people coming to these hearings must come with an entourage.*

David and Travers helped themselves to coffee and sat at the table as a young woman arrived. She said she was on the hearing's staff and wanted to welcome them. She didn't give her name. She apologized for getting them there so early but noted that congressmen don't like to be kept waiting. She indicated that she would be back to escort them to the hearing room and told them they would be sitting at a table with microphones and that the Committee Chairman, Congressman Lyle Reninger of Texas, would be holding the hearing and that they should follow his instructions. David told her he would like to make an introductory statement, and the woman said she would pass that request to the Chairman. She said she would be back for them.

As she left, David thought to himself, *So I won't know anything until this farce begins.*

Travers stirred his coffee more than he needed to. "Did you get hold of the attorney I told you about?"

"Yes. I have an appointment next Wednesday. I've got a draft contract for him to look at."

"Good. I don't know the guy. A good friend of mine recommended him. Hope he works out."

They sat quietly for a while. David asked, "Did you have any trouble getting here?"

"No. I took the Orange Line to the South Capitol Metro Station and had a couple of blocks to walk. I think I arrived about the time everyone came to work. The lobby was packed. Took me about twenty minutes to get in. All hurry up and wait."

"Yeah. I guess they like to make you sweat."

David decided he would like to go to the bathroom before the hearing. He had only drunk half a cup of coffee. He thought that was enough.

Travers joined him, and they wandered down the hallway until they found someone to ask for directions to the bathroom. It turned out it was near where all the reporters had been gathered. Fortunately, they apparently had entered a hearing room. David wondered if it was his hearing room.

One reporter was in the bathroom. He recognized David. "You nervous? Is this going to be a big nothing? Lots of 'with the advice of my attorney, I would like to decline, etc.?'"

David didn't look at him. "We'll see. Don't expect anything dramatic."

"Okay. Best of luck."

They returned to the waiting room and sat. Shortly before nine, the young woman returned and led them to the hearing room. It was, indeed, where the media had gone. David glanced around and saw everyone looking back at him. He noticed Mary Murphy to one side and nodded to her. She looked quickly away, as if hoping no one had seen them making eye contact.

He and Travers sat at the center of a long witness table. A man came over and tapped their microphones. The table faced a desk, if that was what it could be called. It was long and curved so the congressmen could sit behind it. It was raised so that they could look down at David. David imagined the Supreme Court Chambers. This was kind of like a court. He decided they couldn't sentence him, but they could find him guilty. He shivered a little.

There were seats against the wall behind the congressmen's long desk. There were a number of people sitting there or milling about in the area. Two congressmen were already in place, and a couple of more were wending their way to their seats. None of them made eye contact with him.

He noticed the television cameras aimed at him and looked around to see more pointed at the congressmen. He wondered if Linda would know to watch C-Span. Maybe bits of the testimony would appear on the news media.

Everyone started settling down. Congressman Reninger pounded a gavel, and silence prevailed.

Reninger glared out at the audience. "This Hearing of the United States Congressional Committee on Science and Technology will come to order. We are meeting today to investigate a possible use of government time and resources in the conduct of unauthorized experiments and the possible failure of management to identify improper use of government resources. To this end, we will begin today by hearing the testimony of Mr. David Neale, an employee of the National Institutes of Health satellite facility in Fairfax, Virginia. As we know from media reports and from police and FBI investigations, Mr. Neale, a laboratory researcher, was apparently involved in an experiment aimed at modifying the gestation period of the human species. This research, as I firmly believe, was neither authorized nor condoned by anyone in the government. The question before us is whether this research slipped through the crack of lax management and if it used government resources."

Reninger, hardly looking at David, asked him to rise and be sworn in.

Following this procedure, Reninger again addressed the room. "Mr. Neale has asked to make an introductory statement." He looked down at David. "Are you ready, Mr. Neale?"

David swallowed. "Yes, Your Honor."

Reninger frowned and chastised David. "Mr. Neale, do you see me wearing a black robe? I am not a judge, and this is not a court."

David looked at Reninger. "Yes, sir. I know. I only meant to show respect."

"And that, you should. Go ahead."

David had his notebook opened and looked down at it. "Chairman Reninger and Members of the Committee, I welcome this opportunity to speak to you today." He swallowed and looked up. "I wish that I could be here in a marine uniform saying I had done my duty as best I could, but I'm not a marine. I'm a scientist. I wear a lab coat and perform research. I try to discover things. I bring certain skills to my efforts that I have developed through years of education. Again, I am a scientist. I ask questions and seek answers. I ask you to accept me for what I am."

David took a sip of water and continued. "Chairman Reninger has mentioned an experiment. I would like to address that experiment today. Mr. Seth O'Halloran and Dr. Sidney Gill, both deceased, and I were laboratory coworkers at the National Institutes of Health in Fairfax, Virginia, as the Chairman has noted. We did, indeed, conduct an experiment directed at reducing the gestation period of women. The experiment was conceived by Mr. O'Halloran and funded with his lifetime savings. Preliminary experiments were conducted on rats and guinea pigs in Mr. O'Halloran's apartment in Alexandria. The apparent success of those experiments led Mr. O'Halloran to propose conducting similar experiments on human beings. Both Dr. Gill and I cooperated in these experiments.

"The experiments involved employing three women as surrogate mothers. The eggs of these women were modified by replacing their cytoplasm with cytoplasm obtained from cells in the amniotic fluid of gibbons, another primate species. Gibbons have a seven-month gestation cycle. By using this cytoplasm, the goal was to change the timing of cell development in humans to the timing in gibbons or, at a minimum, to reduce the gestation period of the women. Following replacement of the cytoplasm, the women's eggs were fertilized and planted in the surrogate mothers' wombs. All the work with the women took place in a house that was rented at 227 North Pearson Street in Alexandria, Virginia. Dr. Gill, a trained OB-GYN doctor, handled the medical aspects. O'Halloran handled the logistics and recruiting of surrogate mothers, and I handled the processing of the eggs. The experiment was successful in shortening the gestation period of the subjects but unfortunately, resulted in introducing some of the characteristics of the gibbons into the infants born of the process. The experiment was clearly conducted prematurely and not based on sufficient preliminary research."

Reninger was looking at him with an unemotional expression. "Are you finished, Mr. Neale?"

David closed his notebook. "I am, sir."

"We will then proceed with questions from the Committee. For the initial questioning, I'd like to change the order of questioning to ask the Gentleman from Virginia to initiate the procedure."

J. Madison pulled the microphone to him. David noted the congressman's size and cringed.

"Mr. Neale, you have admitted that you participated in an experiment that was ill-conceived and failed. You are a government employee, professionally working on important aspects of medicine. Do you understand that by extending your research in this clearly inappropriate manner, you have become an embarrassment to the federal government?"

David hedged, "I guess I do."

J. Madison's voice hedged on being angry. "What do you mean by 'you guess you do'?"

David looked down and then back up. "Sir, these experiments were done entirely on our personal time. I'm not sure what right the government has to dictate what we do on our personal time."

"Are you trying to be funny, Mr. Neale?"

David looked J. Madison in the eye. "Absolutely not."

"Are you saying that what you did in this experiment has no relation to the kind of activity you perform for the federal government?"

"No, sir, not at all, but simply to say that the government did not pay for the time we spent on the work."

"Completely independent of your government job, Mr. Neale? Are you saying that it was never discussed at work? That no planning went on at work?"

"Well, we did a lot of discussion and planning over lunch in the NIH building's cafe."

"But never during routine work in your lab?"

David was caught. There hadn't been much discussion, but to say "none" would be a lie. "Sir, I would respectfully, on advice of my counsel, decline to answer that question."

J. Madison was pleased. "And I would additionally suggest that there is a close relationship between what you do for the NIH and what you did in the 'experiment.'" While saying the last word, J. Madison made quotation marks with his fingers. "Is that not so, Mr. Neale?"

"It is, sir."

"And so you understand that your conduct in this case is an embarrassment to the government that employs you and pays your salary."

David didn't quite see it but answered, "I guess. I can understand how some people might think that because we are government employees, our experiment might somehow be connected to the government."

J. Madison was partially satisfied. "There's no doubt that people think that way. Now answer this, was your experiment condoned by anyone in government, and second, was it done with anyone in government having knowledge that the experiment was being conducted?"

"No to both questions."

"Should your superiors have been aware that the experiment was occurring?"

David shook his head. "I know of no way they could have known."

"Do your supervisors visit your laboratory on a regular basis?"

"They visit periodically. We provide weekly written reports of our accomplishments and have meetings to discuss what we are doing and where we should be headed."

"But in those reports and meetings, you only report what you wish to?"

David was a little annoyed. "We report what we have done."

J. Madison leaned back and summarized, "I would guess you only report what you have 'officially' done."

He continued. "So your supervisors only periodically visit to visually see what you are doing. Most of the time, they rely on your being, shall we say, *honest* with them."

Again, David weakly defended himself. "Sir, we are *honest*."

"Mr. Neale, I suspect you are not. I suspect that the three of you discussed your 'ill-conceived' experiment on government time and, almost as importantly, spent time thinking about it on government time." He made some notes. "Now, Mr. Neale, you have indicated that it was your job in this experiment to modify the human eggs that were being used. I would view this as being a fairly sophisticated scientific process. Is that not true, Mr. Neale?"

"Yes, sir. It is."

"And I would suspect it requires the use of some fairly sophisticated equipment?"

David knew where this was going. "Yes, sir."

"Like the equipment in your laboratory at NIH?"

"Sir, I can assure you that all the equipment in our laboratory is there—glassware and all."

"That wasn't the question, Mr. Neale. The question asked 'was it like the equipment in your laboratory,' and more specifically, was it the equipment in your laboratory?"

David surrendered. "Sir, on advice of counsel, I respectively decline to answer that question."

"Then I suspect, Mr. Neale, that parts of your experiment were going on during laboratory time. I suspect there were things going on in petri dishes, in incubators, and in cryogenic dewars. Your hands-on work may have been after hours, but I suspect things were happening on their own on government time."

David didn't say anything.

"Am I right, Mr. Neale?"

"Sir, on advice of counsel, I decline to answer that question"

J. Madison again summarized, "And I would expect that a knowledgeable and caring supervisor would have noticed these things happening, if they were paying attention."

David said nothing.

J. Madison looked satisfied. "I would now like to turn the questioning back to our Chairman, the Gentleman from Texas."

Reninger thanked Conroy.

He shuffled some papers. "Mr. Neale, I think my CoChairman, Congressman Conroy, has clearly shown that what you have done is an embarrassment to the National Institutes of Health, which does so much important work for our nation, and to the United States Government as a whole. It is not just an embarrassment because of a possible connection of our facilities to this ill-conceived and failed experiment but also as a poor reflection on the ethics of our entire nation." He looked up at David. "Mr. Neale, are you a Christian, yes or no?"

David was taken aback. "Sir, with all due respect. That's like Joe McCarthy asking people if they are communist or have ever been communist, yes or no."

Reninger glared. "Mr. Neale, are you comparing me to Joe McCarthy?"

David protested, "Heavens, no. What I'm saying is that most questions don't have a yes or no answer. If you ask me if I got out of bed this morning, I can tell you yes, even though I might wish I had stayed in bed." There was a snicker from press. Reninger glared, and David continued. "The simple fact is that most questions have context, and the answers do too. If you demand 'yes or no' answers, you will force me to cite the Fifth Amendment. If you let me answer, I will give the best answer I know how."

Reninger looked a little resigned. "Okay, Mr. Neale. We'll play your game. Are you a Christian?"

David drew in a deep breath. "Obviously, it depends on how you define 'Christian.' Is a Christian someone who goes to church every Sunday, or is he someone who follows the Ten Commandments and the Golden Rule? I view myself as a Christian. But I am not someone who goes to church every Sunday, although I go now and then. What I am is someone who does a fair job of following the Commandments and Golden Rule, though hardly a perfect job. I think I'm a fairly good Christian but not perfect."

Reninger pounced, "Then, Mr. Neale, if you are a Christian, how do you justify challenging the laws of God and the natural order that God has established?"

"Respectfully, sir, I didn't know I was challenging God. I don't know whether or not the Bible says a woman's period of gestation should be nine months, or a gibbon's, seven months, or such. It may. I'm not an expert on the Bible. If it says anything, I suspect it's in a different context rather than being a law."

"Mr. Neale, it's been nine months for all time. It's the way God set it up. As a man, you have no right to challenge God's ordained process."

"Sir, again, respectfully, what you're implying is that, if a woman has a BRCA1 gene mutation, she shouldn't have a mastectomy because that defies the natural order of things."

Reninger was again annoyed. "Mr. Neale, a nine-month period of gestation is in the natural order of things. Cancer is a disease."

"Yes, sir, but I believe our genes are in the natural order of things."

Reninger was disgusted. "Mr. Neale, I don't know if you're playing with this committee or not, but I suggest that you be careful. What we're talking about here, Mr. Neale, is the ethics of what you have done. It is broadly agreed that what you have done is not ethical. Don't you agree?"

"It appears, sir, that you're equating Christianity with ethics, two things about which there is little agreement in this world. I don't know about religion, but I believe ethics are changing faster than the computer. If you don't believe it, ask my grandfather. If you're talking about the ethical approach to gene research, I agree that scientists have tried to establish rules and review processes to ensure the research doesn't do things that we don't want to live with. Many scientists feel that O'Halloran, Gill, and I violated the spirit of those rules. In our defense, we believed that we were not modifying genes in our experiment, only modifying the speed with which cell processes proceed. Perhaps in the process, we did inadvertently modify genes or somehow activated genes that have been recessive or downright dormant for one hundred and fifty thousand years. I don't know, but I understand the concern of scientists who have criticized us."

"So you agree that you have made ethical errors in what you have done, in violation of what Christianity tells us."

"I agree that there are ethical concerns appropriate to what we have done."

"Seems like the same thing to me. You can play games with words, Mr. Neale, but you do realize, don't you, that your experiment failed and led to the deaths of five people?"

David felt that he had been kicked. "I realize it all too well. If that is a fact you're trying to discover in this hearing, I fully acknowledge the horror of those deaths. I also, flatly state, that I didn't kill anyone and did not have any knowledge of the killings. I never intended that there be any deaths, and I did not participate in their happening."

"Just the same, five people are dead."

"Not as a direct result of the experiment."

"Does it matter?"

"It does to me."

Chapter Sixty-Seven

MONDAY - DAVID NEALE

The Hearing continued with many of the same questions. The Congressmen were all trying to make points, hopefully targeting their own constituents.

Then the Gentlemen from Utah asked a surprising question. "Mr. Neale, the chairman has described your experiment as one that was ill-conceived and that it failed. Is this an appropriate description of your experiment?"

David was caught off guard. He hesitated. "Sir, I've spent a lot of time thinking about the experiment. In fact, you might say my mind has dwelled on it. I'd like to address both elements of that description. When you ask if it was ill-conceived, I think there are a couple of elements to address. If you are talking about whether there was enough preliminary work done to justify applying the concept being tested to human beings, I would say that I had reservations from the beginning. In retrospect, the answer is that there was not. If you are talking about the philosophy of the experiment and ethics of the experiment, I think that can be argued in many ways.

"As to the experiment's failure, I would say this. The goal was to shorten the gestation period of the human species.

The experiment did that, so on one level, it was a success. Clearly, it had concurrently aspects that make it, as performed, unacceptable as an approach to achieving the shortening of the gestation period. At the same time, what was done will lead to research to better understand the process that goes on in the cell when a baby begins developing and perhaps to understand why or how different primates went their separate ways in ancient history.

"I would also suspect that the two murdered babies are currently being studied to learn more about human development, perhaps in the labs of the NIH. I daresay that the cells of those babies have probably been frozen for future research."

The Congressman challenged this. "Are you saying that the research you describe justifies you doing the experiment?"

"Not at all. But once the experiment was done, I believe it provides opportunities for research that might not otherwise have been available. I don't view this as a success of the experiment but only as an opportunity it has generated."

"Finally, Mr. Neale, let me ask you how you personally feel about having performed the experiment?"

David wondered if he was talking too much. "Let me separate my answer from the deaths that occurred. They were a terrible and unfortunate aftermath of the experiment, but they are, as I said, not a direct consequence of the technical aspects of the experiment. With that considered, if you are asking me if I'm ashamed of having performed this experiment, I'm afraid I have mixed emotions. I'm sorry we jumped into it without more preliminary work. I'm sorry that the babies had mixed phenotypes. But I must admit that the experiment was exciting from a scientific point of view.

"In performing the experiment, I used skills that I have spent years developing. I found I could do some rather remarkable things. I also had the opportunity to participate in the development of lives. There is little that is more exciting than that. I found the whole process exhilarating. I suspect it's an exhilaration that only a scientist, or perhaps a doctor, can feel. I would love to be involved in similar processes again."

The Congressman nodded. "Mr. Neale, I, in no way, condone what you did, but I do understand a little of what you are saying. If you have an opportunity to pursue research in the future, I would hope that you are more circumspect in your approach to and conduct of your research and that you will seek appropriate peer review before commencing your work. I'm aware that there are both exciting and productive possibilities in what might be done with genetic research. At the same time, the possibilities are frightening. If this hearing does nothing else, I hope it makes the point to all scientists that genetics research is like messing with dynamite—or perhaps even the atom bomb."

When everyone had finished asking their questions, Chairman Reninger summarized, "If no one has any more questions, I'd like to thank the Committee Members for their participation today. I think, after hearing Mr. Neale's testimony, that the experiment that he and his laboratory partners conducted on the gestation of human beings was ill-conceived, both scientifically and ethically, and that their supervisors, had they performed adequate management surveillance of the activities being performed in Mr. Neale's laboratory, should have been able to terminate the experiment early on and thus have prevented the failure of the experiment and probably the deaths of five individuals. Tomorrow, we will meet here again to explore with the Director of the National Institutes of Health why the current system failed and what we can do to prevent this from ever happening again."

With that, Reninger moved to adjourn, was seconded, and everyone got up and filed out. David didn't feel that he had been excused. He and Henry Travers sat there until everyone was gone, and the reporters began to pack up and leave.

Travers turned to David and noted, "I'm exhausted, and I didn't even do anything, even though you gave me credit for counseling you as to when to exercise your Fifth Amendment rights. I didn't do a bad job either, even though I didn't say anything."

David sighed. "Did I hang myself?"

"Not that I can tell. You'll have to see what these guys in the back of the room have to say. At least Chairman Reninger seemed pleased that a lot had been accomplished."

David shook his head. "I didn't agree with the summary."

"No. Well, he wasn't addressing you." Travers stood up and picked up his unopened briefcase. "I hope I was helpful being here. I'll add this to my resume. Another experience in my thirty years of law. Guess there are still things to learn."

David rose and picked up his notebook. "I hope it was worth something to you. I appreciate your support. At least I wasn't alone. And I guess I'm getting more comfortable with all this. But yes, I'm also very tired."

As they left, the reporters tried to ask questions, but David and Travers hurried through the crowd with no comment. They got on the elevator and shook hands as Travers got off at the first floor, and David continued down to the garage.

CHAPTER SIXTY-EIGHT

MONDAY - DAVID NEALE
AND MARY MURPHY

David checked out through security and walked to his car. He found Mary Murphy leaning against the car, her arms folded across her chest and her briefcase by her feet.

"I thought you'd never get here."

"You want my 'after hearing' comments for the Alexandria paper?"

"No, I've got all I need. And thanks to you, I'm now with the *Washington Post*."

David smiled. "Well, congratulations. I'm glad all this was good for someone. How do you think it went?"

"Well, as I understand it, you're sorry in some ways that you performed the experiment, but the world will learn from it, and you got scientific kicks out of the whole thing. And now, you've probably got some federal prosecutors and various scientific ethics committees wondering what to do about it."

"I guess that sums it up."

"So what's next? I came here on the Metro and need a ride. How about taking me some place for a cup of coffee?"

"Gee, I don't know. I've got worries about potential trials, what I do in the future, how I mend things with my famil—"

Mary held up two fingers in front of David's mouth.

"David, I know you've got problems. We're not going to solve them standing in this parking lot."

"Yeah, I know, but—"

"David, it's just a cup of coffee."

ACKNOWLEDGEMENTS

Several novels have been rattling around in my head for sixty years. I finally decided that if I was going to write them, I had better get on with it. I felt some trepidation in actually putting myself out there. Fortunately, my children, J.S. III, Kristie and Michelle, and a few friends encouraged me. It was a fairly limited group and I am grateful to them, especially to my daughter, Michelle Adams, who did my proofing. It justified my paying for her to get a degree in English from the University of Virginia, a degree not used directly by a woman who has become a successful Interior Designer.

I also appreciate the help that Xlibris provided in guiding me through this publication process. At my age I didn't have the patience to seek an agent or a publisher.

Finally, I would note that in writing *Gestation Seven*, I had no illusions that I was writing great literature. I simply wanted to tell a story. I had fun writing it and I hope my readers will enjoy it too.